SS Glasgow Castle

Michael Rymaszewski

Published by Barfly Books, 2023.

SS GLASGOW CASTLE

First edition. October 1, 2023.

ISBN: 979-8223087687

Written by Michael Rymaszewski.

CHAPTER ONE

"There'll be champagne."

"And oysters."

"Plus lots of other delicious food and booze."

"*Free* food and *free* booze."

"And girls."

"Dozens of girls."

"Beautiful girls."

"All panting to meet the Nordic God."

"Now, we know you're a good husband."

"A very good husband."

"In fact, probably a model husband."

"Still, you could probably use some admiration."

"And adoration."

"And fornication."

"Everybody can."

"Oh yes, and there'll be this hot new band—The Sunshine Kids."

"You probably heard them on the radio, performing in the breaks between the commercials."

"Some of which were probably art-directed by yourself."

"Well?"

The Glitter Twins—also known as John and Jim Robinson—grinned at me from inside their Italian suits. They were very big on corporate fun; their vaudeville cross-talk routine was developed because of this overwhelming desire to please everyone and everybody. Once, they'd even brought an ukulele to a presentation, and attempted to perform a proposed advertising jingle in front of a roomful of suits; that was when people started calling them the Glitter Twins. The clients loved them. Everyone else hated them. Well, not everyone; they were account directors now, and rumor had it that before long they would be anointed as account *group* directors.

"I can't come, guys," I told them. "Donna has a company Christmas thing too tonight, and someone's got to take care of the baby."

"Ah, the baby."

"Oh, baby, baby."

"Oh, baby, *baby*, bay."

They got up, strumming imaginary guitars and grinning wider than ever. Jim or John (I couldn't tell them apart) slipped out of my office. John or Jim made as if to leave, then stopped, turned to me.

"Try to come, Oscar," he said softly. "It would be good if you came." He looked serious for a brief moment; then he rearranged his face into the usual mask, and left.

So: you know my name is Oscar, Oscar Hansen. I'm an advertising art director. I wanted to be a painter, but I became an advertising art director because I had to make a living, like everyone else. Painters who actually paint usually can't make a living, and only a very few can make art.

I'm thirty two years old, married to a Donna. Her name is Donna, and she *is* a Donna. She has long black hair, big sad dark eyes, and a wide red mouth; she is suitably willowy, though not very tall. We don't have children, but about a year ago, I made up this lie that we had a daughter. It just happened, just like that. One moment I wanted to take the afternoon off—I was having a really vile day—the next I was telling the secretary that my daughter was having a fit in her expensive day care, and that I had to go, right away.

I wanted to set the record straight later, but I couldn't. Everyone at the office was suddenly looking at me with new respect. It was nice, and I also found that having a little kid and a working wife was the right setup to have if you wanted time off in a hurry.

It was four o'clock, and I had nothing more to do that day, nothing that couldn't wait until the next day. I swivelled round in my chair and picked up the phone and called Rapid Taxi, and asked for Joe, my childhood buddy Joe, the guy I used to play cops-and-robbers with.

"Joe," I said, when he came on the line, "Can you do the usual?"

"I got twenty assholes waiting for cabs," he said.

"Well I want a cab too."

"Asshole." He hung up.

I hung up too, got up, and went to the can with a slow, deliberate step. On the way I caught a glimpse of the Glitter Twins. They were knocking on an open door, grinning at each other. The door belonged to the office that belonged to my partner, Tad. Tad had once wanted to be a writer, but he became a copywriter because he had to make a living, and—as he confided to me one beery evening—he couldn't make art. We got on together famously, me and Tad. We talked only when it was absolutely necessary, and gave each other maximum slack.

The company can was just around the corner from my office, and mercifully it was empty. I combed my hair twice, inspected my teeth, and ran a quick scan of things in general. And then, probably because I was in the can—there's something about the place that invites introspection and reflection—I started thinking about me and Donna. Things weren't well there. They weren't simple, either. They never are when there's guilt on both sides.

I spent two more minutes in the can, repeatedly glancing at my watch. Then I walked out and took the long route back to my room, past the main secretarial desk. The secretary—the constantly smiling Paula Johnson—wasn't there. She smiled at everyone as often as she possibly could, and possibly she had a good reason; rumor had it she was snitching for Schutz. I made another long detour so that I could walk past Daphne, our red-haired receptionist, in a seemingly preoccupied and professional manner.

"Oscar," she sang out, thank God, and waved a pink slip at me. I unrolled it, looked, frowned.

"My daughter's sick again," I told Daphne.

"Your little daughter."

"My little daughter, oh yes. Very little."

She grimaced and bent over her log, her spybook. I noticed a little pile of what looked like cab slips next to her elbow.

"Are these –?"

"Yes. For the party tonight. Don't drink and drive."

"Absolutely," I said, reaching out.

Outside, the street was speckled with Christmas lights and decorations that became gaudier with every passing minute, as the day died. I inhaled the cold, clammy air; solitary snowflakes fell heavily onto the pavement and onto my shoulders. A smudge of orange intruded from the left: Rapid Taxi. Good old Joe. If you know a good old Joe, life is so much easier.

I settled down in the smelly, creaky interior and gave the appropriate directions. I had a car—or rather *we* had a car, me and Donna. We shared it; I usually got it two days in a week (the exact days differed). Life was nice then, because our car was a big BMW. Things were quite pleasant even when I was stuck in the morning traffic, with a steaming styrofoam-cupped coffee clipped to the dashboard and a guy doing his best to entertain me on the radio.

The other three days a week were hell. We lived as close to the suburbs as you can without actually living in the suburbs. Getting to work involved a bus and a fucking *train*. A lot of the perfumed people I met therein didn't wash in the morning. There were legions of the unwashed in my city, even though it deemed itself a world-class city, and the area I lived in—an upscale, world-class area. Maybe the world was unwashed, as a whole.

But now I was riding along in a cab, and the company was paying for the long ride. I enjoyed the approaching headlights slashing across the windscreen, lighting up the thickening snow; I even got used to the smell. It wasn't a *dirty* smell, but –

5

"Nice smell you've got in the cab," I said. "Air freshener?"

"And Mister Clean." He guffawed and bent over the wheel.

"What?"

"Mr. Clean. You know." He paused to negotiate an intersection with sure, flat slaps of the steering wheel. "Hope you don't mind my telling you this," he said, "But a guy threw up all over the back seat earlier today. Started the party early. But I scrubbed everything real careful with Mister Clean. Including the cracks, heh-heh."

I wished I knew how to levitate.

"It's very important to wash in the cracks," I said.

"Yah. Heh-heh."

The driveway was marked by fresh tracks, squeezed black into the thin, melting snow. Upstairs, a light was on. I tipped my honest driver and weaved along the flagstones to the front door. I didn't like this weaving path. I used to cut across on a regular basis, but Donna forbade this. She cares about the grass.

The house was empty. I knew that without trudging up the staircase. I took my shoes off, shed my jacket, and got rid of the fucking tie. I soft-socked it to the booze cupboard and poured a drink. After a while, I poured another. Donna was still absent. She was in her world, a world of professionals dealing with failed love. Donna was a very good divorce lawyer. She specialized in getting minimal settlements for guilty husbands. A long time earlier, when I still had my very own Mustang, I drove round to the cheap, ground level law office that gave Donna her first job, and watched her work.

I stood half-hidden behind a street lamp post, feeling like an idiot; the blinds in the window were up, but a cleverly placed potted cactus obscured the face of her client. I got a good look at Donna, though. Her hair was pulled back in a severe bun; her wide mouth was pursed in solemn concern. Her hand held a pen as if it was a scalpel, the paper beneath—an unsuspecting body. I understood then how she got wronged, furious women to shrink their claims. She'd say yes, he's wrong and you're right, but being right carries a price too. They'd look at her and agree, as they had to.

Donna owned everything; I didn't own a damn. My money paid for the bills—we had an ever-increasing amount of ever-growing bills—and the weekend shopping sprees at the local plaza (very upscale: a fountain masquerading as a waterfall, tons of plants in ceramic tubs, guys and gals in fancy dress smiling as if their life depended on it—maybe it did—while pushing assorted flyers and leaflets into the shoppers' hands; donation boxes for at least three different charities on each checkout counter; and let's not forget the string quartet serenading the shoppers—*two* string quartets and a choir at Christmas. In short, everything you could think of to make the act of spending money—*consuming*—a moral experience).

When Donna and I moved in together, I covered rent, the car, and entertainment, and she got the groceries and the bills. Now it was the other way around, and she went to Christmas parties without waiting for me to tell her I wasn't going to mine. You could say I had plenty of material for deep thinking sessions in the office can.

We'd *met* at a Christmas party, several years earlier. It wasn't a corporate get-together, but a friendly booze-up thrown by my neighbours, a married couple who were increasingly worried by my single state. Donna was invited to meet me and another unmarried holdout, a rich real estate agent called Frank Mahoney. Frank Mahoney has tufts of hair sticking out of his nose, a pot belly, and a beery laugh, while I, as John and Jim Robinson had observed, I am a Nordic god. Donna looked like a Barbarian princess in artistically torn suede and net stockings; we hit it off at once, while Frank pensively dipped his nose hair in large glasses of whisky.

Donna and I got married on a rainy May day; her Hispanic aunt observed mystically that rain on wedding day meant plenty of married good luck. I changed jobs for a 50% raise three months later. In September we bought a house in a new housing development. The developer had used a talented architect, and the house—a two-storey affair of grey brick, black slates, and white window frames—looked good inside and out. I didn't like the synthetic bluish-grey carpeting everywhere, but Donna did, and she was totally won over by the Italian kitchen. She thought she'd be doing a lot of cooking, back then. But our married good luck continued unabated: she got promoted, changed jobs, got promoted again, and eventually became a junior partner in her law firm, working eighty-hour weeks and pulling in two hundred grand a year. You can't deal with cooking when you make money like that.

It was good she did. My own job situation was—let's call it insecure. The recent personal computer revolution was claiming plenty of casualties. Now that anyone could put together an ad on their own computer, they were firing people left, right, and centre in all the ad agencies in the city. I'd heard that S&S Unlimited body-bagged six media and four creative people just the other week. And you could feel it, you could feel it every day, cruising down the corridor—there would be this waft of cold air on the back of your neck in spite of all the expensive air-conditioning, and if you looked around quickly enough you'd see a door closing, a shadow disappearing around a corner, someone swiftly averting their eyes.

Night had fallen; the pool of light from the standing lamp turned a bright yellow. I decided against having a third drink and went upstairs to take a long shower.

I caught a whiff of perfume when I entered the bathroom. There was a thin trail of talcum powder near the basin's pedestal, and a few drops of hairspray frozen in the corner of the mirror. I felt a tug of jealousy at the thought of Donna making herself pretty for other people and squinted at my reflection, suddenly ashamed of my thoughts, my nakedness, and at the way things were between me and Donna.

She had written me a couple of love notes on the mirror soon after we'd started living together. I should have felt happy, but instead I felt embarrassed. To start with, I was uncomfortable with the mirror: I knew the man inside was no Nordic god. Also, the very thought of *my* writing a note like that practically made me gag. I regretted feeling that way, and actually forced myself to think about writing Donna back, so to speak. But I couldn't very well use lipstick, and once I started thinking about writing materials (shaving foam? No, it would run. Soapy finger? No, it would simply look as if the mirror was dirty) the whole thing ceased to have anything in common with love or affection and became like art-directing an ad. So I dropped it and became embarrassed instead, and eventually Donna became embarrassed too, and there were no more love notes.

I took my shower, went to the bedroom to dress in something comfortable, and found the kind of note Donna and I wrote each other nowadays. She'd gone to her Christmas party; she hoped I'd enjoy mine.

I reached for the phone.

"Joe," I said, when he came on the line, "I need a cab."

Bollicker's was founded in 1936 by Herman Volcker, an Austrian butcher who sold smoked horsemeat as pastrami and quickly became rich. Following the inevitable discovery of his little fraud, he departed for the sunny shores of Florida. His son Joachim renamed and redecorated the delicatessen, turning it into an upscale restaurant. That was in 1940; fifty years later, Bollicker's was one of the most chic establishments in town. Its heavy black doors hissed shut behind many a celebrated back; its interior was liberally wallpapered with signed photographs of politicians, movie stars, and millionaire salesmen.

I strode up to the door and put my hand on one of the heavy chromed handles, the shape and size of a policeman's truncheon. I hesitated for a short moment, pretending to watch the cab I'd been in pull out into the traffic. When its red tail lights became undistinguishable from all the others, I went inside.

"Crystal Room," I said curtly to the smiling, tall teenager that had been lurking behind a potted palm next to the entrance.

"Yes, sir." He seemed dismayed I did not have an overcoat to hand over. "This way." I followed his bobbing blond head down the corridor.

I was late; the party had begun at seven, now it was almost eight. I entered the dining room. It was the best of Bollicker's three rooms: there was a Brass Room, read bar, a Golden Room, read ordinary dining room, and the Crystal Room, which served as a banquet room and was usually reserved by parties for parties. The last of my fellow workers were drifting away from a large sideboard littered with the debris of assorted appetizers, taking their seats at the small round dining tables. I felt a stab of dismay: I didn't know where I was supposed to sit. I scanned faces and heads perched atop unfamiliar evening costumes, looking for Tad's shaggy head. I couldn't find him.

"You made it," a voice breathed into my left ear. I turned. Jim or John Robinson was grinning as usual, left hand discreetly adjusting the crotch of his pants. He was wearing a tuxedo. When you wore a suit every day to work, a tuxedo was the least you could do on special occasions.

"Yeah, Donna decided to stay and take care of Bonnie."
Bonnie was the name of my imaginary daughter. "I have no
idea where I'm supposed to sit." I glanced around the room
and saw that most of the guys, not just the top brass and the
perennially elegant Robinsons, were wearing tuxedos.

"The creatives are there, in the left corner." He extended
a manicured finger, and turned away with a final flash of
faultless teeth. I cut across the empty center of the room. No
one looked up, no one shouted a greeting. Maybe they all
were really hungry.

I slowed my step as I approached the group of tables in
the indicated corner. Peter Haslam, Creative Director and
king of all creative types, was there; his shaved head was
bowed attentively as he listened to the whispering Paula
Johnson, the departmental secretary. Kurt Kenner, Associate
Creative Director, sat on Haslam's left, staring moodily at an
empty wineglass. There was an empty seat at their table, but
I didn't think it was intended for me. I always sat next to Tad
on these occasions.

Where was Tad? I stopped and swivelled on my heel,
and caught Joan's eye. She was a senior art director that
somehow seemed threatened by my presence from the day
I was hired; now she smiled and waved, the puffy sleeve of
her golden, shimmering blouse fluttering above her elbow,
like a flag. She was seated with three junior types; there were
no free seats at her table, either. There weren't any free seats
at any of the creative tables, except Haslam's and Kenner's.
Where was Tad?

"Oscar." Haslam had actually got his two hundred and eighty pounds up; he was standing a few feet away, breathing through his mouth, blue eyes bulging with belligerent worry. He gave me a come-hither wave, and retreated towards his table. I followed uncertainly.

"Sorry I'm late," I began, sitting down. "Bonnie – "

Haslam silenced me with an upraised fat palm.

"Not to worry, not to worry," he said softly. His eyes said otherwise. Kenner and Paula Johnson were silent, looking at me with something akin to new appreciation. I noticed, with a small shock, that Paula Johnson wasn't smiling. I nervously checked my appearance with a couple of glances. No, there were no stains on the lapels, and my shirt collar felt correct. I fingered the knot of my tie; it seemed straight.

"Avocados with tiger shrimp," Kenner said luxuriously, licking his chops. I had lunch with him once, soon after joining the agency. I came over from Delta Communications, a small shop with a reputation for firecracker creative; Schutz, Bellamy, and Berger was a big place that was trying to spiff up its grey, solid image with an infusion of new blood. Kenner was the designated interrogator of new talent; he would take everyone to Swiss Chalet, where he would order an extra plate of fries in addition to the mound that came with his chicken.

He would ask questions only after he had dealt with the primary plate, picking up the fries one by one, dipping them in sauce, and stuffing them thoughtfully into his round mouth while he listened to the answers. He and Haslam made a good pair; at one time, there'd been a bet who wears larger pants, and it was meant very literally.

A white-sleeved arm deposited the advertised avocado in front of my nose. I picked up a spoon and started digging, trying to avoid looking at the others. Haslam and Kenner don't eat; they devour. I felt a tingle of dread pass down the back of my neck, and decided not to ask about Tad.

"Delicious," I said, instead. Haslam and Kenner agreed with enthusiastic grunts; Paula gave me a beautiful smile. I felt much relieved.

"Where's the wine?" Haslam asked plaintively. Kenner jerked in his chair as if he had received a mild and not unpleasant electric jolt.

"Peter, you're a genius. A fucking genius. This is it. It's exactly what we need for Petouche." Petouche Wineries were one of SB&B's small but prestigious clients. "I can see it. It's right here. Same setting. Elegant couple gets served, pan of the beautiful food, closeup of white wine chilling in a bucket. Man looks at it, asks: where's the wine?"

"No. The *woman* looks and says, 'Where's the wine?'"

"Fucking genius."

Haslam nodded slowly.

"It ain't totally bad," he said. "Give it to Greg tomorrow—no, tomorrow's half-day—shit, give it to him anyway to storyboard it for the twenty-eighth. When are we meeting those people, twenty-eighth or ninth?"

"'Eighth. Want me to write the copy?"

"Why not—you did most of it already."

"That's really brilliant," said Paula Johnson, smiling brilliantly. Her tone reminded me of a mother complimenting a retarded child.

14

"It's good," I said, with sincerity. Kenner beamed, and attacked his food with fresh enthusiasm.

I was still halfway through the avocado when, once again, I felt unexpected dread. You develop a kind of a sixth sense when working in advertising—after all, you are working in communications, with special emphasis on subtle insinuation, veiled suggestion, and innuendo. I looked up from my plate; there was a lone figure standing in the entrance to the Crystal Room. I quickly identified it as one John MacArthur, a freelancer occasionally hired to help with new business pitches. His glasses flashed as he looked around –

"John's here," Paula Johnson, always the efficient secretary, said matter-of-factly. Haslam's spoon froze halfway to his mouth, dribbling Thousand Island sauce onto the white tablecloth. His eyes met mine, and they said I'm sorry, I'm really sorry, and suddenly I understood why Tad wasn't with us.

"You left early today," Kenner said softly. I stared at him; my cheeks and ears were starting to burn. "Berger came in at quarter to five. His wife works out at Sunnyside Spa, and she happened to run into yours just yesterday. She asked about the delicate health of your daughter." Kenner paused to cough, raising the back of his hand to his mouth.

"They told me to get rid of a team by New Year's," said Haslam. "I didn't want to. It was still up in the air, I think, but this – "

"It was very embarrassing for old Penny Berger. There were all those people listening. She had to say she made a mistake, and she hates making mistakes." That was Kenner.

"She hates admitting she made one even more." Haslam.

"And then you left early—you weren't there when Berger wanted to bawl you out."

"He just told me, Peter, either it's you and Kurt, today, or Hansen and Kornik." Me and Tad. "I tried to get him to let it be for a couple of weeks. I reminded him we're a writer short as it is. He picked up my phone and told MacArthur he was hired full-time, asked him to come to the do tonight. Then he went and fired Tad."

"The Robinsons said you weren't planning to come tonight, otherwise we would've set up an extra table." Kenner. Paula Johnson didn't say anything; she just kept on smiling.

I got up awkwardly. The chair legs made a hideous screeching noise on the parquet floor.

"Good night, Peter," I said. "Good night, Kurt."

"I'll make sure you get a good package," said Haslam. Kenner said something too, but I didn't hear him. I was already walking to the door, concentrating hard so as not to trip over my own feet. I stopped by MacArthur.

"Your seat's there, John," I said, pointing. "Welcome to SB&B." His mouth moved soundlessly. I patted his tuxedoed arm, and walked out.

CHAPTER TWO

I woke up when I fell off the sofa in my living room. I lay on the carpet for a while, eyes closed. When I opened them, I saw my mud-caked evening shoes about an inch from my nose. I groaned and got up, an act that necessitated sitting down very quickly on the sofa.

The clock over the fireplace told me it was ten past eleven, and I felt a surge of panic—I was late for work. Then I remembered that there wasn't work to be late for any more.

"Donna!" I shouted hoarsely. But she was gone, she had things to do. That was good, because I needed to think things over, and do a few too: there was a trail of mud leading from the front door to the sofa.

I staggered to the famous Italian kitchen and made myself a mug of coffee, drank a scalding sip, ran to the bathroom, and threw up. Then I went through the remaining morning ablutions. The hairspray was gone from the mirror—Donna was very particular about keeping the mirror clean nowadays—but the thin trail of talcum powder was still there. She was one of those people that rarely look under their feet.

The coffee was cold by the time I got back to the kitchen. I made a fresh mug, and then made an effort to think about the previous night's events. I remembered flagging a cab from Bollicker's and riding halfway home, changing my mind and telling the driver to head downtown. I faintly recalled going into Pompeii, a trendy bar, consuming several drinks there, and deciding to go in search of Tad. The drinks had made me confident that I'd find him sooner or later, bent over a table while a chick with a pierced nostril whispered something into his hair.

I was determined to find him and apologize; my lies had cost him his job. I visited many bars; I had a dim memory of the curious stares I drew, in my jacket-and-tie ensemble, and of being mistaken for a producer in search of new talent. This mistake led to more drinks in the company of two, possibly three chicks, one of whom might have even had a pierced nostril. The rest was blackness, a blank, which was just as well.

It was a beautiful day outside. The strong sun lit the fresh snow with a thousand lights, green, purple, orange, constantly changing, some coming on, others going out. I watched this friendly winking and didn't feel so bad about getting fired any more. I knew I didn't have a chance of landing another job in the very near future, not with agencies firing people left, right, and centre. But I decided I'd let Stuart Jerome Stuart, the adbiz agent who'd fixed the SB&B job for me, worry about that. I also quickly decided I'd put the whole business aside for at least a couple of weeks. Christmas was coming. Maybe I could use some of my free time to improve things with Donna. I'd be able to find a job sooner or later, and in the meantime she was making twice as much as I did, anyway.

The sunshine made me confine my cleanup effort to dropping the muddy shoes onto the shoe mat. Then I got dressed, and went out. The sun felt almost as hot as in the summer. Birds twittered busily on the naked, wet branches; everything looked so pretty. Even the ragged old crow sitting on a nearby tree looked good, although its plumage resembled a well-worn overcoat: matted here, smooth and shiny there.

I walked to the nearest corner, turned, and realized with a little start that I hadn't been on that particular street since the day Donna and I toured the neighbourhood when buying the goddamn house. It was just a hundred yards from where I lived, but it was off the route to work. I looked around with interest: everything was strange yet familiar. Well, the houses were practically the same—what could you expect, after all they all were part of the same housing development.

The houses were silent, their interiors hidden by blinds and curtains. Their inhabitants were all at work. This was a residential area; there was nothing to do here but reside.

I shook my head, stopped, swivelled round on my heel, and looked around, taking in the curtained, blinded windows. I was the only person on the street. It was a fucking ghost town. Everyone who lived around here—well, they didn't *live*, they just slept and spent weekends here. Not all weekends: we were all the kind of people that go away for the weekend; mostly childless, hard-working couples. Working at work, working out, working on relationships... Fucking work again.

I was standing there with hands thrust into my pockets, thinking strange new thoughts, when a little figure strode silently into view around a corner at the far end of the street. It approached with odd, jerky movements that resembled a speed-walker's gait. Then it turned briskly into a driveway and mounted the front steps of a faraway house. Metal clinked and rattled, the sound somehow rusty and dirty as it spread over the glittering snow. The toy man ran down the steps and cut across the white lawn like a trapper in a hurry; I made out the outline of a big shoulder bag. Of course! The postman.

I set off in his direction, timing things so that we met at the intersection. I asked him about mail; he frowned, dug his hand into the bag, and pulled out a slim wedge of envelopes held together by a rubber band.

"Here you go," he said, thrusting it at me. "Rubber courtesy of Canada Post."

I faked a smile, said goodbye, and slipped the band off. Donna's book club, the bank, a couple of solicitations from charities (I thought I knew the guy who wrote one of those—he liked writing copy for charities—he claimed they paid well). Finally, a standard office envelope with my name on it. So soon? And that wasn't SB&B stationery –

I ripped it open and pulled out a single sheet of paper, blank except for this:

Your wife is fucking someone else

The envelopes slipped from my hand and fluttered down to the already melting snow. I bent and scrabbled around for them, finding astonishing comfort in the activity. I almost wished I'd dropped more.

I folded the single letter that I'd opened and stuffed it back into its envelope, then put all the mail in a pocket and started walking away from home.

So.

She was fucking someone else. Or was she?

I kicked a lump of dirty snow and it exploded with a wet, gritty sound. If only I could feel shamelessly angry. But I couldn't, because I was guilty too. I did it just once, but once is enough.

I kept walking as if in a trance. In the end, after a few minutes of residential streets, I came to a big collector road. The visible traffic consisted of two vehicles, and that was counting the bicycle freak riding along the siding, the bike slicing through snow and water like a motorboat. I looked left and right, trying to decide where to go next. I was quite sure I didn't want to go back home, not just yet.

There was a small building on the corner that had a sign saying 'The Big One', and under that, 'Restaurant'. I crossed the road and looked at the placards stuck to the windows from the inside. One of these, a cheap mass-produced nightmare of orange letters on black background, claimed The Big One was home to the best hamburgers and steaks in town; every greasy-spoon restaurant made a claim like that—if it wasn't the best steak in town, it was the best pizza or whatever. I went inside.

I was hit by a sour smell of old beer and smoke mixed with pine air freshener. A couple of older guys were sitting at the bar, half-full beer mugs in front of them; their poses suggested they'd been sitting like that for quite a while. I glanced at the beer mugs as I passed: the foam on the inside rims had dried in a frost-like pattern; these guys were going at half a beer per hour, and it didn't look as if they could afford to drink any faster.

I caught the barmaid's eye in the mirror; she was hunched over the cash register, her back to the room, examining her right hand with suspicion and distaste. She held it with the fingertips of her other hand as if it was a bag of dogshit, and peered at it like a concerned dog-owner looking for evidence of worms. I waited patiently. Eventually, the register drawer clanged shut.

"I blew ten bucks on that sad excuse of a manicure," she said. Then she added, as an afterthought:

"What would you like?"

I ordered a beer—a Heineken—and sat down in an orange plastic chair at a small steel table, suddenly gripped by acute awareness of my jobless status; it was paying for the beer that did it. In a way it was a relief, because it made me stop thinking about Donna sucking strange cocks and fucking faceless men. I stared at the old guys at the bar instead, wondering if that was the future I was headed for: nursing a mug of tap slop for hours on end, silent, eyes woodenly fixed on the TV set suspended above the bar...

The guy nearer me must have felt my gaze burning through his dirty green nylon windbreaker. He looked at me over his shoulder; he was too far away for me to see his eyes, but when our gazes met I got the impression his was watchful and alert. He had thin hair dyed black and sculpted into a withered Presley pompadour. He grinned at me; his mouth was a war zone; countless tank divisions had gone hither and thither as the front lines shifted, leaving a few crooked yellow stumps. His grin seemed to say, well hi there pal. Glad you could join me in the Big One.

I drank up quickly and went home, to deal with the mud.

Donna was already home, at least temporarily; the black BMW glistened in the driveway. The garage doors were closed; maybe she'd just dropped in for a bit, and would be leaving soon. I found myself stepping increasingly softly as I walked up to the front door: maybe it was a good idea to turn around, and hide somewhere until the coast was clear. But that would make me feel like a total loser, so I gritted my teeth and grasped the handle and froze: there was a regular, swishing sound coming from the inside—Christ, she was cleaning *my* mud! I opened the door very energetically, eager to apologize and take over. It slammed into something soft; there was a cry and the sound of a fall. She had been right behind the door. I was afraid to push it open any further. I put my mouth to the opening.

"Donna? Are you all right?"

"You asshole," she said. A few seconds ticked by; I stared dumbly at the door jamb.

"I'm sorry," I said finally. "I didn't know you were right behind the door."

She didn't answer. I opened the door wider, and peered inside. She was squatting on the floor, holding a carpet brush in one hand; from time to time, she wobbled a little and

23

steadied herself with the end of the brush. I saw she was still wearing her office high heels; she must have thrown herself onto that mud of mine the moment she'd walked in.

"May I come in?" There was an exaggerated, exasperated sigh. I gingerly pushed the door open wider and stepped right onto the rubber mat by the wall, feeling like a helicopter pilot landing on the roof of a skyscraper. I took off my boots and my jacket, waiting for her to say something. She watched me silently, most likely waiting for the same thing.

"I'm sorry," I said again.

"You'd better be." There was a pause. "Couldn't you have at least cleaned up what you'd brought in?"

"I intended to," I said. "But I felt really rough after last night and thought I'd manage to have a short walk first, and then tidy up before you came back."

"Yeah, last night. That's another story." Donna stood up, dropping the brush on the floor. She walked to the kitchen, wobbling on her high heels. I looked down at the brush; a dustpan sprinkled with dark sand lay by the door. There was only one thing to do.

The mud had completely dried out, crumbling away under the brush; there were faint yellowish stains left here and there, but they would come off under a wet sponge. I brushed away, squatting, kneeling, and finally sitting on the floor. I ventured into the kitchen once to empty the dustpan. Donna was standing by the window, waiting for the coffee maker to do its business, smoking one of her very rare cigarettes—a thin toy tube of tobacco called More; approximately a third of it was cellulose filter.

I had to squat down next to Donna in order to put away the dustpan and the brush in their designated and officially approved spot. I shoved them in and hesitated. Donna's legs were maybe six inches from my face. She wore her office pantyhose, a silvery grey, which went well with all of the half dozen or so of her business suits. I felt an impulse to reach out, to run my hand along that beautiful, shiny leg. A year earlier, I would have. Now, it seemed the wrong thing to do.

"Coffee?" asked Donna.

"Yes," I said, straightening up.

The teaspoon clanked a couple of times, and she handed me my mug. It really is my very own mug; I bought it at a garage sale when I was still a student. It has a Scots grenadier painted on one side, and a French fusilier on the other—I'd leafed through a couple of books to establish these identities. If you hold it in your right hand, you see the Scot, skirt and all; if you hold it in your left, you see the fusilier. Both are charging away from the handle, spiky bayonets atop the raised muskets, destined to meet but never making it round the bend.

For some reason Donna had always showed a slight distaste for that mug, and bought me another one: it was decorated with cartoony, happy cows in a field of flowers. I dropped it one nervous morning and it broke. She thought I'd done it on purpose. I told her it was an accident. She wasn't convinced, although she pretended to believe me.

Donna had this talent for finding hidden motives, the rotten seeds that germinate into monstrosities. I suspected that was how she got all those cheated wives to settle so easily. She sought out and tuned into all the ugliness they

25

felt, all the rage and the hate, and she let them know that she *knew*. They instantly felt guilty, and settled for less: an act of nobility to convince themselves they weren't really *that* bad.

"We have to talk," Donna said.

I became very interested in my coffee. It was bitter. Donna thought sugar and salt were death in disguise.

"I lost my job," I said.

"I know you did. You told me a hundred times, last night."

I thought about it for a little while. I couldn't remember talking to Donna upon getting home, but then I couldn't remember getting home either.

"I was pretty drunk last night," I said cautiously.

"You were stinking drunk. But somehow, what you said made quite a lot of sense." I wished fervently I could remember *something* I'd said, especially since it reportedly had been so wise.

"Look," I said, "Why don't we forget last night and have that talk as if last night didn't take place. I was pissed and unhappy."

"I have no intention of forgetting last night," said Donna. There was a pause. "But you seem to have."

There was no use trying to outfox her. She was too smart. That was one of the things which had initially attracted me to her. It's funny how often the very things that attract you to another person become the things you fear or detest, after a while.

"I'll refresh your memory," said Donna the lawyer. "You came in drunk, told me about the job, and that you don't have a snowball's chance in hell of finding another one. I asked you what induced you to spin that fantastic lie about a nonexistent daughter. Then you called me a cold-hearted bitch that's only interested in money. I asked you if you wanted children, Oscar, both before and after we got married. You never said you did."

I called her a cold-hearted bitch that was only interested in money? That was news. I didn't even think that way. Or did I?

It happens sometimes that someone spits out a ridiculous accusation like that, an accusation that can't be proved or disproved—how do you prove you never *thought* something?—and, having initially recoiled with horror and denial, you realize it's true. I looked at Donna, smartly efficient in her business suit. She was eyeing me coldly; there wasn't a trace of sympathy visible on her face. Things had definitely changed since, since oh God, since a fucking long time ago.

"I didn't want a daughter," I said. I cleared my throat. "We. We didn't want children. Not right away."

"That's correct. We didn't. We talked about it. I thought we had an agreement."

"We did have an agreement," I said. "That thing at the office was just a stupid joke that got out of hand." I took a reluctant sip of the coffee. It was still very bitter.

"Some joke." I shrugged and looked at the floor.

"Oscar," said Donna, after a pause. "The past year, we've been seeming to drift further and further apart. Don't you think so?"

"We've both been very busy."

"We've always been very busy. But it didn't seem to matter, previously. Do you realize we haven't made love for nearly three months now?"

Now that was a dirty blow. We'd stopped making love because I thought, I felt Donna wasn't so crazy about it any more. She never initiated anything; that was always up to me, and lately, okay, for some time now, there was this reluctance... Donna never refused me. There were no not-tonight-I've-a-headache situations. But I could sense the reluctance, and became reluctant too. Add the fact that after a while things become too familiar to be exciting, and you've got the picture.

"Oscar, are you having an affair?" I nearly dropped my favourite mug. I prophylactically set it down on the counter; some coffee slopped over the rim.

"Wait a sec," I said. Then I did something incredibly foolish. I went to the hallway and got the anonymous letter from the inside pocket of my jacket. I returned to the kitchen and handed Donna the envelope without a word. I picked up my mug and sipped my coffee, heard the whisper of that mostly blank sheet of paper being pulled out –

"You believe that." It was a statement, not a question.

"Should I?" I asked. I didn't look at her.

She didn't answer. I heard the rustle of paper being folded back inside the envelope, a soft slap as the envelope landed on the kitchen counter, then the click of Donna's heels on the floor tile as she walked out, leaving me alone.

A nd so it went.

As usual, we spent Christmas with Donna's family, whose members tended to become religious on designated holidays. I had my job cut out acting as if I was confident about finding another job, which I wasn't. It was either an excellent effort or a wasted one; no one seemed to care. Donna's family was deeply into the life, death, and impending burial of an aunt called Consuela, who had inconveniently expired the day before Christmas. There was also the question of what would become of Consuela's Floridian condo; she hadn't left a will. It was a fascinating problem for all those gathered at the Christmas table.

It certainly wouldn't have been better to spend Christmas with *my* family. My father is a former sailor and rarely utters more than twenty words a day, maybe forty if he's had a couple of drinks. My mother is similarly outspoken; they are true Scandinavians, with their ability to sit there in total silence and make the air buzz. My younger brother Todd is positively extroverted by comparison, but he thinks I'm a bit of a pansy, pussy-whipped by Donna to be quite blunt, and anyway it wasn't one of those instances of undying brotherly love. Todd is a professional hockey player; not a great star, but not an unknown either. Once in a while, he gets himself into a group shot on the sports pages of national newspapers, waving his stick in celebration of a goal he hadn't scored. He is a bachelor, and has no idea of what goes on in married life.

You might suspect I'm the kind of guy who asks his wife's permission to go to the can. This isn't true. For instance, that particular year it was I who'd made the plans for New Year's Eve. I'd bought tickets to a big bash at a classy club, and was hoping to spring a little surprise on Donna. I knew she would only remember about New Year's Eve during Christmas week, and then bring the subject up together with a couple of names of people who would be throwing a party. That would be when I'd wave the tickets: surprise, surprise.

As it happened, we practically had no personal contact until Christmas was over. Donna's father had retired to a palatial house in the so-called country, and we'd been staying there for three very long days. The daily seance at the food-laden table took around six hours, and preparations for this grand event took up all morning. The evenings were spent in what was called the family room, where I sulked silently in a corner with a glass of sweet sherry while Donna and her family discussed aunt Consuela's Floridian condo, uncle Alberto's liver, young Fabio's tendency to get caught speeding with a joint sticking out of his shirt pocket, and other subjects of family interest. The rich food and the sherry usually knocked me out by ten, at which time the conversation was just starting to get lively. I would retire politely and sleep like a log for ten hours; by the time I woke up, Donna would have been and gone—she got up at seven to help with the ongoing battle in the kitchen.

The trouble began the moment we'd finished unpacking the trunkful of food that we'd been obliged to take home. Donna poured herself a glass of Dubonnet, lit one of her toy cigarettes and said:

"Well, you really outdid yourself this time."

"Could I have a drink, too?"

"Sure. Go ahead and help yourself. You didn't mind helping yourself the last three days. You must have gone through at least two bottles of Bristol Cream."

"Jesus Christ," I said, and went to the bar and poured myself a big scotch. Donna frowned.

"That's just like you, to blaspheme two days after Christmas."

"Don't get Catholic on me, Donna," I said. I mean, she didn't even go near a church on Sundays. I took a hefty swig from my glass, forgetting that I hadn't put in any ice.

"Could you elaborate on what you meant by saying I really outdid myself?" I asked, when I could speak again. Donna snorted.

"Don't be ridiculous. You know very well what I meant. Sitting there with a face like thunder and swigging sherry like, like a homicidal lumberjack in a backwoods bar."

"I don't think homicidal lumberjacks drink sherry," I said. "I apologize for the face. But that was because I was dying of boredom. If only anyone took the trouble to talk to me – "

"They didn't talk to you because you were sitting there with that face."

There was no answer to that one. I drank some more whisky and took a deep breath.

"I'm sorry," I said. There was another muted snort.

"I just hope things will work out better at the party," she said.

"What party?"

"New Year's Eve. Don't tell me you've forgotten?"

31

I took another deep breath. I seemed to need lots of oxygen.

"Donna," I said, "You never told me about any party."

"I did." I had the absolute, total certainty she was trying to pull a fast one. I never forgot stuff like that; but Donna did, and that made her think everyone else did, too.

"You didn't. And anyway, I've made plans for us for New Year's Eve. I've bought tickets to a ball at a club."

"A club? And what the hell are we going to do at a club?"

"We could dance," I said.

Donna laughed.

"Oscar," she said, "You dance like a disabled ape."

That did it.

"You nasty little bitch," I said.

CHAPTER THREE

L ittle words can lead to big things, given enough time.

It's now exactly a year since I called my wife a nasty little bitch. I'm living in a rented room, one of many (twelve) in a sprawling mansion originally built for a meat magnate at the beginning of this century (there are also two small, one-bedroom flats tucked into the front corners of the house). The grimy tiles in the huge communal kitchen are painted with portraits of what had made the magnate's fortune: smiling cattle, joyful chicken, and contented pigs. Presumably, the meat was good.

Eventually, it bought the magnate a two-storey house with a spindly turret adorning each roof corner, a wide oak staircase, and gas lighting in all of its rooms. The gas piping was buried in the brickwork, so ripping it out would have been lots of trouble. Instead, a later owner turned each gas light into an electric lamp after feeding wires through the embedded pipes. This means that pressing an ear against the lamp's brass arm—the thin pipe that connects the light to the wall mounting— allows one to spy efficiently. Predictably, it's a very quiet house.

My room measures six paces by five. I have a bed, a bookcase, a table, and two chairs. I also have a narrow wardrobe by the door; its shape, size, and unique odour suggests it has been used, at one time, for storing mops and brooms. I keep most of my clothes in my two suitcases.

When I arrived here for the first time, my clothes caused a minor sensation. I came to see the advertised room, but the caretaker couple (elderly East Indians; the house is owned by a retired shadow in sunny Florida) insisted on showing me one of the flats (the caretakers live in the other). They were very disappointed when I turned it down. Their hopes had been raised by my designer togs. In here, everyone over forty wears Zellers and K-Mart; everyone under thirty—Salvation Army and Goodwill. Between thirty and forty there's only myself, me and my fading, shrinking assortment of designer gear.

For neighbours, I have an old guy that appears to be dying of tuberculosis (to the left of the entrance to my room), and one of the three communal toilets (to the right). Initially I was horrified by the neighbourhood to the right. However, my fears turned out to be groundless. The occupants of the house conduct their bodily business next door with a great delicacy—one could say secrecy. They creep up to that door on soundless feet—the top hinge squeaks faintly—there is a soft, barely audible thump as the door closes, then a moist click as the latch is slipped. You have to be listening hard for sounds from that quarter to hear any action. So far I've heard only a single loud fart. And I suspect that once, someone threw up—not because of the associated noise, but from the smell when I went in there to do some business of my own.

Of course, whenever I do go there myself I creep like a trained commando, and operate the latch as if I were setting a delayed fuse. I don't want anyone thinking I'm a supporter of loud self-expression in the toilet. I live next door, after all.

Life has a way of being brutally just; the noiseless can came with a tubercular geezer on the other side. He limits himself to four or five fits a day and two a night, which isn't too bad.

But – let's face it, let's be brave now – things *are* bad.

It all began on a better note, though not an especially happy one. I moved out of my world-class, not-quite-suburban home in the first week of February. Donna and I had spent most of the preceding month on discussions, during which we established beyond any doubt that we didn't care for each other as much as we used to.

There was no hate or anger or anything like that, but I did feel really shitty. Of course, I didn't even bother to look for work. It's no use calling about a job when feeling like that. If people are to hire you, you have to make them feel good. They want to hear confidence and hope, not a guy sounding like a depressed actor in a Russian drama. You can't make people feel good when your manner suggests that grandpa has just hanged himself in the barn.

My manner was well suited to the conversations I had with Donna, though; hers was much the same. We agreed despondently that our busy professional lives prevented us from getting to really know each other, but somehow neither she nor I showed much enthusiasm for the process of mutual re-discovery. We agreed on several more issues in the same vein; eventually, we also agreed we should separate, and see what transpired.

Somehow, it went without saying I would be the one to move out. Donna graciously released me from the obligation of paying the house bills; she said she would rent a room out to a car-owning, university-going cousin of hers (she had at least a dozen cousins, and I didn't bother to delve into the details). The nearest college or university was so far away Donna's cousin would be spending a fortune on gas, but maybe Donna's cousin had the ambition to live in a world-class area.

As it turned out, finding a place for myself was surprisingly easy. I dug up an old real estate agency card that had been tossing around in a drawer for several years, and dialled the number. I was connected to no other than Frank Mahoney, the one with the whiskered nostrils. The shock made me honest about the reasons behind my call, and an overjoyed Mahoney found me a very nice, inexpensive studio within forty-eight hours. I wondered whether he'd wait another forty-eight hours before he called Donna.

Mahoney's efficiency resulted in my moving out much sooner than I thought I would. I packed in a state of slight stupor, mechanically selecting only things I was sure to use over the coming twelve months. They came to embarrassingly little; the only large items were my drawing board and my computer. I couldn't very well take chairs from the dining set, my half of the double bed, and so on.

After I saw the studio that was to become my new home, I visited IKEA and a couple of antique shops (on my continent, anything older than sixty years is classified as an antique, people included), and bought everything I needed relatively cheaply. It gave me a big boost, buying new furniture, partly because I hadn't liked the world-class furniture that I owned with Donna. For example, we had this big dining table that we used for dinner parties (when on our own, we ate in the kitchen). That table was topped with glass, and summer barbecues were particularly tough. You've no idea what an array of bare human legs, many of them hairy, can do to the appetite. You can't look at the plate without flinching.

I also had a bit of money, too. I had a few thousand stashed away in government bonds, plus a few grand more that I received upon terminating my company pension plan. Add the dole money, and I had a guaranteed minimum of ten months' painless existence even if I hadn't managed to find a single gig.

The building I moved into contained studios inhabited by relatively young, relatively independent professionals and artists. There was this silent consensus hanging in the conditioned air: since we live here, we're independent, intelligent, and interesting. All this made me think I'd weather the sad developments in my personal life without too much pain. I even fancied I was on the verge of starting a new life, which was total bullshit. It's one life apiece, no returns, refunds, rainchecks, or repeat orders.

I gave myself a month to settle in before looking for work. But before the month was up, the crisis struck. I spent the next few weeks wallowing in self-pity. I constantly felt on the edge of breaking out in tears, and several times I did. It made me feel even worse, although in the meantime I'd purchased and read a book which claimed crying would make me feel better.

I found I couldn't really talk to anyone. Losing your job and then your marriage effectively banned looking for human sympathy. I mean, you've just lost your job and your spouse, and now you're there snivelling and pawing a sleeve.

What eventually cured me was talking to Donna. It was a Thursday evening, and there was a party going on in the studio next door to mine. There even had been an invitation slipped under my door, which I promptly tossed in the trash. It reminded me, unnecessarily, that it was St. Valentine's. Every shop and store in the city had been sporting the appropriate decorations for the previous three weeks—even the nearby butcher, with paper red hearts suspended over bloody red flesh waiting to be bought and eaten.

I felt compelled to call Donna. If I *didn't* call her on Valentine's Day, I would feel bad about it later. I went out and bought booze: two bottles of wine, some beer, and a half-bottle of vodka. I didn't expect her rushing over for a drink in response to my call; I was partly inspired by the festivities next door, and partly by a nameless fear.

I got home, had a beer, and a quick slug of fairly warm vodka right before picking up the phone. I dialled my old number carefully clearing my mind of any bad thoughts. Needless effort; she wasn't in.

I had another beer and tried again, with the same result. And again. And again.

By the time I managed to speak to Donna, I was already on the wine. She was displeased, then pleased, then displeased again. Overall, she was displeased. After that, I proceeded to drink all the booze I had. I woke up at five in the morning feeling dead, but the crisis was over.

I gave myself a couple more days to relax, as it was the weekend anyway. Then, come Monday morning, I called Stuart Jerome Stuart. As I mentioned earlier, Stuart Jerome Stuart was a personnel agent specializing in the turbulent world of advertising, and had gotten me hired at Schutz *et al* in the first place. He was both a charmer and a terrible snob; he often wore a ghastly tartan tie that I checked on, and found to feature traditional Stuart tartan. Like all good Scots, they have their own pattern.

Stuart Jerome Stuart did not sound happy that winter Monday morning. He sounded particularly sober when he realized it was me, on the other end. However, we agreed to do lunch middle of the week.

The lunch started on an optimistic note: Stuart insisted it's on him, and kicked off the proceedings by ordering cocktails; I had a humble Bloody Mary. Then, over the meal, he treated me to a summary of all the gossip currently making rounds. Things turned serious together with the coffee.

"I'll tell you this, Ossie," Stuart Jerome Stuart said, fingering his cup in a reflective manner, "Things are fucking bad. You know how I'm making money these days?"

"Shovelling snow?"

"Well there's a bit of that. Unavoidable, even though it fucks up my sinuses for days. Clinches a deal, sometimes. No, but truly? I find young shitheads starving in little studios and printing houses and hire them away for as little as thirty a year to replace the guys that have been fired, the guys that used to make a hundred a year. And the way things are going, I'd say that's how things are gonna stay for the next few months. Maybe by next Christmas..." I remember feeling my lip sag over the remains of my meal.

"You don't feel I qualify as a young shithead?" I said. Stuart Jerome Stuart became horrified.

"My God, no. Don't even fucking think about it. Nobody would ever hire you for that money anyway. They'd be too ashamed."

"Part-time? Contracts?" Stuart shook his clever, curly head.

"Just hang in there," he said, "And I'll get you something good. But not before Christmas. In the meantime, why don't you freelance? They're firing all these people but there's still work to be done, and some gets handed out."

"Yeah, I'll try," I said gloomily. Stuart Jerome Stuart emitted a royal sigh.

"Look," he said, fingering his tie, "You know why I wear that?" The tartan didn't go too badly with the dark wool jacket he was wearing that day.

"Yeah, I do," I said, giving him the knowing eye.

"Right," he said. "Fucking art director. But you know something? I'm half Jewish, half Greek." He grinned, and politely waited for me to finish laughing.

"You know what the moral is?" he asked. I shrugged helplessly.

"Appearances are important," said Stuart Jerome Stuart. And with this final pearl of wisdom, he slid back his chair.

Weeks went by. I awoke one day startled by hot sunshine. As the air got warmer its perfume changed, taking on a whiff of last year's decay. Perversely, my daily routine changed in the other direction; I slept in later and later behind drawn blinds, and spent increasingly long evenings roaming around the place, doing a bit of this and a bit of that, occasionally going out on an invented errand for an hour or so. Predictably, I also found out that a drink or two helps ward off the melancholy that lurks in the lengthening shadows of a dying day.

I also moved on the job front in a firm and decisive manner. I refused to accept Stuart Jerome Stuart's words of gloom. I quickly found they were true. And although there was a respectable amount of freelance work floating around, there were fifty mouths claiming every gig available. There also were a couple of people who were impressed by my looks as well as talent, and made vague promises if anticipated new business pitches became reality. Finally, a creative god with a fashionably shaved head, a hotshot imported from Australia, liked my stuff. But there was a snag: he told me that he was looking for an art director/copywriter team. Solitary art directors didn't interest him.

The following evening, having mulled things over a glass of wine, I resolved to track down Tad, my copywriting partner at Shit, Bullshit, and Balls. Stuart Jerome Stuart had no idea what became of him. Tad always had been a bit of a mystery man: he tended to hide behind his long hair, bushy beard, and vague pronouncements on spiritual values. He'd have been fired within thirty eight seconds if it wasn't for the fact he also wrote brilliant advertising copy.

I finally had a go at the telephone directory and called him on a long, sunny, late-spring afternoon. Partly rationally and partly irrationally, I was expecting an answering machine. I got Tad in person.

He didn't seem to be surprised I called—but then, it was Tad's policy not to be surprised by anything. He was pretty busy for the next couple of days. Would Friday afternoon be all right? The best idea was to come down to his place for a drink; he was sure we both wouldn't mind saving a dollar without any pain. I wasn't quite sure whether Tad's place wouldn't cause any, but I agreed.

The appointed Friday came under a blanket of slate-grey clouds. It rained very wetly throughout the morning, and I was surprised at the amount of concern it caused me until I traced it to the fact I was afraid of having to spend money on a cab. The rain stopped by two in the afternoon, and soon after it did I ventured out with a grimly determined step; I was to present myself at Tad's at three. He didn't live very far—I thought I'd simply walk there. I calculated it wouldn't take more than ten minutes.

It took twenty, in spite of the hurried trot I occasionally broke into when I realized I would be late. I had a stitch in my side from speed-walking while clutching a magnum of cheap Beaujolais under my arm.

Tad rented out a flat in a fake Victorian townhouse on a modestly elegant street. I pushed the upper of the two buttons by the door. Steps creaked and groaned; a dim shape shimmered behind the frosted glass. The lock clicked –

I was speechless for a moment. Tad had shaved his beard! His face was small and childlike in its frame of frizzy hair. The clean-shaven look didn't suit him: he had thin, bloodless lips whose corners drooped sadly.

"Oscar," he said. Then he turned round and marched off and up a long flight of narrow stairs.

I followed, the stairs moaning as if my presence moved them to new heights of sadness. Tad's flat consisted of an upper floor that had been divided into two rooms, a kitchen, and a bathroom; there was a faint smell of pot. It seemed Tad could afford drugs, which was promising.

Tad dived into a nook I took to be the kitchen, and emerged with a wineglass and two fresh bottles of beer. I had to ask him to get a corkscrew. There was no furniture at all in the living room, so we settled down in his bedroom. It contained one of those sofas that unfold into a bed, a desk dominated by a computer, two chairs, and a bookcase overstuffed with paperbacks and magazines.

I pulled up a chair to the side of the desk and pushed the mousepad behind the monitor to create some space. Tad opened the wine with well-practiced deftness and poured me a glass. I toasted him silently, and took a sip of the wine. It tasted of cork.

"So," Tad said. "I finally get to thank the guy who got me fired."

I'd completely forgotten that angle. My cheeks and ears felt hot. I drank my wine and poured more, looking for my voice; it had disappeared somewhere.

"I'm sorry," I said eventually.

"Fuck," said Tad, "You actually look sorry. Red like a fucking tomato. Relax." He patted my arm; I grimaced, which was misinterpreted.

"Forget I brought it up. It's been on my mind," he said. He looked at the bottle in his hand as if he'd just noticed it for the first time, and took a hefty swig.

"Understandably," I said.

"You know, you actually did me a favour. But tell me: why the fuck did you get a *daughter* into it?"

I shrugged.

"I overheard a secretary use that excuse to take off," I said. "It sounded good."

"Yeah," said Tad. "It's good, all right." He giggled and rolled his eyes.

"What do you mean by saying I did you a favour?" I asked, after a cautious pause.

Tad sighed. He swished the slops round in his bottle, staring at it as if seeking inspiration.

"You remember the time I was crying in my beer and telling you I can't write?" he asked eventually.

"You did that many times, Tad," I reminded him. "Which one do you have in mind?" It was his turn to look like a fucking tomato.

"Yeah. Well, it was bullshit. I can write."

"That's what I always told you," I said patiently.

"Truth is, it's easier to write a couple of clever lines selling toothpaste or beer than it is to write a poem. And they pay so much money for writing about beer." I realized that Tad must have had a few before I arrived: he was slightly drunk already.

"So you've decided to go the artist route?" I asked, and drank some wine to hide the sneer I felt breaking out on my face.

"Fucking right I've decided to go the artist route." He sounded childishly defiant. "I'm tired of selling shit. Have you ever thought we're actually causing social harm?"

I raised an eyebrow. I put the wineglass to my lips and discovered that it was empty.

"I clearly remember you saying that we perform a social service," I said, pouring more wine. "That by helping sell stuff, we guarantee increased production and so, increased employment. Or something like that."

Tad waved a weary hand.

"These were the bullshit days," he said. "I needed that bullshit to reconcile reality with my own ideals. It didn't work."

"I'm glad it didn't work," I said.

"I think you're taking the mickey out of me."

45

"You don't even have a mickey I could take."

"That's because you've taken it already."

I waved my hands, palms out.

"I surrender," I said. My glass was empty again. I refilled it.

"Listen, Tad," I said. "When I called you, I... um... I've been looking around for a job, and there's a chance that someone who doesn't want a single art director might be interested in a team. But from what you say it doesn't sound like you're interested?" I made it a question, because Tad had started to grin.

"What, work with a guy who has imaginary children?" If he was going to get never-ending mileage out of that one, maybe working together wasn't a good idea.

Tad shook his head.

"No, Oscar. I'm through." He was enjoying himself, rejecting a job that wasn't his yet. "I'm not going back to that shit."

"What shit?" I said, exasperated.

"The fucking politics. The constant backstabbing. And the nature of the job. I tell you, we're hurting people."

"Tad, gimme a break."

"No. I mean it. We are. Look at the dumb fucks out there." Obviously, he didn't consider himself to be one. "You know what they're like. You sell them stuff, right? They're so fucking stupid half the time you want to cry. But they want to be happy. How the hell can they be happy?" Tad asked of the ceiling.

"They should drink exclusively Happy Lemonade, trade mark registered," I said wearily.

"Exactly. When in doubt, spend some money. And *we* are there to tell them what to spend it on. Drink this beer and you'll have a dick like a horse. Wash your hair with this shampoo and every guy will have your cunt on his mind while all the other women go green with envy. And they believe us. They'd eat horseshit if you told them it was full of vitamins and natural fibre. I don't want any more of that shit. I'm finished with this." He looked at me expectantly but I drank the wine silently, reflecting that smoking pot while unemployed could harm one's mental health.

"Did you notice I shaved my face?" Tad asked suddenly. I laughed and nodded.

"It's because I don't grimace any more. Well, maybe when I've got a headache. At the office, it felt like I was constantly fighting muscle spasms."

"And what made you grimace so much?" I asked, slowly.

"Things we all said and did. Particularly things I said and did."

"You didn't say much, and did even less," I pointed out.

"Thank God. Otherwise I wouldn't have a face left, by now."

I looked down at my wineglass and twirled it around. It increasingly seemed I could drop any idea of getting myself and Tad hired as a team.

"But Tad," I said imploringly. "You've got to live on something, haven't you? I mean, what do you get for a good poem—ten free copies of the magazine?"

"I can find all the work I need through here," he said, waving at the computer with the flourish of a magician pointing at the rabbit he'd just pulled out of someone's ear.

47

"You must be good with this box," I said wonderingly. There was what's popularly known as a pregnant pause.

"Tell me, Tad," I said, voicing a thought that suddenly popped into my head as I sat looking at the cramped room, "Tell me something. What do you use the other room for—taking long, after-dinner walks?"

"It used to be my girlfriend's room," said Tad. "She split soon after I, after you and I got fired."

"How disgusting," I said. Tad looked uncomfortable.

"Actually, it was worse than that," he said, after a while. "I told her to move it myself. She was constantly at my throat about getting a new job. And while I still had a job, she was always telling me how she pined for the days when I was but a penniless poet."

"Yes, but what's with the room?"

"She accused me of coveting it for myself. Told me that was the main reason I told her to shove off. So naturally I can't use it now. She visits, sometimes."

"I see," I said.

There was a long pause, and it wasn't one of those pregnant pauses. It was a singularly barren pause; neither of us had anything left to say. Tad stared at his bottle and after maybe half a minute made the discovery that he'd ran out of fuel. He excused himself and got up. The refrigerator door wouldn't close the first time around and I heard him spit out a curse and kick it shut.

I left the new, holy Tad alone with his beer very soon after that.

48

The Australian hotshot had made it crystal-clear he wanted a team; I didn't even bother calling him again. Instead, I set my sights on the Christmas season, remembering Jerome Stuart's assertion that things would change then.

Mindful of Stuart's wisdom, I also spared no effort continuing to look for freelance work. However, my efforts were mostly unsuccessful, although I did get a tour of a Girdle Museum set up by a manufacturer of hosiery. I'd actually contacted him because I'd heard he wanted a catalogue; I got the tour instead.

The manager and owner of the hosiery operation took me around the museum's three rooms in person. He was a tall, lanky man with big bony wrists and a shock of short blond hair that contrasted oddly with the frown ploughed into his forehead. He only needed a dog collar to look every part the disapproving parson. While we stood in front of one of the cabinets and looked at the complicated webbing meant to envelop a woman's waist and hips, he told me, in a reverential tone, that all the girdles had been designed and made by men—older men. He sounded as if it was deeply significant. In the end, he didn't want me to do his catalogue.

Then, Christmas came. The anticipated flood of hirings turned out to be a trickle from a half-closed tap. Some people got hired; others got fired. Jerome Stuart got me two interviews; neither went well.

Donna clustered round: she invited me to dinner on Boxing Day. We ate her family's Christmas leftovers and talked about a lot of things without actually talking about anything. She told me that she'd actually managed to rent out a room—my former study—to one of her numerous cousins.

"He needs an inexpensive place to stay, and I can use some help around the house," she said. I just nodded silently.

When we got to coffee, I got to meet the cousin who'd decided to rent a room from Donna. It was none other than the infamous Fabio, the guy with the flair for turning speeding tickets into drug possession charges. He was a handsome young man; tall, well built, with long black hair slicked back with gel. He passed through on his way to his room; but when he paused briefly to shake hands and introduce himself, he shot me a very knowing look from the bottom of his dark eyes. I had the impression he knew secret things about me, all deduced from clues I'd inadvertently left behind.

When I was leaving, Donna pressed a big buff envelope into my hand, saying it contained papers of mine. I opened it on the train home. There were some old letters, old work samples, and a slim wad of hundred dollar notes held together by a paper clip. I felt doubly humiliated: because she gave me the money, and because I couldn't afford to give it back.

On the first day of the new year—1986—I left my studio and moved into the meat merchant's former house, next to the toilet. The unemployment money was in its last month. I was so broke I was thinking about cancelling the answering service I'd hired on the chance of someone calling with a job offer.

The very next day, I was woken up by a big engine rumbling nearby. My room faced the back; I got up, mystified, and peered out. It had snowed again during the night; everything stood out in stark black and white. The back gate—wrought iron like the fence, likely dating back to the meat merchant days—the back gate was wide open, and there were fresh tire tracks in the snow.

There was a blue van parked right under my window. Its side door was open and as I watched a man emerged, carrying a large carton. He jumped to the ground and carefully placed the carton on the lip of the loading floor, wiped his palms on his hips, and took out a pack of cigarettes. He had thick blond hair cut very short, and as he slid a cigarette out he looked up at my window, squinting. I saw a wide, lined forehead with pale eyebrows, had a fleeting flash of pale eyes, square jaw, and a determined thin mouth. Then he bent his head down to light his cigarette.

It was Kross.

CHAPTER FOUR

Kross's arrival caused a small flurry of excitement in the house. He took the other, empty flat! What was more, the very next, very ugly day the men from Bell arrived and valiantly connected a private phone line, which involved climbing a pole in rain mixed with hail. A private phone line, even though there was a payphone conveniently installed on the ground floor! Clearly, we had aristocracy in our midst.

Living in a house that has a web of brass pipes linking all the rooms means overhearing fellow residents a hundred times a day. In the days following Kross's arrival, I repeatedly heard a note of indignant thrill. People laughed too often and too loud, broadcasting the fact that they were happy in their single rooms; happy with the shared toilets, bathrooms, the communal kitchen decorated with smiling cows and pigs.

No one heard Kross laugh. I neither heard nor saw him throughout the first few days following his grand arrival. I did learn his name one morning, while going through the house mail by the front door. An envelope caught my eye because of the Swiss stamp; the sender's name implied a financial institution—it included the word 'Kredit'. It was addressed to an unfamiliar Mark Kross, and by then I knew all of the names living in my house; most received government cheques twice a month (it had made me feel relieved my own government cheques had ceased to arrive; at the studio I'd previously inhabited they were discreetly tucked away in an elegant brass mailbox).

Mark Kross: it was the kind of name Tad would've thought up for what we used to call a lifestyle representative. He had business with a Swiss Kredit institution, too—with solemn, suited gentlemen in wire-rimmed spectacles, keys snicking in well-oiled locks, bricks of cash hidden in steel vaults. I was curious. I wanted to meet him.

I literally ran into him the very next day.

It was a historical day in its own right, for I had just decided to take up jogging. I'd woken up feeling fucked up beyond repair. If only I could run away from all this, leave all this behind—but of course I couldn't, so I did the next best thing, and went out for a morning run for the first time ever. At least I wasn't wearing the latest in designer kiddie gear: I'd retrieved a pair of shorts I used to wear when playing soccer, back in the early pleistocene. They pinched my waist.

So: I'd just left the house and was running towards the nearest intersection, maybe a hundred paces away. I'd noticed two construction guys in blue overalls examining the dilapidated mansion on the corner: not unlike the meat magnate's, but on a smaller scale, and in a terrible state of disrepair. It didn't look lived in; it looked haunted.

The construction guys were wearing white hardtops; as I approached, I saw that one of the helmets featured a marijuana leaf and the motto 'Born to Build' deftly executed in black marker. The guy under the helmet had a beard and an incipient beer belly, and seemed to be frowning at the ruin on the corner—as I passed, he scratched the back of his neck in a doubtful manner. Parked nearby was what I took to be the guys' runabout: a four-wheel drive on an elevated chassis, with all sorts of grim-looking odds and ends attached: it only lacked a machine gun mounted on top. It was an interesting vehicle, and I didn't notice Kross until he was right in front of my face.

He was running along the street intersecting mine; he was about to cross the road. He wasn't wearing kiddie gear. He wore long camo pants with big, floppy pockets on the sides, the pant legs tucked into the ankle cuffs of brown leather boots that resembled the paratrooper footwear some of the stylish crowd had taken to wearing recently. His upper half was clad in a grey sweatshirt, and I caught a glimpse of a wide dark strap on his left wrist as his arm swung down. He ran past without a glance, splashing snow and water.

I wanted to speak to him, even if it was to be something as inane as a shouted greeting. I turned and started following him. I could tell he became aware of me right away. He lengthened his long, loping stride still more and practically left me standing within half a block. I stopped, gasping and wheezing, my joke Jello legs burning and twitching; I had to claw at a wire fence for support. Fortunately, no one was watching. After a while, I moved off in a chastened trot, heading home.

I made it with teeth bared from pain. As I stood by the front door, wondering whether the molten lead in my thighs would let me make it up the stairs, the door to the caretaker's flat opened with a sharp crack. Mister Natarajan, superintending officer (that's what it said on the card pinned to his door) came bounding out, waving a FedEx envelope in an agitated manner.

"Mister Hansen! Mister Hansen!" he warbled excitedly. "Special delivery for you." I nodded wordlessly—I still hadn't gotten my breathing right—and extended a hand.

"I do hope it's good news," gurgled the Natarajan. His dark eyes implored me to let him in on the secret.

"I hope so too," I wheezed, and crawled up the stairs.

I examined the FedEx waybill before opening the envelope. It had been sent by Donna. The company was listed as Abner, Hansen, & Gutowski—Donna had been made a full partner, and I tore the envelope open rather savagely.

There was another envelope inside: a hand-addressed, heavy cream paper, *personal* envelope. Inside this second envelope was a handwritten, personal letter. It spoke warmly of all my virtues as a man and human being. It regretted that my positive qualities, and Donna's too, failed to bloom fully in what the letter called the greenhouse of our marriage. Donna had always been very fond of colourful similes and metaphors that teetered on the edge of good sense, and I'd always disliked that. It was one of the reasons we talked less and less as time went on.

Anyway, the upshot of all this stunted growth was that Donna wanted a divorce. We had been separated for a year, so we met the legal requirement. She proposed a simple, no-fault divorce without any messy asset-splitting or alimony-setting (her words). She proposed to keep the house and offered me the car (empty offer; I couldn't afford it). She thought it would be only fair if we split the divorce costs in half.

The whole process would be handled by a lawyer she knew at another legal firm. He was a genius whose divorces were minor works of art, and had magnanimously agreed to handle the case for only $1,000—a tiny fraction of his usual fee. I reflected that I'd seen ads touting divorces from $200, but of course Donna wouldn't agree to a divorce handled by any less than one of the best law firms in the city (and it was a big city). Anyway, the bottom line was that my share of the whole thing would come to five hundred dollars, which I didn't have.

I sank down on to the edge of my bed and rubbed my face, as if that would produce a solution. There was a ponderous, tentative cough from across the wall, followed by a scratchy retching noise; the old man next door was conducting exploratory fire prior to the main bombardment. His unseen hand turned on the radio; there was a blare of tinny music. Like all the inhabitants of the house, he was the soul of discretion; he preferred to cough his lungs out under the cover of pop rock.

The music ended abruptly and a cheerful male announcer came on. He informed everyone it was a beautiful day, and proceeded to enumerate some of the attractions available to the paying consumer. The newest Cannes Festival winner was opening at five movie theatres. There was a hockey match today that promised to be a grand spectacle –

I tuned out, my mind working on this last piece of information.

My brother Todd was in town.

It was dark by the time I arrived outside the arena where Todd was making several thousands of dollars per hour for chasing and occasionally hitting a puck with a stick. I timed things so I would arrive about twenty minutes before the end of the match, and activated a long chain reaction by informing the doorman that I was Todd's brother, and had to speak to him about an urgent family matter immediately following the game (here, I prodded him with a driver's license which identified me as a Hansen). Then I waited, watching.

The doorman—a tall, middle-aged guy with a crafty look—sauntered over to a guy wearing a tie, a blue blazer, and a look of satisfied boredom. The blue blazer tilted his head to listen to the doorman's short speech; then he nodded, his expression changing to that of displeased boredom. He looked around and bent an upraised finger to someone out of my field of vision. A sweeper in blue overalls appeared, broom in one hand, shovel in the other. The blue blazer briefed him on the situation and sent him scurrying away at a half-trot. I hoped that after another five or ten relays the message would get to the shower attendants before Todd finished washing after the match, and disappeared into his usual maelstrom of post-game debauchery that would keep him incommunicado for the next few days.

I moved a few steps away from the big glass doors and stared at the traffic. It was a warm evening; the southern wind was rapidly whittling down the miniature icebergs lining the road to small black lumps of city dirt. The wet asphalt gleamed and glittered and there was a certain shrillness in all the street voices, almost as if it were spring already.

"Tickets?" an anxious voice rasped right at my side. I gave a start.

The guy by my side was the ultimate in human weasels. He was barely over five feet, with thin bow-shaped legs encased in crusty jeans. He had a leather jacket that was at least a size too small, with cuffs halfway up his forearms and its waist flopping around his ribs. He wore a red baseball cap, and dirty sneakers at the other end; his pointed, whiskered mug was split in a wide smile—he obviously enjoyed startling people, even though at his life level it could be a dangerous pastime.

"Tickets?" he repeated urgently. "Golds. Incredible deal. Just fifty bucks each."

I looked down on the two printed slips he was thrusting at me. He had long, cracked, dirty fingernails. His hand resembled an animal paw.

"Golds," he repeated. "Best seats in the fucking house. A real trip."

I half-turned and looked at the entrance to the arena. There were unexpectedly many people behind the glass doors; some were coming out. I turned back to the Weasel.

"Look, pal," I said, "The game's over."

It was as if I had called his mother a bad name. He shrank away, his half-open mouth curving into a horseshoe of fear and loathing; he raised his shoulder as if he was expecting to be struck. Then he turned and walked away, muttering something, slapping the tickets against his leg.

"Made a new friend?" said Todd. I jerked round, irritated; I had been crept up on yet again.

Todd looked every inch the sports superstar, with blond locks freshly coiffed into an insouciant lion's mane, the tips brushing his shoulders. He was wearing a stylish, long black cashmere overcoat and a big boyish grin that revealed perfect teeth. I knew many were false; he'd lost a few while making a living. Nevertheless, there wasn't the slightest doubt who was the real Nordic god.

"You look great," I said.

"You don't," he said. You get the idea why I don't see Todd often, right? Of course I could have effortlessly demolished him with a couple of well-chosen words—I was his older brother, after all. But I needed something from him that night and as they say, it pays to be civil. So I remained silent, although sorely tempted to remind him of the time I'd caught him trying to eat his own shit (my vigilance had been sparked by the absence of the usual bawling for someone to wipe his two-year-old ass).

He looked left, he looked right, he looked back at me. He said:

"Why all this messaging? Why didn't you just call me?"

"I don't have a cellphone anymore. And I didn't copy the directory to a notebook. Sorry."

"No big deal. Let's go and get a drink," he said. He started walking without waiting for an answer, and I fell in obediently.

"Did you guys win, tonight?" I asked, as we waited for the light to change. Todd grimaced lightly and made a small, dismissive gesture with his black-gloved hand.

"A tie," he said. After a pause, he added:

"I scored one."

"Hey," I said, surprised and impressed. "Congratulations."

We didn't speak again until we'd sat down in the bar Todd had led us to. It was a ritzy glass-and-metal place called Stars and Bars. I told Todd I thought there was a book or a movie called Stars and Bars.

"A lot of Americans come here," he said, as if that settled everything. He got a double scotch for me (ignoring my request for a beer), and a double vodka and tonic for himself. He was on his third drink by the time we'd gone through the family small talk and got to the real issues. I updated him as to my professional status, financial status, and also the upcoming change in my marital status. It was tiring business.

"Glad to hear the news ain't all bad," Todd said thoughtfully. He was silent for a while, searching for the right phrase, the right compromise between what he really thought and what he thought he should say.

"Look," he said eventually, "How much do you need?"

I reddened a little.

"I still haven't found a job." I said.

"You told me. But you know what? It's not the end of the fucking world." Todd toasted that thought with half the contents of his glass.

"The only enemy you've got is yourself," he announced pompously.

"Oh yeah?"

"Yeah. You wanted to be a painter, right? But you chickened out, and became a sort of sophisticated salesman of toilet paper instead." Thus spake Thor, I mean Todd, and finished his vodka and tonic.

"I've never done any ads for toilet paper," I said patiently, "Just face tissue."

"Let's not fuck around, Oscar. Point is, sometimes you gotta take a chance, you know?"

"Let's not fuck around," I agreed. "Point is, you just don't know how fucking lucky you are." Todd shook his mane determinedly.

"Luck has nothing to do with it," he said. "I knew what I wanted, and I went for it."

"Well, what I wanted was some security," I told him. Todd nodded agreeably, as if I'd just made his point for him.

"Cheers," he said, hoisting a freshly arrived vodka and tonic.

"You're not letting these get warm, are you."

"I've got two days off."

"What will you be doing?"

"Going to a cottage with a girl."

"Boy," I said, "Some guys *do* live."

"Yeah," said Todd. "You should give it a try, too. Sometime."

"Maybe I will," I agreed. I was drinking my third free whisky, and besides I couldn't afford to be disagreeable.

Todd refreshed himself again with the remaining contents of his glass, then dug out a very large black wallet and started pulling out brown hundred-dollar bills. He ran out rather quickly and peered inside the wallet as if there was a stash of notes hidden in a secret compartment.

"Shit," he said, slipped his fingers inside, and extracted a wrinkled, bent joint. He put it carelessly in his overcoat pocket. He had been wearing his Dracula-style overcoat throughout the evening, unbuttoned to show a ritzy cream silk scarf. Apart from that, he wore a simple white T- shirt and black jeans bottomed out by a pair of sleek ankle boots.

"Here's six hundred," he said. I noticed he'd kept a couple of bills back. "You still haven't told me how much you need."

"Just something to tide me over for a month or two." Todd nodded thoughtfully, and produced a chequebook from the inside pocket of his coat. It was like a magic cloak, this overcoat; he'd probably have another dozen items distributed among its well-cut, invisible pockets, ranging from condoms to cocaine. He wrote busily, tore the cheque off with one decisive tug, and handed it to me.

"Here," he said. "That do you?" He'd made it out for two thousand dollars. I knew it wouldn't cause him any particular pain—he'd told me he was currently getting six hundred thousand a season, plus bonuses and miscellaneous advertising deals on top of that.

"That's terrific, Todd," I said. "It's more than I need."

"Use it to live a little." Todd grinned and slapped me on the arm.

We had one more drink apiece before Todd said that he had to link up with the girl to whose cottage he was going the next day. He revealed that he'd been supposed to meet her earlier, put her off for a couple of hours in order to help out his older brother.

By that time, we were standing just outside the entrance to Stars and Bars. It was noticeably colder than when we went in.

"You gonna be all right?" Todd asked, sniffing out the street like an impatient dog.

"Thanks to you," I said. "I'll try and give it back as soon as I can."

Todd shrugged and winked, pulling on his gloves.

"Wait a couple of years," he said and grinned, raising his black leather hand in farewell. I stared at his receding back for a while. Wait a couple of years. That was what I used to say to him, a long time earlier, when he was still a couple of years younger than me.

CHAPTER FIVE

On the way back home, I stopped at the liquor store and purchased the biggest, most expensive scotch I could find ($146.50, tax *compris*, for forty ounces of single malt with one of those Scot names that sound like someone throwing up). Possibly the purchase was caused by Todd's exhortation to live a little. And of course the whiskies I'd drunk with Todd had made me feel better, so having more was the natural thing to do. Nevertheless, the rustling paper bag with its sloshing contents somehow made me furtive. When I got back to the meat merchant's house I opened the front door as if I were a burglar, and crept up the stairs every inch the Invisible Man.

There was a light on in Kross's flat: a soft golden mist lined the bottom of his door. I stood in front of mine, key ready. I didn't want to drink alone; there's no such thing as drinking alone, anyway. When you drink alone you end up talking in your head to long-forgotten people, sometimes even writing letters to girlfriends ditched with relief half a lifetime earlier. I looked at the light, hesitating; then I slipped the key back into my pocket and crept up to Kross's door.

I made almost no sound; one disgruntled floorboard gave out a muted fart. I stopped maybe a foot away from the door, still clutching the big bottle of whisky in its paper bag. I listened; someone was talking in one of the rooms downstairs; there was a muffled voice—I made out the word 'rosebud'—and a soft giggle. It reminded me why I hadn't wanted to socialize with any of the other tenants. Until now.

I strained to hear anything from behind the door in front of my face, but Kross's flat was as still and quiet as the proverbial tomb. I raised my free fist to knock, and hesitated. Somewhere in the house, an old, tired beam groaned softly.

"Come in."

I stared at the door with a sagged lip.

"Come in. Don't make me get up to get you."

I went in.

Kross was seated in the seedy armchair that was part of the flat's rented furnishings, in front of a scarred coffee table that featured a large tin ashtray and a cigarette unrolling a ribbon of smoke. He had an open magazine propped up on his lap; one of his hands was hidden behind it, as if he had been masturbating secretly. He wore black jeans and a thick grey handknit sweater with a cable motif. His feet were resting on the coffee table, and his socks didn't match: one was black, the other grey.

"Your socks don't match," I said. "Isn't it odd how washing machines seem to feed on socks?"

"You a launderette owner?"

"No, I'm an unemployed art director," I said. "I thought that being fellow inmates and all we could share a nightcap. Unless you have art that needs directing right this minute."

I made the paper bag rustle promisingly. He watched me without smiling for a couple of seconds, but that didn't shake me. I'd become used to the fact that people didn't smile at me as often as they used to when I was gainfully employed, and lived in a world-class area.

"Sure. I'll get some ice," he said finally. He got up and I noticed a slight awkwardness in the way he handled the thick magazine—I had the impression he didn't want me to see what it was about. He took it with him into the kitchen; maybe it was a porn mag, and he *had* been giving his gonads the occasional friendly rub. I went up to the coffee table and deposited the bottle, twisting the bag into a paper truncheon and smacking my leg with it as I turned around, searching for a receptacle to toss it in and giving the room the once-over at the same time.

That was when I noticed Kross had made an addition to the rented furniture: a big table that effectively took up one end of the room. It definitely hadn't been there when I was shown the flat. It was a makeshift affair, consisting of a piece of white particleboard laid across a pair of wooden trestles, and it featured an interesting item: a small statue, perched atop the matte black case of a laptop computer as if on a pedestal. I moved a step closer to examine it.

It was about a foot high, sculpted from dark, almost black wood that I thought might be ebony: a tall, spindly statue or rather statuette of a man with what I initially took for a goat's head. But its eyes—narrow, slanted nicks in the dark wood—were both at the front; and the round, sucker-like mouth at the end of the long, curved jaw displayed human teeth. The wrists of the long thin arms were joined to the hips; two huge flat hands thrust out on both sides of the smooth pubis, fingers fused into blades. There were no genitals. I picked the statuette up; it was slightly sticky to the touch, and heavier than I expected.

"Put that down."

I did. Then I made a show of depositing the paper truncheon into the wastepaper basket by the table before turning round. Kross was standing in the kitchen doorway with a mug in each hand. One mug was very red, the other vividly green: very Christmassy.

"Sorry. It's an arresting piece," I said, and did Kross's eyes narrow slightly?

"Sit down." It was more or less a command, and I obeyed. I sank into the flat's other armchair; it groaned and wheezed; my knees pretty much touched my chin when I reached out to take the mug Kross offered me. It was the red one. I shook it experimentally, and the ice inside chuckled.

"Sorry about the glasses." He didn't sound sorry. He picked up the bottle I'd brought and whistled softly. "My, my," he said. "Purveyors to the royal family, no less. Judging by the way they've been carrying on, we should be careful with that stuff." He expertly twisted off the cap and poured himself a nearly full mug before handing the bottle to me.

"Oh, I don't mind the glassware at all," I said, pouring. "Though it's probably sacrilege to drink this stuff with ice. I mean, not as far as I'm concerned. But some people..." I let my voice drift away. Kross picked up his smouldering cigarette and looked at it for a moment. Then he said:

"So. What does someone with such a fine taste in scotch do in this fucking dump?"

"It's my fine taste that put me here," I said, and took a swig. It *was* very good scotch. In fact, it was probably the best whisky I'd ever drunk.

"I saw a FedEx employee asking about an Oscar Hansen earlier today," remarked Kross.

"That's me."

"Mark Kross, with a K." He made an odd little bow from the waist.

"I know. I saw an envelope from a Swiss financial institution asking about Mark Kross the other day."

"*Very* nice." Kross smiled and nodded, and there was a new kind of appreciation in his eyes. "Well," he gestured with his mug-less hand, "As you can guess from these surroundings, my promising envelope didn't contain good news."

"Neither did mine," I said, and took another good swig.

"You said you are an unemployed art director?"

"That's who I am," I said gravely. "Special emphasis on the word unemployed." Kross snorted softly.

"Should I bring a box of tissues?" he asked, and I liked him instantly. You're familiar with the routine that follows confessing to a misfortune, aren't you? Your interlocutor's eyes darken with sympathy or dread or both; they touch your sleeve gently, as if you were made of something very brittle, and begin assuring you everything will be all right in the end. It's not true; endings are bad by definition. Anyway, I found Kross's reaction refreshing.

I suppose that was partly why I told him everything, starting with the day I invented a daughter named Bonnie, and going on to describe all the stuff you know already.

And then there was the scotch; it definitely played a decisive role. The Prince of Wales must have been drinking the very same stuff when he expressed his desire to swap places with a tampon.

Kross listened well; I had the impression that he'd done a lot of listening in his lifetime, and it probably made me more candid than I intended. I was on air for quite a while; although my memories of the later part of that evening aren't crystal-clear, I recall glancing at the whisky bottle when I'd finished and noticing that it was half empty. More than half empty, in fact.

I can also recall that when I'd finished, we were both silent for a while. Then I said:

"And you—what do *you* do?"

"Do?"

"For money. How do you make your living, for fuck's sake."

"Oh, that. I'm a security consultant."

"A security consultant? What's that? You walk around in a uniform, looking for broken windows and torn fencing? No, waitamoment," I think I said, probably waving a correcting forefinger. "That's a security *guard*."

"Well, you might say I'm an advisor to the people in charge of the security guards."

"Change the flashlights for more powerful models? Purchase longer nightsticks?" A little sarcastic, but I needed to change my tone after my confession. Kross understood, and nodded amiably.

"Something like that," he said, and activated the whisky bottle.

"Business flat at the moment? I expect that's a good sign. We should all be happy and grateful things are safe and secure," I said darkly. "You've been doing your job too well, Mark."

"Don't call me Mark." I looked at him and he shrugged. "I never liked that name," he said. "It sounds like something dangling from a nostril."

"Yes," I said. "Isn't it sad how we all get named without prior consent. I keep hearing all those stupid jokes about the Academy Awards." Kross didn't laugh or smile, and I liked him that much better.

"So what do I call you then?" I asked. He shrugged again.

"Kross is fine," he said.

"Ah, I see. You're a Christian type of guy." We drank in silence for a while. Then I said:

"I saw my younger brother today in order to borrow some money."

"You've told me already."

I sighed.

"He told me I'm a coward. That I'm afraid of taking risks."

"You've told me that, too."

I sighed again, and said:

"My younger brother is still very young. He thinks life is just a big adventure. Oh, I admit that if someone showed up right now and invited me to look for Blackbeard's treasure or something like that I'd jump at the chance. But that's not *life*."

Kross straightened out in his armchair and lit a cigarette. He watched me through the smoke for a while, and said:

"Well, what is it then?"

I didn't even attempt to answer that. I stared at the melting ice cubes in my mug. Kross flicked the lid on his Zippo lighter a couple of times. Eventually he said:

"Let me tell you a story."

Is it cheerful? I could use a cheerful story."

"It's entertaining for sure."

"Then go right ahead."

"In the summer of 1812," Kross said after a dramatic pause, "Around the time Napoleon was marching on Moscow with his Grand Army, a thirty-gun British frigate named *Swallow* left Plymouth, and set sail for the African coast." He took a long drag on his cigarette, and blew smoke at the ceiling.

"The *Swallow* wasn't a very nice ship," he resumed. "In fact, in those days life aboard *any* ship was hell. And it was even more hellish on board of the *Swallow*, because her crew consisted of possibly the worst bunch of ruffians in the whole Royal Navy. Practically all of the men aboard had been press-ganged—you know what that means? No? It means they were kidnapped by a marine patrol, dragged on board of the ship, and kept in irons until it left port.

"The captain, a guy called Connacher, wasn't much better. He believed war was an opportunity for personal profit, and stole much more than was customary from the money he received for provisioning the ship. He also took bribes, and that was a particularly lucrative sideline just then. Britain had recently outlawed slave trade. The *Swallow* had been specifically sent out on slaver patrol, but somehow she failed to stop a single slave ship. And of course Connacher

72

took advantage of every opportunity to trade the proverbial glass beads for gold and gems. And now we come to an important point. Connacher kept his loot in a trunk, right in his cabin on the ship. This was found out by his first lieutenant, a freshly promoted young man called Avery."

"I know that name. Wasn't he a famous pirate?" I said.

"No, the Avery I'm talking about was not related to the pirate. Now shut up and listen," said Kross, pouring more booze, which silenced me very effectively.

"The *Swallow* had hardly taken station off the African coast," he resumed, "When the crew started to grumble. There was the food, or rather the lack of it. Also, when the ship was overhauled before before the journey, some of the rotten oak was replaced with teak. Teak is as hard as oak—but its splinters are poisonous. And in a battle between wooden ships, most wounds..." Kross shrugged, and I remember envisioning a hedgehog-like sailor. He lit a fresh cigarette, and continued:

"Every month or so, the *Swallow* stopped to pick up fresh water, fruit, and vegetables at an anchorage off a place called Dixon's Cove, which featured a fishing village and a British fort. It wasn't always possible to put to shore right away, especially once the rainy season had started. And on one of these occasions, the shit hit the fan.

"The *Swallow* threw down her anchor off Dixon's Cove just before midnight, in a sea that was boiling under the pounding rain. Avery recorded this fact in the ship's log, then gritted his teeth and went for a final round of the decks. He heard raised voices, and ended up eavesdropping outside the crew's quarters in the forecastle. The sailors were preparing to mutiny; the *Swallow* was moments away from becoming a pirate ship."

"You said your Avery wasn't a pirate."

"Shut up. Avery ran to warn Connacher, who panicked. He ordered Avery to lock the ship's steering wheel and lower the stern dinghy. He intended to go ashore, and return in the morning with a boatload of troops from the fort.

"Avery did what he was told to. No one noticed him; the rain had swept the decks clean. Then he went to get the captain, and got a surprise. Connacher insisted on taking along a large, heavy trunk. Avery protested: speed and stealth were important, and they were to return to the ship anyway in the morning. But Connacher refused to budge without the trunk, and finally bought Avery's agreement with a gold guinea. He had to open the trunk to get the money, and that was when Avery realized that it contained Connacher's life savings. The stolen Navy money, the bribes, profit from Connacher's private transactions—it had all added up to quite a lot by that time."

"So now that Avery knew his secret, Connacher had to kill him. Right?"

"Shut up and listen. The next morning, the colonel in command of the garrison at Dixon's Cove was told a man claiming to be a British naval officer wanted to speak to him. The man introduced himself as lieutenant Avery, but couldn't produce any proof of his identity—he was naked except for a pair of breeches. He told the colonel there had been a mutiny offshore, and that he and the ship's captain had barely escaped with their lives. Unfortunately, Avery added, shortly thereafter their boat capsized, and the captain drowned.

"The colonel was suspicious. The fort's guards hadn't reported any ships offshore. True, it was still raining heavily, and visibility was very poor; according to Avery, that was why Connacher had been afraid to anchor closer to shore. But no explanation could alter the fact that allowing a mutiny wasn't what was expected of a naval officer. The colonel stopped short of putting Avery under arrest; instead, he had him promise he would not venture outside the fort. Later that day, when the rain eased, he sent out a sloop to look for the *Swallow*. But it wasn't there, and no one ever saw the *Swallow* again. A search of the coast yielded nothing, not even Connacher's body. And within a fortnight, Avery broke his parole and disappeared into the jungle."

"I bet he recovered all that money from a hiding place and became a local sultan or chief or whatever, with a harem of hot chicks and so on," I said.

"Not quite. Now let's fast-forward twenty years, to the eighteen thirties. France is conquering northwestern Africa. In the process, French troops liberate a white slave. It's our friend Avery, and he's not well—in fact he's close to dying. He makes it to England, but dies just a year or so later in a Sussex village. Before he dies, however, he has many long conversations with the local vicar. He tells the vicar about himself, and about the fabulous treasure he'd left hidden on the West African coast. If the vicar helps him, body and soul—settling the outstanding bill at the inn, taking care of the funeral, and so on—Avery swears to reveal the exact whereabouts of this treasure. It's all yours, he tells the vicar. Do whatever you like with it. Build a new church, fund an orphanage, maybe start eating a little better."

"How noble of him," I sneered. "He knew he wouldn't live to spend it."

"Greenbottle—that was the vicar's name—wasn't excited by Avery's offer. He'd been the shepherd of his little flock for over thirty years, and had already listened to a lot of deathbed pledges, received many donations from dying people hoping to buy a blissful eternity. A gold mine in Brazil and a castle in Scotland, to mention a couple. So he simply added Avery's African treasure to the list."

"Wise man. Say, how do you know all this?"

Kross allowed himself a smile of superiority.

"Because something about Avery must have impressed the vicar," he told me. "A few years later, he decided he'd like to continue providing spiritual guidance even after death, and wrote a long manuscript consisting of moral teachings thickly spiced with real-life examples. When he'd finished, he had the manuscript bound into a book.

"The vicar duly died, and his book was stuck in a drawer. Probably everyone was sick of his sermonizing, and had no desire to read what they'd already heard a thousand times. The book stayed in the drawer, and the chest of drawers stayed in the vicarage for nearly two hundred years. Then, quite recently, the vicarage had a jumble sale. Greenbottle's masterpiece was bought by a tourist: a nice Canadian girl bicycling through Sussex. She did try to read it, but didn't get far. I don't blame her. *I* read it, and I'm glad I wasn't a member of Greenbottle's flock. Mind you, he did a pretty racy piece on adultery."

"You *read* it?"

"Yes. We sort of lived together until just recently. Me and the girl, not Greenbottle. Obviously."

"And that book's where you read about the treasure." Kross nodded slowly, and said:

"He used it as an example in a sermon on the evils of making false promises. The Brazilian gold mine and the Scottish castle both rated a mention. Avery's treasure filled five pages. Somehow, Greenbottle didn't neglect to include a full description of its location."

"You mean to say the treasure's really there? Still there?"

"Sure it is. I even know the exact spot."

"But what stopped Avery from picking it up after he left the fort? It doesn't make sense."

"He *did* pick up the money and the gold. He hoped to buy his way home. Uncut diamonds weren't exactly a viable currency, so he left them behind, to collect later. But the locals who were supposed to help took his money and the gold, then sold him to Arab slave traders. Arabs had been buying African slaves long before Europeans showed up on the scene. And the local people, the black Africans—who do you think sold the slaves to the traders, in the first place? A tribe would raid a neighbour, capture as many people as they could, and sell the slaves they didn't want to keep for themselves. Black Africans were as complicit in the whole business as the Arabs and the Europeans."

"I find that really hard to believe."

"Unpleasant truths are always hard to believe."

"But why didn't you pick up those diamonds by yourself already, if you know the exact spot?"

"Because I found out about the treasure just recently. Gave me a shock. Fifteen years earlier, I was standing right next to it, totally unaware of its existence."

"Fifteen years earlier? I don't understand."

"After my discharge from the army, I signed a contract to help train the Ghanaian military. Scored a bullseye: good pay, plenty of free time. Been doing that kind of thing ever since. Anyway, while I was in Ghana I visited the spot where Avery hid his treasure. It's a very special place. Shunned by the locals, they think it's haunted. And it isn't mentioned in any tourist guides."

"You're absolutely sure those diamonds are still there?"

"Yes, I'm sure. Want to go and get them?"

CHAPTER SIX

I didn't really get it until the next day. It started badly.

I woke up and just managed to make it to the toilet next door where I proceeded to wear the toilet seat the way a horse wears its collar. When I'd finished retching, I sprinkled the place with my aftershave and returned to my room and sat on my bed, holding my head in my hands—it felt as if it was falling apart. Once I'd gotten my breathing right, I got the electric kettle going and made myself a mug of instant coffee, which was a mistake: it necessitated another hurried trip to the can. After that, I sat down on the bed again and tried to remember what had happened in Kross's flat.

After a while, I recalled that there was a second bottle present at the scene: something really toxic that Kross had extracted from his fridge once we'd run out of scotch. I remembered following him into the flat's tiny kitchen, and seeing the magazine lying on the sideboard: the magazine Kross had been reading when I made my entrance. It was a fucking gun magazine.

I jumped up from the bed as if it had bitten me on the ass and started pacing my cell. It all came back: I remembered Kross telling me how, after five years in the army, he did a stint in the Republic of Ghana, training members of its armed forces on armoured cars. He even said he'd been to the place where it was hidden—unaware of its existence!

And now, many years later, he couldn't enter the country for some reason—there was something fishy there—I couldn't remember what he'd said, but remembered my disbelief. He'd also told me he needed someone who could go and pick the loot up for him in exchange for a share, something in the upper five figures, and that I volunteered.

"Fuck. *Fuck!* " I said.

There were two sharp, decisive knocks on my door. I froze in mid-step. Then I slowly sat down on the bed again, trying to make no sound.

Unfortunately, I'd forgotten to lock the door. It opened and Kross marched in. He was holding a familiar red mug, and I flinched instinctively.

"You're alive," he said. I smiled weakly.

He marched up to the window and deposited the mug on the sill; it was full of liquid that made sloshing sounds. Then he unwrapped a piece of silver foil to reveal a large, flat white tablet. He dropped it in the mug—plop, fizz, hiss. He said:

"Drink this up, get your passport, and let's go."

"But why me?" I said, straining to keep pace with Kross as we hurried down a busy downtown street. "I know you told me. I want to hear it again. Why me, not one of your bosom pals? Surely you have plenty."

"Not any more."

"Why?"

"Some have retired, and some are dead. "

That shut me up, but shortly I tried again.

"But you only met me yesterday."

"Doesn't bother me. I'm a good judge of people." I was probably expected to take this as a compliment, and dissolve in smiles and curtsies.

"I'm not," I said. Kross stopped and looked at me.

"Well if that's so it's lucky I'm around, isn't it?" he said, and pushed open the door to the airline office.

I watched him approach the counter, slap down our passports, and enter negotiations. I lingered by the entrance in a state of mild panic.

Of course I'd tried to think of a way to wriggle out of this while I was looking for my passport. But I only had a couple of minutes because there already was a cab waiting, and couldn't come up with any good excuses in that short time. In the cab, Kross finally explained that we were going to the Ivory Coast consulate to get visas, and once that was done—to get airline tickets. That was reassuring because I'd heard, at one time or other, that obtaining a visa for an African country required filling out innumerable forms and a long wait, sometimes weeks and weeks. Plenty of time to think of a way to make a graceful exit.

I was disabused of this notion very quickly. Kross had a magic track to the consul, and after conducting a short and pleasant-sounding conversation in French with the receptionist he was almost immediately admitted into some inner diplomatic sanctum, leaving me wriggling on the cushions of the reception sofa. I tried to think of a good excuse to at least slow down the proceedings a little, but before ten minutes had passed Kross reappeared, triumphantly bearing our passports stamped with the visas.

Following that, we hurried straight to the Air France office—Kross insisted on booking our flight through official airline channels: no fucking around with travel agents for this guy. I followed him making weak bleating sounds and eventually attempted to halt the proceedings by informing Kross that I was broke. But Kross told me that the issue had already been discussed in detail the previous night, and that he was handling the initial investment, as he put it.

And so I stood by the entrance to the Air France office, watching Kross work his magic. Following a short conversation with the clerk, he barely had the time to turn his head and grin at me before he was whisked off to a back office by an older guy wearing a suit. He was gone for a long time. I paced back and forth by the entrance, too uptight to sit down, fighting a growing panic. What was happening felt unreal. The worst thing was that I couldn't find a way to stop it without making a complete ass out of myself. But then I thought: why not? I'd already made a complete ass out of myself the previous night. I'd be consistent, and consistency was a virtue.

I began to work on a list of illnesses that could knock me out at short notice, making any travel plans null and void. It wasn't easy because I'd have to convincingly fake the symptoms. Kross reappeared by my elbow just as I was contemplating acquiring a head cold—it wouldn't be hard at this time of the year—and claiming life-threatening influenza.

"We're booked for the fifteenth," he said, handing me my passport together with an airline ticket wallet.

"But that's a week from now!"

"Correct. Get vaccinated in the meantime—the sooner the better, you might feel lousy for a couple of days. Make sure you've got the right gear to wear, especially footwear. I strongly recommend desert boots; no runners, basketball hightops, or any of that city sportsman shit. I'll be back by the weekend, so we'll still have time to sort out the details."

"Wait," I said, extremely alarmed. "What's this—you're going away?"

Kross laughed.

"You can definitely hold your liquor," he said. "You didn't seem to be that far gone, last night. In fact, you kept insisting you want more."

"I did?"

"You also insisted you have to see Greenbottle's book with your own eyes before we leave, so now I'm going to get it. And Sharon—the girl who's got it—lives on the west coast. Remember now? Hello? Anybody there?"

He was going to get Greenbottle's book!

"Can't she just courier it over?" I asked.

"Sharon's a moody chick. She appreciates subtlety," Kross told me. He dug out his keys and slipped one off the ring. "Look," he said, "Why don't you use my flat while I'm away? I don't want you sitting in that hole of yours and getting depressed. Help yourself to the aguardiente if you feel like it." So *that* was the name of the poison that did me in. I stared stupidly at the key Kross was offering me; eventually, I reached out and took it.

83

"Don't drink and blab, and don't forget to get your stake together," Kross said.

"My what?!"

"Christ. Your stake. Five thousand American, three in cash. You're getting at least a quarter million in return, right? Fuck. You *were* wiped." Kross's eyes narrowed with suspicion. He said:

"This is the last possible moment for you to change your mind. I'll restate the basics. You're getting a third of whatever we find. Between a quarter and half a million American dollars. All you'll have to do is take a six-hour drive, and spend maybe an hour walking through bush. You're getting a generous cut. It's my gig and I'm in charge, which means I'm the one who has to make sure we don't have any trouble along the way. And that includes taking care of customs, and converting whatever we find into cash. Finally, I'm putting up ten grand, and you're putting up five. We need five each for food and transportation and so on, and another five for bribes. So. You invest a third and get a third of the proceeds. Fair and square. In or out?"

This was exactly what I'd been waiting for. I opened my mouth to say 'out' and said instead:

"I'm in."

"Good," grinned Kross. "Go easy on the rocket fuel. See you Friday."

And he was gone before I could tell him I was only joking, that I was out, that there was no way in hell I could raise five thousand American dollars in a few days.

I wondered why the fuck I'd told Kross what I did all the way home. That was a long time, because I got off the streetcar early and then walked: I needed to clear my head. I only understood why I'd said what I said when I reached the house. I looked at the spindly turrets decorating the corners of its roof and felt as if I were returning to jail, after a short pass.

I'd agreed to join Kross in his madcap scheme because *not* agreeing would've been even worse. I'd be running around in a growing panic trying to find a job while my money ran out. I definitely wasn't going on welfare. Having my mail handed to me with a knowing grin—I'd sooner sweep, mop, and scrub the toilets at a bar like The Big One, just so I could afford my rented room.

It would be that or visiting people I knew with hat in hand. I would be going through one hell of a humiliation and each fresh kick in the ass would make me regret very deeply turning down an opportunity to make a ton of money. Maybe as much as half a million American. It was no contest.

As I entered my room, I had the thought it might be wise to find out more about Kross.

Late afternoon found me in Kross's bathroom, conducting a thorough investigation that included the inside and back of the toilet's water tank. I found nothing there. I moved on to examine the contents of his bathroom cabinet; I'd learned this advanced search technique from a woman who claimed she could instantly decipher a man's personality from his cabinet contents: she dove into people's bathrooms the way a cat dives into garbage. But all I found was a small bottle of Bayer's Aspirin, a big bottle of Dettol, some cotton wool, and a box of Band-Aids.

I re-emerged into the living room, blinking at the yellow glare from the western window. I had already looked around the big room, and knew that Kross's laptop was missing, which didn't distress me: I was far from a computer expert, and he was bound to use a password anyway. There wasn't a lot to examine: a telephone book, a notebook-sized blank writing pad, BIC pen, the familiar gun magazine, and a couple of paperback thrillers.

The top page of the writing pad featured light indentations, and I thought about tearing it out and giving it the charcoal treatment in order to work out what had been written on the preceding, missing page. But I wasn't really eager to get into any dirty work, and in any case the dents in the paper were very shallow and disjointed.

I spent a couple of minutes standing in the centre of the room, looking around and becoming increasingly convinced I wouldn't find anything of interest in the flat. Kross wouldn't have given me the key otherwise, would he?

I ran a perfunctory check on the kitchen and found nothing interesting there except for a spider that ran up my arm when I stuck my hand behind the fridge in case something was taped there. It gave me a scare and I slapped it with such fury that it took me a good couple of minutes to wash off the mashed remains. While I was busy doing that, I thought I'd better get used to that kind of thing: from what I knew, Africa had a thriving insect population.

That left the bedroom. I hadn't felt bad about poking around in the public and semi-public parts of Kross's flat, but the bedroom—this definitely was private space. I hesitated for a while. Searching the bedroom didn't feel right, but leaving the job incomplete didn't feel right either. I had the brief hope that the bedroom door would be locked, absolving me from further action. But it swung in freely when I turned the doorknob, and I stepped inside.

It was dark in there: the curtains were drawn. The first thing I focused on was a huge ancient-looking wardrobe made of dark wood. It was complemented by an equally ancient chest of drawers. There was no bed, and for a silly moment I imagined Kross sleeping while reclining in mid-air, just like all the top witch doctors in Africa.

I went over to the window, pulled the curtains back, and noticed an evil-looking hook screwed into the wall right next to the window, about hip height. I turned round and immediately saw the netting of a folded hammock hanging from another hook screwed into the opposing wall. Kross slept in a hammock! It had to be some sort of clue.

The rest of the room wasn't interesting. There was a small table—actually an ancient card table, its top was inset with green felt. A big ugly wooden chair was set against the wall by the chest of drawers: when I examined it from close range, I noticed a very long black hair hanging from the top backrest bar. It definitely hadn't been left there by Kross. It put me on alert, and before opening any drawers I examined them for hairs strategically trapped between the drawer lip and the chest frame, as recommended by James Bond.

I remembered that Bond also recommended searching a chest of drawers bottom to top, so that's what I did. The bottom drawer was empty, and so was the next one. The third one up contained maybe half a dozen T-shirts in white, black, and olive green, plus a number of spotlessly white jockey underpants. This confirmed Kross's superhero status, since I verified they weren't brand new—I checked for things hidden under each item in the drawer, sliding my hand in for a gentle feel. Finally, the top drawer contained socks, around a dozen pairs tied in efficient flat knots; they were all knee-length hose, which was interesting, but then it was winter. The colours—black, grey, khaki—fit a range of military uniforms, but were also popular in a general sense. So, nothing.

The wardrobe's contents were similarly unexciting. They consisted of the pair of camo pants I'd seen him jogging in, two pairs of jeans (blue and black), six long-sleeved shirts (four white, one powder grey, one light blue), a couple of sweatshirts (black, grey) and the grey cable-knit sweater he'd worn the previous night. A thin fistful of ties hung from the clothes hook on the inside of the wardrobe door: one plain black, one dark blue with faint red-gold stripes, and two variations on the black knit mode. There were no suits or jackets of any kind; maybe they were all at a drycleaner's.

I wondered about that for a little while, and while so engaged recalled that Kross had told me he came to Toronto on a job: planning and overseeing the update of the security system of a small company somewhere in the suburbs. It wasn't a well-paying contract, but there was little work around. I remembered vehemently agreeing to that last point, and raising the red mug in a toast to our treasure-finding enterprise.

Finally, I lay down on the floor and looked under the chest of drawers and the wardrobe, just in case.

There was nothing under the chest, and the wardrobe had a curvy, curlicued wooden skirt; I couldn't see a thing. I gritted my teeth and thrust my hand into the darkness, expecting another spider. But none ran out; instead, my fingers encountered something unusual. I palpated gently: a small thin rectangle of something—paper?—had been taped to the underside of the wardrobe. I memorized its exact location, and pulled it free.

It was a business card. The front identified Mark Kross as a Consultant with Vanguard Security Services of 5 Ash Lane, WC1, London, United Kingdom. The logo—a blade cutting through darkness—could equally well represent a manufacturer of lawnmowers. I decided I would call the phone number listed and ask a couple of discreet questions, but when I turned the card over I changed my mind.

The back of the card featured a single word in big blue capitals:

GOTCHA!

After I'd replaced the card Kross had left for me, I returned to my room burning with shame. But within a minute I had a brilliant idea: instead of trying to learn something more about Kross, I could find out more about James Avery, Connacher, and the *Swallow*. The obvious thing to do was look for information on the internet. I hit the communal payphone to ask myself over to Tad's place. I told him I urgently needed help with something and promised to bring beer. That did it.

"I'm doing a bit of personal research," I told Tad, after I'd followed him up the stairs to his flat. "It's not a big deal. I just wondered whether you could look for something for me on the web."

"No problem," said Tad. He seemed to be in high spirits. In fact, the moment I saw him it was evident I was dealing with a new, improved, longer-lasting Tad. He was wearing brand new jeans, a suspiciously crisp cream shirt, and even smelled of good aftershave.

"You look good, Tad," I told him while he was putting the six-pack I'd brought in the fridge. "You look like the man of success."

"That's because I *am* a man of success. I scored a big brochure for an investment fund. Say, do you mind if we start with my Amstel? Let the stuff you brought chill a little."

"Sure. Are you saying someone was naïve enough to give you a commission?"

"Your feeble sarcasm is misplaced. Not someone, an investment fund. A client with really deep pockets. Forty pages of compelling copy for their flagship brochure. I gotta interview a few people, too. A hundred hours easy. And a hundred hours at freelance rates equals three months of regular pay at Shit, Bullshit, and Balls."

"I guess they aren't looking for an art director?"

"They've got an in-house designer. But they thought they could write the copy themselves. After months of trying and failing they saw sense. They'll gladly pay a small fortune just so someone takes it off their hands."

"I'm green with envy," I said, and figuratively speaking it was true.

Tad sat down at his desk, took a hefty swig from his bottle, and fired up his computer.

"Hey," I said, "Sorry to bother you with this."

"Who says I'm bothered?" The modem emitted a series of melodious peeps, then twanged ominously.

"What am I supposed to be looking for?" I'd been thinking about that one all the way to Tad's place—over half an hour—so my delivery was smooth, crisp, and professional.

"Two guys: Jan Hansen, J-A-N, and James Avery. I've found out that one of my great-greats was quite a character."

"That might be difficult," Tad said, typing swiftly. "Didn't you tell me that Hansens were dime a dozen in Scandinavia?"

"That's why I'd like to additionally check out this James Avery. Family lore has it they were close pals. Fellow naval officers and so on. And there's a specific time frame: we're looking at the first half of the eighteenth century. Less than half actually, make it the first thirty years."

"Okay. Anything else?"

"As a matter of fact, yes. See whether you come across any mentions of a Royal Navy frigate called the *Swallow*. Same time frame."

"This won't be easy. There must've been hundreds of ships called the *Swallow*."

"You really don't have to do this right this moment." My tone implied that, nonetheless, he should get it done the very next moment. Tad heard it loud and clear; after all, he'd heard it a hundred times in the three years we'd spent fruitfully working together.

"Just a quick look to have an idea of what's involved." I couldn't see the screen from where I was sitting, but I saw Tad's face being washed by a succession of different lights. The hard drive chirruped and clicked. I drank some beer.

"Wow," Tad said suddenly, "A link to some sort of a pirate fan club. The Brotherhood of the Coast, they call themselves. Sounds like a beach bum trade union." My ears suddenly felt hot: hadn't Kross told me the mutineers intended to turn the *Swallow* into a pirate ship? Tad took his time, clicking languidly and emitting interested grunts and generally being extremely irritating.

"Found something?" I said finally.

"This is far out. The greatest pirate treasure of all times. Hey, you on a treasure hunt or something? May I join?" I ignored his question; I was busy moving my seat alongside his.

"What's this?" I said, jabbing an aggressive finger at the screen, just as if he'd written a particularly silly headline, and obediently he started explaining:

"This guy is answering a query about the circumstances surrounding the death of Bartholomew Roberts—one of the most famous pirates ever, that guy robbed hundreds of ships. Seems his loot has never been found."

"Oh, just shut up and scroll to the beginning," I said. Tad sighed in that special martyred way of his and did as I asked. This is what I read:

"The frigate *Swallow*, under Chaloner Ogle, ended Bartholomew Roberts' pirate career on the 10th of February, 1722, in a sea battle off the Gold Coast (today's Ghana)." Ghana! Kross had spent time in Ghana. I said:

"Seventeen twenty-two? What the fuck is this?"

"You said eighteenth century."

"I said... Oh fuck it. So I did. But you know I always mislabel the eighteen hundreds as the eighteenth century." Tad shrugged innocently.

"Shall I exit this?" he asked, and I almost said yes. Then it hit me: what if Kross *had* lied—a little? Changed the date, a few names—Greenbottle's book? Fuck, that could be faked. And I still had to see proof of its existence.

"I wouldn't mind reading all of this," I said. "It's interesting." And so I read on:

"Ogle had a lot of luck: Roberts commanded a fleet of three ships, which had split up right before the engagement. Even then his flagship, the *Royal Fortune*, with forty guns and a hundred and sixty men aboard, could have proven to be more than a frigate could handle.

"The *Swallow* opened fire with two salvoes of grapeshot, intended to sweep the deck and rigging of the pirate crew. Roberts was on deck of the *Royal Fortune*; according to Daniel Defoe's second-hand account, he 'made a gallant Figure, being dressed in a rich crimson Damask Waistcoat and Breeches, a red Feather in his Hat, a Gold Chain round his Neck, with a Diamond Cross hanging to it, a Sword in his Hand, and Two Pair of Pistols hanging at the End of a Silk Sling (according to the Fashion of the Pyrates;) and is said to have given his Orders with Boldness, and Spirit.'

"Defoe writes that a piece of shrapnel from the second salvo struck Roberts in the throat, killing him instantly. The pirate crew panicked and surrendered, though not before they 'threw him over-board, with his Arms and Ornaments on, according to the repeated Request he made in his Life-time.'

"The marines boarding the 'Royal Fortune' found two thousand pounds of gold dust in her holds. They didn't find any of the precious stones and jewelry Roberts had stolen over the preceding forty months, to say nothing of gold and silver coinage. AFAIK, the value of that treasure is estimated at between twenty and forty million pounds sterling. That makes it the richest pirate hoard in existence—somewhere.

"See also Idiotboy's earlier thread about Long Ben Avery. Defoe insists that he'd been swindled by accomplices who handled the conversion of his jewels into cash, but there is a persistent rumor that the bulk of the treasure he'd stolen from the Grand Moghul of India is hidden somewhere off the East African coast, most probably Madagascar."

"Avery!" I said. "What does AFAIK mean?"

"As far as I know. Yes, Avery and *Swallow*—two matches. That's why this page came up. But your Avery was a James, right? And no mention of Jan Hansen. What I'm gonna do, I'll post a few queries and check on them in a few days. That do you? And hey—what's all this about?"

"Oh, just family folklore," I said. "I visited my folks the other day and the old man told me this story."

"Your old man told you a story? I thought he was practically mute."

"He had a few drinks," I said. Lies are like cockroaches; you start with a couple and they just keep multiplying forever.

"That reminds me," said Tad, rising from his seat and picking up his empty bottle. I said:

"Tad. Do you have any coffee?"

CHAPTER SEVEN

Who was Kross? Why had he chosen me? What was the real origin of the treasure? These three questions kept me awake a long time into the night. Upon returning from Tad's I locked the door, unplugged the phone, and worried my head until I came up with three answers.

One: Kross was an intelligent, efficient security consultant. He'd led me up the path very nicely. He literally had me crawling on the floor right before he slapped me in the face with his business card.

Two: he needed someone to go fetch the loot, and couldn't ask/didn't trust any of his buddies. He could certainly trust me not to cheat him; I wouldn't know *how*, for fuck's sake.

Three: I didn't really care where the treasure came from as long as there actually was one, and I got my cut.

I was cautiously optimistic about staying out of an African jail. Kross had impressed me with his ability to get things done as well as his planning: setting aside money for bribes was smart. I felt that many African customs officers would briefly look the other way for a discreet five hundred or a thousand. It was a question of identifying the right guy, and after all Kross's job was largely concerned with identifying the right guys when required, sometimes before they even showed up on the scene.

I was going on a treasure hunt in Africa! Had someone told me a few months—weeks, days!—earlier I'd be doing something like that, I'd probably call the police.

The very next morning, having shaved and showered and breakfasted, I went to cash Todd's cheque. I checked the current exchange rate at the bank, and found that five thousand American translated into over sixty-seven hundred Canadian. I still had to raise nearly five thousand dollars of the inferior Canadian variety, and I cursed the fact that I'd already made a pass at Todd. I could have hit him for five grand instead of two and a half, and I was sure I could get a couple of thousand from my parents. After all, money is the glue that binds most families.

I kept thinking about how to raise all that extra money all the way back home. I was still trying to solve this problem, as common and pleasant as the flu, when I turned the final corner and saw a familiar black BMW parked in front of the meat magnate's house. Modelling my behaviour on the late Bartholomew Roberts, I smoothed my hair, gave my jacket a straightening tug, and walked on with a purposeful step.

As I passed the car, I heard the ticking of the cooling engine; Donna had just arrived. I turned towards the house and was maybe ten steps away from the front door when it opened, and an elegant Donna emerged. She didn't notice me right away. She was talking over her shoulder to an unctuous Natarajan, whose teeth were bared in a permanent grin as he bobbed and nodded, shoulders rolling as if he was wringing his hands behind Donna's cashmere-clad back. He was both awe-struck and delighted; his world didn't usually include beautiful, elegant women driving expensive cars.

"Hello, Donna," I said, and stopped. I ignored Natarajan; he was just a moustache wriggling on the periphery of my vision.

"Oscar," she said. She turned to dismiss Natarajan with a regal nod. When the front door had thumped shut, Donna said:

"We need to talk. Could we go somewhere?"

A trickle of dread ran down my back; a conversation with Donna was unlikely to be pleasant. I glanced over her shoulder while fishing for an answer, and saw that the grinning Natarajan was eavesdropping right behind the front door: I could clearly see his teeth and moustache through the frosted glass. I said:

"Okay. Lead the way."

As we were approaching the car, Donna said:

"I've been trying to reach you for the past two days. I must have called at least ten times."

"I've been pretty busy trying to find work, Donna. It's not easy."

"You're looking for work, but you aren't collecting messages from your answering service?"

That was it: game over. I said:

"Well, I did spend some time farting around with Tad. There's a chance someone will hire us as a team, and I wanted to make sure he was in the right frame of mind."

"You drink too much, Oscar." Donna leaned forward to unlock the door and got into the driver's seat while I was busy unclenching my jaw—she was the main reason I drank too much. She pressed the button for the passenger door; the lock coughed dangerously. I didn't want to go for a car ride with Donna. I stood by her window until it slid open, then leaned down with an elbow on the roof.

"You didn't tell me why you've been trying to reach me," I said.

"I asked you to call, in the letter. You got my letter, didn't you? I sent it by courier to make sure you did." Of course, she'd have already checked with FedEx.

"Yeah, I got it, but that item must have slipped my mind," I said. "Todd was in town the day before yesterday and I was hurrying to meet up with him." She stiffened; as I might have mentioned, there was no love lost between her and Todd.

"You were too busy to call me," she said. "You can't call me once in months even when I ask you to. Okay. I came here today hoping we could talk. Go somewhere and have a long, meaningful conversation. But you're probably too busy for that, too."

I flinched, and said:

"Talk about what, Donna? You said it all in your letter. You even went ahead and cut us a great deal on the divorce with a hotshot lawyer. Is there anything left to talk about?"

She was silent. She let her hands slide off the wheel and folded them in her lap. Then she looked up at me, squinting oddly, and said:

"Have you got five hundred dollars?"

It was a beautiful shot, but it missed. She should have guessed I hadn't been seeing Todd just for the fun of it.

I straightened up, dug out the roll of hundreds and started counting.

"As a matter of fact, I do have five hundred," I said. "And I also remember I owe you another seven hundred. Here." I put my arm through the window and dropped most of my wad into her folded hands. She reached down beside her seat and pulled out a grey envelope.

"Here," she said, and thrust it at me. I took it reflexively, and she leaned forward and started the engine.

"Goodbye, Donna," I said. She shifted into gear and pressed down the switch to shut the window. I stepped back and watched her drive away. Then I turned round and went home, tapping my thigh with the grey envelope.

I regretted my grand gesture bitterly the moment I returned to my room and to my senses. Twelve hundred dollars! It practically wiped me out; given next month's rent and everyday expenses, I basically had zero of the seven thousand Canadian I needed. I stomped around my cage for a little while before redirecting my attention to the grey envelope.

The envelope hadn't been glued or otherwise fastened shut, and I impatiently spilled the contents onto my bed. They included, to wit: one single-page letter from Donna to myself; one Petition for a Divorce; and finally a receipt from an institution called Hercules Security and Storage. This last document listed all the items I had left in Donna's garage, and informed me the said items were safe in a luxury, air-conditioned cubicle, on premises patrolled by Doberman dogs with diplomas in biting people. Donna had paid around two thousand dollars for a year's storage, including a hefty insurance premium. She'd really wanted my stuff out very badly.

I turned to the letter. It had been carefully crafted: it began with an expression of regret that we could not have a face-to-face talk. It understood my hostility, and forgave me for it. It informed me that it was time to move on so that we could both progress with our individual development, and it detailed the various practical arrangements involved, including the role played by Hercules Security and Storage. The letter ended with the hope that I would take good care of myself and find new happiness and love and luck and all that crap. I nearly shouted with anger, and tore it into confetti.

I subsequently spent a little time tidying things up, and a lot of time sitting on my bed and thinking about money. Then I sprang into action.

I got plenty of change at the corner store and hit the payphone. I called my doctor's office and set up an appointment for noon the next day. Then I talked to my father and advised him I'd be visiting him in the immediate future. He didn't ask why; he just emitted a series of affirmative grunts. I also called my answering service to collect messages and erased them without playing any back. I had no desire to listen to Donna getting shrewish. I had no desire to listen to Donna ever again.

I also made an excursion to purchase some art supplies, and inhale plenty of calories fast at a McDonald's. Then I spent the rest of the afternoon and the whole evening making ads.

Next morning saw me rising at the crack of dawn; around half past seven at this time of the year, so not very painful. I proceeded to brush, shave and shower with special care, conscientiously cleaning all my orifices. Then I spent three hours running around downtown, putting up the posters I'd drawn the previous evening. Flawlessly rendered by my professional wrist, the posters in question advertised an absolutely unique opportunity to acquire a top of the line drafting table, a powerful Mac, and an assortment of functional modern furniture.

I hit the university campus downtown first, targeting all the bulletin boards I could find. I raided vocational colleges and libraries, schools of design and computer training centres, prepared for any eventuality with my small roll of tape and a box of pushpins. I penetrated into a school board building, scandalizing a couple of patrolling matrons. I even buzzed briefly into the no-fly zone around Donna's law office building to score a hit on the promising arts college just a block away.

At twelve sharp, I presented myself and my orifices at my doctor's. My physician is an elderly East Indian gentleman who had spent the first half of his life in Uganda, moving to Canada when Idi Amin began slitting throats. When he heard that I proposed to visit Africa, he shook his head sadly: the water... the food...

He had a wonder vaccine right in his office: a lethal cocktail guaranteed to immunize the adventurous traveller against pretty much everything but AIDS. However, he urged me to satisfy my yearning for tropical delights by visiting the Caribbean instead of Africa—he recommended Aruba. Eventually, he sighed deeply and proceeded with a meticulous examination (including selected orifices) and with the vaccine. He warned I might not feel so good over the next couple of days. Happily, he didn't say I drank too much.

Two o'clock found me aboard a mostly empty bus bound for Peterborough. This unpretentious city is where my parents chose to spend the rest of their lives. My old man likes its inland Ontario location because after forty years of looking at the sea he doesn't ever want to see it again (he doesn't mind lakes). My mother likes it because, as she says a little too often, it reminds her of her childhood home in southern Norway ('only there is so many more trees and bushes here'). They even both claim they like the horrific winters.

It was getting dark when I arrived at their bungalow, half-hidden behind the advertised trees and bushes; it stood in the back half of a large lot surrounded by a white picket fence. I disliked that fence. I had been made to paint it every other summer, which meant not only applying a new coat but also being responsible for the irresponsible Todd. As I opened the gate, I gave the post a sliding kick with the side of my shoe. Hopefully it left a smudge.

There was no light showing in any of the windows. After I had pressed the doorbell a few times at civilized intervals, I heard footsteps shuffling towards the front door; it sounded like all the ghosts of my past approaching.

He had been asleep; the hair on one side of his head was turned the wrong way by the pillow. He opened the door, saw it was me, grunted, and went to the kitchen. By the time I joined him, he'd already poured two half pints of coffee. His hand hovered by the cupboard in which he kept brandy, which suggested my mother wasn't home.

"You hungry?" he asked. I shook my head. He nodded thoughtfully, and took out the brandy. I'd promised myself I *would* cut down on alcohol, but what could I do? I'd come to ask my father for a lot of money. No discordant notes—that was the recommended policy, and anyway my old man never had more than three drinks in one sitting. He did make each one count, though.

"Thanks," I said, accepting a glass with what looked like a triple. "Where's mum?" He had a sip of the brandy and looked out of the window, maybe to check the weather, before he could bring himself to speak.

"Frieda's had a stroke," he said finally. "She'll be staying with her for a while." Frieda was my mother's sister. Properly speaking, my aunt, but she didn't feel like one: I'd never even met her. She lived in Narvik, Norway; judging by the photographs I'd seen, one of the most desolate spots on earth. To make things even more depressing, she'd married a mining engineer. He went in too deep one day, and she'd been a widow for some time. I said:

"I'm sorry to hear that. Are you managing okay?" He nodded and had more brandy. I had some too in order to lubricate my throat for what I had to say.

"Well," I said eventually, "I'm not doing great myself. It looks like I've fucked up. I'm sorry, Dad." He waited, sipping. "Donna and I are divorcing, and I still haven't found a job," I said.

"That's sad," he said. There was a longish silence, punctuated by the dripping of the kitchen tap. He was out of his chair before I could move, twisting it properly shut. He sat down again.

"Have you got another woman?" he asked. I shook my head.

"You should get another woman," he told me.

"I probably will. Eventually. Right now I don't feel like getting involved with anyone, if you know what I mean."

"You should get laid," he told me. That was rich, coming from a guy who went about the marital business at most once a month; I could watch, listen, and count no worse than any other adolescent.

"Right now I'm getting along fine with a wank every Sunday," I said. "I know they told you it makes hair grow on your palms, but it's not true. And I find it's less demeaning than fucking someone I don't really want to fuck just so I get my rocks off. It's also less expensive."

"It's sad you don't want anyone," he said.

"I don't need anyone in my life right now."

"It's sad you don't need anyone."

I took a swig, took a deep breath, and said:

"Dad, what I need is money. Can you help me out?"

My parents are thrifty people. They always manage to keep a couple of thousand in their chequing account, and another six-seven in readily accessible savings (the bulk of the family fortune is salted away in long-term government bonds). I had grounds to hope I'd be able to borrow a few thousand. Unfortunately, the family till had been cleared out by my mother's unexpected trip to the side of the ailing Frieda. I asked for six grand but got four. My father valiantly offered to cash one of the bonds, but I couldn't agree to that because then he'd start to be truly concerned, and maybe ask a couple of questions. It's impossible to lie to my old man; he has an uncanny knack for picking up on lies. He doesn't comment, but he *knows*. I had a very trying childhood, and I spent that night in Peterborough sleeping on the front room sofa, although I'd been offered my old room.

We paid a visit to the bank first thing in the morning, and then I caught a bus back home feeling fucking awful. It couldn't be booze: I'd just had the one triple brandy. It took me a while to work out that these were likely the after-effects of the germ cocktail I'd been injected with the previous day.

I spent the bus ride suffering silently, and counting and recounting the money. I kept coming up with the same result: forty-five hundred if I didn't put aside anything towards the rent. There was still a chance I could raise the balance by selling the stuff guarded by the vigilant dogs of Hercules Security and Storage.

I made a point of calling my answering service the moment I was off the bus in Toronto. There were over a dozen messages, heartening proof of my ad-making talents. I liked the message left by a man called Rory best; it was brisk and to the point and without any I-have-to-see-whether-I-like-it bullshit. I called him back right away; he offered to pick me up at home in his van, and we arranged to visit Hercules Security and Storage that very afternoon. Then I went home and lay down on the bed and finally allowed myself to feel really bad. In a way it was a relief when I had to get up and leave in order to get a bite before I met up with Rory.

Rory turned out to be a tall, gruff, flannel-shirted and pony-tailed man in his thirties. His van was an ancient Dodge; painted light grey, it resembled and sounded like a small tank. We drove down to Hercules Security and Storage without talking, the silent Rory chain-smoking unfiltered Lucky Strikes and changing the station on the car radio every couple of tunes. When we got close to our destination, it became apparent that I'd never been there before. I felt stupid, but Rory wasn't puzzled or curious; he patiently drove around the suburban industrial park until we found Hercules. I liked Rory: his calm patience was reassuring.

The number of my cubicle was attached to the key I got from Donna. The Hercules representative on duty—a fat, pimpled young man who had been reading a paperback novel when we came in—quickly identified the location of my luxury cubicle, pointing it out on a convenient wall map. It was then that I finally took in the Hercules logo and saw that it showed Hermes, the ancient Greek god of merchants and thieves. Somehow, this seemed promising.

My luxury cubicle was one of many arranged in a row behind iron bars; my stuff looked as if it was in prison. We spent half an hour going through it; my possessions seemed more numerous and interesting than I remembered them: there was a nice oxidized steel Anglepoise lamp, for instance. Rory liked it too; I watched him covertly, and most of the time he was nodding in a very encouraging manner. He seemed mildly disappointed that we couldn't hook the computer up to see how it worked, but I made it up by putting on a five-minute demonstration of the advanced gadgetry of my top-notch drafting table (original price: $1695 plus tax). Then I said:

"Well?"

Rory nodded thoughtfully.

"I'll take your word that the computer, monitor, printer and scanner work," he said.

"They do. Absolutely."

"Great. I'll give you fifteen hundred."

"For the computer stuff?"

"For everything."

"What?!"

"Everything. Cash. I've got it right here." Rory paused to pat his hip and finally registered my dismay. "Okay, sixteen hundred. But that's it. Can't afford more."

"I need at least twenty eight hundred," I said slowly, and then I had a brainwave. Donna had paid a small fortune for a year up front, and I was vacating the space after a couple of weeks. Surely I could get some money back?

"Wait," I said to Rory, who was already in the process of turning away. "I just realized that since I won't be needing this space any more, I might be able to get a refund. It's paid up for a year."

"Sure you can get a refund," said Rory.

"Seventeen hundred."

"Sixteen. We can clean this out in twenty minutes, and I'll give you a ride back."

"Done."

We shook hands and got down to work. Rory was very efficient, swiftly negotiating entry for his car and loading the van with an expertise that bespoke much experience. We were done in fifteen minutes, not twenty; on the way out, I asked Rory to wait a little and went to ask about a refund. The pimply Hercules told me he didn't deal with any complicated stuff; that was the province of the manager, an important man who only came in twice a week. I was advised to see him on Monday, and I was supposed to be flying to Africa on Wednesday. It made me nervous.

"Got your refund?" asked Rory as we drove out.

"I have to see the manager Monday," I said. "It might not be easy." Rory pondered this with great gravity, looking wise beyond his years. Even his pony-tail was full of wisdom. Eventually he said:

"You gotta show them you mean it, man. That will work."

CHAPTER EIGHT

Kross was due back that evening. I'd assumed he would show up quite late, given the three-hour difference between Toronto and Vancouver. But when it was nearing ten o'clock and he still hadn't arrived, I checked my answering service. I had about a dozen fresh enquiries about the stuff I'd just sold to Rory. At least a couple had the I-definitely-want-something quality, and I briefly regretted moving so fast. But this was a Saturday, and on Wednesday I was supposed to be flying over the Atlantic.

Kross's message was last. He had unexpected trouble laying his hands on Greenbottle's book; he made a reference to a message left earlier, which I must have erased along with Donna's instalment drama. He proposed to stay in Vancouver until Monday; he wanted me to see the book, he wanted me confident and convinced I was doing the right thing.

He instructed me to keep going at my end and to make sure I got my stake together; his Vancouver visit was getting expensive. His coming back on Monday wasn't a bad development. I'd have a chance to accost Hercules management for a refund before Kross asked me to put my money where my mouth was.

I was still feeling like shit from the vaccine. I spent most of Sunday drawing up battle plans for the Hercules showdown while lying in bed. I also speculated on my chances of getting another loan from Todd, but he was bound to be playing a match in another city. I simply had to score with Hercules. I definitely wasn't going back to ask my old man to cash a bond.

It was lucky I still had the keys to the BMW. I had no doubt that if I asked Donna, she'd have gladly let me use it as needed; she wouldn't have missed this chance to prove how noble she was, compared to me. Maybe that was why I chose another way of doing things on Monday.

Monday morning began on an optimistic note: I was feeling much better, the effects of the vaccine had passed. I showered and shaved and dressed with extra care, as if I were going to attend a job interview. I unwrapped a clean shirt I'd been saving for that very purpose, and spent a few minutes polishing my best shoes. I put on the only suit I'd kept—a versatile black Italian number that fit funerals, parties, and job interviews equally well. I tied a narrow black tie, repeatedly combed my hair, applied aftershave, and generally primped myself like a courtesan before a tryst with the king. I felt I shouldn't underestimate the Hercules manager. He was bound to be at least as good as his diplomaed dogs.

I arrived at Donna's office building at a conservative twenty past ten. The big ground floor lobby was deserted: there were just two junior exec types standing by the elevator doors. One of them threw me a glance when I pressed the 'down' button; they were waiting for the elevator going up, of course. Their elevator arrived first, and I was temporarily left standing alone. I could feel the curious gaze of the security guard on the back of my neck: his little fortress was facing the elevators, as if this was in fact the preferred means of access for villains.

I rode down to the second level of the underground parking lot. I thought I knew exactly where Donna's parking spot was, having been there with her many times, but I forgot she'd been promoted. I spent an anxious two minutes before I located the BMW right next to the elevator door I had emerged from. It looked very modest in its new company, which consisted of a Mercedes, two Porsches, and a Maserati.

I got into the car and spent a minute or so sitting still before I started the engine. The car smelled differently than I remembered it, and I fancied I caught a very faint whiff of an unfamiliar but distinctly male aftershave. I thought about it for a while, and ended up shrugging. I backed the car out very smartly, and drove it to the exit with appropriate dash and elan.

It worked. The attendant guarding the exit started to raise the barrier almost as soon as I swung into view. I gave the gas pedal a final prod before taking my foot off, coasting past the steel and glass kiosk with a throaty burble. I caught a glimpse of a pale, startled face that failed to match me with the car. Then I was accelerating up the ramp to the street, locking all thoughts of traffic accidents out of my head, and allowing myself just a brief stop to get used to the sunlight before darting into the mid-morning traffic.

It was nearing eleven when I parked right in front of the Hercules entrance. I went in and there was a different guy moving around inside, definitely a managerial type of guy: short, bald, stout, forty plus, wearing gold wire frame glasses. He didn't look as if he exercised much, which was good.

I paused to straighten my tie before I approached the reception counter. Old Tubby, who had been pottering around so busily when I entered, quickly sat down at the desk in the back and began reading a document. I had to say good morning twice just to get him to look at me. I was getting his number fast, and he made me angry.

"Are you the manager?" I asked, with intentional incredulity. He puffed up instantly, swelled so strongly he just had to stand up. He was wearing a dark blue blazer with the Hercules/Hermes logo and a pair of dusty black slacks; he probably resented my suit instead of being impressed. He said:

"I am the owner."

"I'm one of your customers," I said. This put him on automatic, and he walked up to the counter. He had a very stately walk. He wasn't even distantly related to Kross; the only security he was concerned with was his own. I decided I was dealing with a small-potatoes millionaire, maybe a real estate hustler who got some money together and started a business of his own. In short, he was a guy who needed all the highly trained Dobermans he could get, and it seemed there weren't any around. This was good.

"And what can I help you with," he said. His tone suggested there wasn't much, and he peered at me over his glasses with what he probably thought was a piercing gaze. He had big, wet eyes, the eyes of a poseur. I said:

"I think you can help me with plenty. Eleven days ago, someone rented a cubicle here under my name for a full year, without my knowledge or consent. I don't need it. I already have lots of storage space, and I don't see why I should pay for something I never wanted and won't use. I'd like a refund." I put my receipt and the cubicle key on the counter. He picked up the receipt and studied it.

"Is this your signature?" he said. Damn Donna, and her insistence on signing her full name, with an extra big, rounded D at the beginning (the H in Hansen is half the size). I said:

"As I just finished telling you, this cubicle was rented out for me by someone else, without my approval." He nodded several times, and smiled: he was enjoying himself. I was sure he was going to refuse me, and I was right. He said:

"I'm sorry. I can only discuss a refund with the person who actually signed the agreement. And in any case, this agreement constitutes a binding contract. Refunds on a change of mind aren't part of our policy." He put the receipt back on the counter. Then he walked back to his desk and sat down.

The counter reached my ribs but I was over it in a flash, as if I'd been vaulting counters all my life. I was by his chair before he had time to get up. I grabbed his lapels and dragged him out and, partly because I was about to lose my balance, swung him into the wall. He hit it with a satisfying

115

double thump with both his back and his head; an alarmed file cabinet clattered briefly. He tried to grab my wrists, and I used a tried and true schoolyard tactic: I kicked his shin. His face screwed up and he dropped his arms to his sides. I released one lapel and took a handful of his shirt, pulling the collar tight. His glasses slid off and dangled on one earpiece. He had bad breath.

"Listen, you dumb asshole," I said, and saw my spittle landing on his face. "I told you I want a refund." I tightened my grip on the shirt. "Eleven months' worth. You still get a full month's fee, and I'll go easy on you: I'll make it an even eighteen hundred. And spare me any whining about the insurance premium: we both know you own the broker, too. Now get busy writing cheques."

I swung him over and threw him at the desk. I was getting good at this: it was surprisingly easy. He offered no resistance at all. He nearly fell down and had to grab the desk for support, his glasses finally falling off.

"Get going, you sad clown," I said. I took a couple of steps towards him and he got into his chair very quickly. He threw a forlorn glance at the telephone, opened a drawer—I tensed—and pulled out a big, corporate chequebook. He blinked, and I obligingly tossed his glasses onto the desk.

"Get writing," I said. He did, and paused almost instantly. He asked:

"Who do I make this to?"

"Leave that blank. Just eighteen hundred dollars, and your signature. And countersign it on the back. What the fuck are you waiting for?" I made a move as if to grab him, and he got going. It took him three tugs to tear the cheque out.

I examined it carefully before folding it into my wallet. My wallet was a present from Donna, so it was fairly posh. She invariably bought me a new wallet each Christmas: a bit of innocent black magic that failed to work. I let the fallen god of Hercules see my wallet; he was sure to know all about wallets, and get the message. I said:

"I'll be back if there's any trouble with that cheque."

When I made it to the car, I had to use both hands to get the key into the ignition lock. My feet kept sliding off the pedals. I began to drive back to Donna's office, going very slowly. I managed to stop shaking and collect my thoughts after a couple of minutes, and consulted the city road map that was always kept in the glove compartment. The bank branch on which the cheque was drawn was nearby, as I suspected, and twenty minutes later I had eighteen hundred in cash in my pocket. I had to show my driving licence at the bank, but this didn't bother me. I was feeling a little invincible by then.

I made it back downtown without any fuss, and turned down the ramp into Donna's official parking lot with a confident flick of the wrist. I pulled up smoothly right next to the attendant, and we looked at each other. He couldn't have been much more than twenty; he would likely have to show his driving licence when getting a drink in a darkly-lit bar. He winked at me, and raised the barrier.

I put the car back in its spot and left the keys in the ignition lock. The elevator came almost right away. The ground floor lobby contained a scattering of early lunch-goers; the clock that hung over the security guard's little fortress showed five to twelve. I joined the outgoing trickle of people processed by the glass paddlewheel and, feeling flush, caught a cab to my bank. I made a big deposit and checked the exchange rate again. It turned out I had my stake plus just enough to tide me over the next couple of days, and purchase a bottle of duty-free booze on the plane.

I spent the whole afternoon waiting for Kross. Around four, the house got busy. It started with excited coming-and-goings up and down the stairs; a few moments later, I saw the chubby young female living down the hall open the gate to the backyard. A Rent-a-Wreck van backed in, and I retreated from the window. I sat down on my bed, and spent the next few minutes listening to the sound show staged in the stairwell: there was a female voice insisting 'no, this way', plus assorted bumps, thumps, and muffled curses. When someone knocked on my door I thought it would be my chubby housemate, asking for help.

But when I answered the door I saw that it was Kross. He smiled at the surprise on my face, and said:

"I'm back. Can you give me an hour or so before we talk?"

"Sure." He began to turn away and I added: "Wait. Aren't you forgetting something?" and held out the key to his flat. It had been in my pocket throughout the afternoon.

"Oh that," he said. "I've got another. See you in an hour, then." And he fucked off.

It proved to be one of the longest hours of my life. When it was finally up and I went to see Kross, he knocked me off balance right away.

"I haven't got Greenbottle's book," he said, the moment I entered and closed the door behind me.

"Why?"

"Sharon had lent it to a friend, and the friend left town for a while. Two weeks in Cancun. It seems she took it with her."

"She took Greenbottle's book to read on the beach? Come on. How do you know, anyway?"

"It wasn't in her apartment."

"You broke into her apartment?"

"No. Sharon visits it once a week to water the plants. I hung around until she did, and went along with her."

"She let you toss her friend's apartment?"

"I didn't *toss* it," he said impatiently. "I'd told Sharon I wanted the book, right? So I looked around, which she didn't mind. Are we happy now?"

"Not quite," I said. There was a pause.

"Okay," he said eventually. "Seeing the book was part of the deal. So, do you want out? Just remember to keep your mouth shut about the whole business."

I only realized how deeply I was committed to that business at that exact moment. It was no longer a question of it being an option; it was the only way to go. I couldn't even imagine backing out. So I said:

"I have to think about it."

"Fine. But make up your mind by tomorrow afternoon, all right? By three o'clock at the latest. I have to be at the airline office by four to get a refund on your ticket."

"Okay. Can I ask a question?"

"Ask away."

"Who are you going to take along in my place if I don't go?"

Kross shrugged.

"I'll just have to improvise. Find someone on the spot to help me out."

"And you really can't just go yourself?"

"No. It's too risky. I could run into someone I know, and I left the country on pretty bad terms with a lot of people there. A long time ago, yes, but those guys have very long memories."

"I'm not sure I remember what you told me about that. I remember you did tell me something. You got involved in a mutiny?"

Kross laughed.

"No, that was Avery," he said. "Basically, there was a change of government. A coup. The new guys didn't like foreigners signed on by the previous government. I left before they could throw me in jail."

"Did you do stuff that could put you in jail? Like shoot someone, for example?"

Kross didn't answer. He just stared at me in a way that clearly communicated I could be the one to get shot.

"Never mind," I said. "Stupid joke. Here's your key."

He took it from me, still without saying anything.

"I'll let you know how things stand by two o'clock tomorrow, at the latest," I promised.

"Great. You sure you don't want to ask me about something else?"

"It can wait."

I returned to my room feeling that I should really get some advice before confirming my involvement. But getting advice meant describing the problem to somebody, and I couldn't do that. I didn't even want to imagine what Kross would do when he learned that I'd told someone about our plan.

Tad was the only person somewhat involved in the whole business, even though he knew nothing about it. So in the end I called Tad. He wasn't answering his phone. I waited for ten minutes, and called him again. He wasn't there. I forced myself to wait another five minutes, then dragged things out for an extra couple of minutes by promising myself repeatedly that it was really going to be my last attempt to reach Tad.

This time, he answered the phone.

"Finally," I said. "I've been trying to reach you for nearly half an hour. Where the fuck have you been? It's late. Decent people are in bed this time of night."

Tad informed me that he was a free man, free to come and go as he pleased. He went on to ask me what was up, then quickly answered the question himself. The Australian hotshot with the shaved head was insisting on Kornik and Hansen, the sharpest creative team in town! He was offering remuneration in the six figures, company cars ('And I won't take anything less than a Lexus,' warned Tad), comprehensive health, dental, and life insurance, plus immunity from prosecution should we murder one of the market research people. I said:

"Tad, please. Tad. Tad?"

"Separate suites when we have to travel," said Tad. "First class, naturally. Plus complimentary limousines, Cristal champagne—none of this Moet Chandon or Dom Perignon bullshit, and I mean it—and of course grand-a-fuck whores and premium cocaine." I finally twigged Tad was high on coke on top of being stoned and drunk. He seemed to be doing well, since this was a Monday. I was pleased for Tad. I said:

"Actually, I'm calling about that stuff we were looking for on the web the other day—you know, Jan Hansen, a ship called the *Swallow*. Manage to find out anything?"

Tad informed me he hadn't. He was busy searching for more meaningful things, such as true knowledge. Unlike everyone else, he was aware of the fact that he knew nothing, and was proud of it. He –

"You stole that line from Socrates," I interrupted. "You fucking writers are always stealing from someone. So: you didn't look, or you looked and didn't find anything?

"I looked and didn't find anything," said Tad with dignity. "Plenty of swallows. Plenty, but none featuring a Hansen. Very odd."

"What about Avery?"

"Big pirate. Big, big pirate. Very rich. Died of starvation. Very sad. Anorexia doesn't choose... this means you!" said Tad.

"Tad," I said patiently, "Can we talk seriously for a minute?"

"Tomorrow," said Tad. Then he started singing: tomorrow, tomorrow, I love you tomorrow, you're always a day away—little orphan Annie on nose candy.

"I'll call you again tomorrow," I said, and hung up.

CHAPTER NINE

I spent a largely sleepless night, thinking about the very many good reasons for backing out of my African adventure. This treasure business was just too fantastic to be real. There was a silver lining: it had spurred me to do a round of fund-raising, and I now had some money to live on while I looked for work.

That was the sensible thing to do, no two words about it. And there wasn't any sense in attempting to get anyone's advice. When anyone heard *that* story, they'd call an ambulance or the police or both. An unemployed, soon-to-be-divorced, soon-to-be-bankrupt art director looking for treasure in Africa! Please.

But deep down, I knew I had to do it anyway. I'd never forgive myself if I didn't give it a try. I'd regret that to the end of my fucking days.

I left the house as soon as it was light. I needed a walk to clear my head. Luckily it promised to be one of those sparkling sunny winter days. Some fresh snow fell during the night, and my footsteps squeaked eerily in the empty street. I realized that I was walking to Tad's place when I reached the first crossroads.

Yes, it was a good idea to visit Tad. I wanted him to run another search for me, a search on someone called Mark Kross. It really was surprising that I hadn't thought of it earlier. I wasn't expecting to find something. I wasn't even *hoping* to find something. Because if I did find something, it would probably be bad news.

I knew it was way too early to visit Tad, especially after he'd spent most of the night bombed out of his mind. So I detoured to the local main street and found a place called The Pioneer Grille that was serving breakfasts. All that walking made me hungry so I went in and treated myself to their Pioneer's Special. The Pioneer's Special had three of everything: three eggs, three large, thick slices of bacon, three sausages, and a three-scoop-sized mound of French fries. I drank three coffees with that.

Feeling both rejuvenated and groggy from all that food, I resumed my journey to see Tad. It still wasn't even nine in the morning, but it would be by the time I arrived. I was sure this was going to be too early for Tad anyway, but so what? Life was tough sometimes. I did decide to show some mercy and got a couple of takeaway coffees from a corner store near Tad's place.

It felt pretty stupid, walking with a Styrofoam cup of coffee in each hand. As I got closer to the corner that marked the turnoff into Tad's street, I saw there was a guy standing there. And there was something funny about the scene—it was being lit up red at regular intervals—I broke into a trot, coffee sloshing in the cups.

The guy on the corner had gone out to walk his dog. It was a miniature pinscher and it was cowering by his ankle, snout raised imploringly. But its master was ignoring this mute appeal to move on; he was totally motionless, staring down Tad's street. He was wearing an olive-green parka and a toque pushed back far enough to reveal longish dirty grey hair. He hadn't shaved that morning and something told me that he was unemployed, just like me.

I stopped beside him and looked and saw an ambulance parked right in front of Tad's house. The rooftop disco and the open back doors suggested an intervention was in progress. I was about to walk over and hopefully get confirmation that they hadn't come for Tad when I noticed the police cruiser parked a little further on. It stopped me in my tracks.

"The fire brigade have already been and gone," the guy with the dog said. "They were the first to show up. Biggest vehicle, but arrived here first." He seemed to find this deeply significant. His gravelly voice suggested plenty of booze and cigarettes.

"You have any idea what's happened?"

He gave me a blank look. He had watery blue eyes with pouches that stretched down to his cheekbones. He said:

"Are those coffees?"

I saw movement at Tad's front door and didn't answer. Two guys emerged carrying a stretcher. The person on the stretcher had a clear plastic oxygen mask over his nose and mouth but there was no mistaking that frizzy hair. It was Tad.

"Oh fuck," I said.

"What?"

I turned to the dog guy and handed him the coffees. It caught him by surprise, even though he'd been eyeing them all along. He said:

"Why, I... Thank you. But won't you keep one for yourself?"

"Give it to the dog," I said. "It looks like it could use one."

I pushed the cups into his awkward embrace, and walked away.

I think it was the Pioneer's Special that kept me from freaking out. Things can't be that bad, my body told me; we just got ourselves literally a shitload of nutrients. I kept walking on automatic, and somehow, in my mind, Tad on a stretcher became myself on a stretcher. It had to be a warning, an omen.

Nonsense, my body said. That's what happens when you poison yourself with booze and drugs. And you, us, we just had the Pioneer's Special. Things are cool.

And then I suddenly saw Rory.

I'd reached the local main drag again by then, and like all main drags everywhere it was lined with storefronts of all sorts and sizes. Rory was prominently displayed in the medium-sized storefront window of a company called Ace Office & Computer Supplies. His ponytail was gone, replaced by a Jesus-style parting and a beaded headband. He wore black leather jeans and a printed white T-shirt; its lettering appealed to Save Something or Other.

As I watched, Rory knelt down right next to my former drafting table—it was occupying a premium spot on the display—gave its leg a loving rub with a duster, and affixed a big card to the board. It advertised my table as A STEAL! $1299. A steal was correct, I thought; as I passed unnoticed just a few feet away, I saw that his T-shirt pleaded to Save the Wolves. He obviously thought himself an endangered species.

I actually checked the time it took me to walk from Rory's store to my house. It was less than fifteen minutes, and it made clear his courtesies—picking me up, and dropping me back home after our Hercules voyage—hadn't given him much bother.

Upon arriving home, I was greeted by Mr. Natarajan. He was polishing the frosted glass set in the front door, his moustache bristling with indignation; he informed me someone had come looking for me, and that Mr. Kross had had a talk with the gentleman. It was obvious that the mysterious gentleman hadn't met with Natarajan's approval. He was looking at me with a new hostility.

I loped up the stairs and went to my room and tried to guess who might have come to see me. I had no idea. It couldn't have been Todd or my old man. It obviously couldn't have been Tad. Could it have been Donna's divorce lawyer? No, because he was likely to look sharp and radiate wealth, and would have won me new admiration in Natarajan's eyes, not suspicious hostility.

After banging my head against the wall in this manner for nearly half an hour, I went to see Kross. I hoped he could provide me with a clue as to who had come to see me.

He did so even before I managed to ask him.

"There was a private dick here looking for you," he informed me right away.

"A what!?"

"Private eye. Private investigator. What have you been up to?"

"How do you know he was a private investigator?"

"He showed me his license. Would've thrown him down the stairs otherwise. What the fuck have you been doing?"

"It must be Donna," I said with false conviction.

"It isn't your wife. He was sent by a guy called Bob Wagner. A businessman. Seems Bob's taken offense at the way you've handled things last time he saw you. Now, are you going to tell me what's all this about?"

"It's no big deal," I said. "All I did was collect some money I was owed. I didn't have five big ones sitting around." Kross tensed, and said:

"You didn't tell him what you needed the money for?"

"I didn't tell him a fucking thing," I said. "I just slapped him around a little." I thought this would improve my standing with Kross, but he wasn't impressed.

"You want to be careful about going around slapping people," he said. "This dick of his wasn't a nice guy. He was a frightener."

"But you cross-examined him with effortless skill."

"Frighteners don't frighten me," Kross said. "Okay. Let's get back to business. Are you in or out?"

I allowed myself a pause. I looked him in the eye. Then I said:

"I'm in. But first, show me the fucking money."

Kross showed me his money without any ado. His stake included a fat wad of American dollars and a couple of rather nifty gold coins he called napoleons. Bribes that featured a napoleon on top of a stack of the world's most popular currency were simply irresistible; it was the magic of the gold, he said.

Following that he became very businesslike and grilled me about my own preparations. They were found lacking and I was sent out to get my money, including a couple of thousand in traveller's cheques. There was a problem with those; it seemed I needed to order them in advance. I was directed to a big bank downtown that catered to tourists. I spent the remainder of the afternoon wandering around downtown, buying clothes plus a pair of the recommended desert boots. They promised to be very comfortable, but overall everything felt strange and I emitted a hysterical little giggle when I was paying, alarming the checkout girl.

Upon returning home, I didn't even bother to unpack some of my purchases. Instead, I packed two bags: a big duffel bag and my photographer's shoulder bag, with stiff edges and metal corners. Then I went to see Kross. He was pleased to see the traveller's cheques, and to hear that I followed his advice and purchased a pair of desert boots.

"You did good," he told me. "Time for me to brief you."

"Brief me?"

"Don't you want to know some details?"

"Of course I want to know the details. I assumed they were top secret."

"They are. Which is why I'm going to reveal them now, too late for an opportunity to blab something to somebody."

"Thank you for your trust," I said, with maximum sarcasm. It was water off a duck's back; he didn't notice.

"Let me fix some coffee and get a map," he said. "Make yourself at home."

"Kross?"

"Yeah?"

"Do you think there's a chance this private dick guy will come around again?"

"None."

"None?"

"None."

"What did you tell him—what did you do to him?"

"None of your business," he said, and went to the kitchen. I heard him fill the kettle from the tap.

The African statuette was standing on the front window sill. I walked over and looked at its slitted eyes. Suddenly, I realized that I had stepped into another world. In this new world, longtime friends were carried away on stretchers; hired toughs were sent out after me; and my new partner wasn't a poet prostituting himself in advertising, my new partner was a mercenary soldier. I wasn't sure how I felt about all that.

I did my best to keep my composure during what Kross called a briefing; it had a strong military note, which made me nervous. We were to leave at three in the afternoon. Six would see us aboard a plane to Paris; fifteen hours later, we would be flying to Abidjan in Ivory Coast, right next to the Gold Coast—Ghana's old colonial name.

After a couple of days ('you'll be getting acclimatized while I set things up'), I'd rent a car and embark on the short drive to the Ghanaian border. I'd get a short-term tourist visa right there, no problem, provided I had the necessary papers: a few hundred-dollar bills.

"What if they don't like my face and refuse me entry?" I asked.

"No matter how much they hate your face, they love Ben Franklin's."

"You hundred percent sure?"

"No," Kross said. "I'm making all this up. I have this hobby: I make up expensive plans and put them in motion just so I can fail and have a good cry afterwards. It's so cleansing. Stop being a moron, okay? I'll go to the border with you to make sure everything works out. And later you'll just follow my instructions, and all will be fine."

After crossing the border, I was to drive for two hours along the coast to the town of Dixcove, known as Dixon's Cove in Avery's time. Nowadays its perfectly preserved fort made it a popular tourist destination; Kross assured me that I wasn't going to draw any attention other than that given to any other tourist. He wouldn't tell me exactly how and where the treasure was hidden ('need to know, old boy, need to know'), but I gathered I'd have to leave the car and go on foot into the fucking jungle. He assured me there would be a path, but being a well-read person I knew jungle paths were exactly the spots where hungry carnivores liked to congregate. From their point of view, it was like sitting down in a restaurant and waiting for the meal to come along.

After I'd recovered the treasure—which could require a small shovel, already purchased by Kross—I was to drive back at maximum speed, so that I would cross the border with the same guards still around. Having been told I was on a day trip to see the Dixcove fort and nothing else, they would expect me, and I would get waved through without a problem.

"But wait a moment," I protested. "Suppose the treasure turns out to be contained in a big trunk that's falling apart and the whole thing weighs a hundred pounds."

"It won't. The treasure consists of a few handfuls of diamonds, in a leather pouch that's inside an air-tight, metal tobacco box. It will easily fit into your pocket."

"It might take some finding if it's so small."

"It won't. Not more than ten-fifteen minutes."

"I assume you'll give me all the required details later."

"You assume correctly."

Kross also took special care to explain that in Africa, corruption was a fact of life. It wasn't even perceived as corruption. It simply was appropriate to include a gift along with a request. If the gift fit the request size-wise, the request was granted. Most of the five grand earmarked for bribes would be spent on our way back to Europe, when we would be hopefully carrying the diamonds. Kross had numerous European contacts that would help convert them into cash.

I spent the rest of the day re-packing my stuff over and over again, and worrying about Tad. Eventually I convinced myself that Tad was doing fine. A short stay and detox in a hospital was exactly what he needed. He'd emerge bright-eyed and bushy-tailed, ready to conquer the world.

Next day I woke up late. I repacked my suitcase yet again, this time including my snazzy black suit; that way I could be buried wearing something decent. I went out and walked all the way to The Pioneer Grill and treated myself to a Pioneer's Special.

When I got back, Kross informed me he'd already ordered a cab. I was to go to my room and stay there. And in the future, when I wanted to take a leave of absence, I was tell Kross about it in advance and get his permission. I didn't think this merited an answer. I gave Kross a scowl and went back to my room and lay down on my bed and before I knew it, I was asleep.

And then Kross was knocking on my door, and I was struggling with my bags on the stairs and pushing past a suspicious Natarajan who asked if we were coming back soon—he meant before rent due day. I told him we'd be back within a couple of days so that he would fret a little.

It had turned really cold again, and my breath smoked as I spoke. The Natarajan had sprinkled fresh salt in front of the house and it crunched and crackled under my feet as I carried my suitcase to the cab, waiting with steam rising from its hot yellow bonnet.

CHAPTER TEN

We flew over the sea at night. It lay unseen somewhere within the black void, many miles under our brightly lit flying bus. I was hoping to see the sun rise, but fell asleep soon after the in-flight meal plus beer. When I woke up the aircraft was casting a spindly, flickering shadow onto a layer of light grey clouds, and Kross told me we were already over Europe.

We landed at half past six in the morning, local time. Paris, France smelled of burnt kerosene and consisted of long concrete ramps and a single pallid, sour Frenchman in his forties who inspected our passports and tickets and directed us to the transit lounge. We had a four-hour wait for our next flight. The lounge featured a bar which featured yet another Frenchman, a discouraged-looking character smoking a cigarette and reading a newspaper; his remaining hair had been carefully assembled into a Napoleonic lock valiantly struggling for survival among the vast open steppes.

Kross bought coffee and pastries from him while I seated myself on an uncomfortable stool welded to a circular table. I looked round and saw the lounge also featured a conspicuously quiet Middle Eastern family and a couple of suited, self-contained businessmen. There was a notable shortage of French women. I had hoped to see some. I'd gathered we'd be stuck in the lounge throughout our wait because Kross wanted to touch bases with someone he knew, someone who worked at the airport.

"Is it a woman?" I asked, after we'd spent a mostly silent ten minutes drinking coffee and picking at the flaky pastries. Kross said:

"No, it's a guy. Met him through work. We're friends."

"Good friends?"

"Fairly good," he said. "Be nice to him. He'll be flying our plane."

"I've always wanted to meet a real pilot."

"Now you will."

The advertised pilot finally showed up just half an hour before our scheduled departure; I'd already begun to repeatedly glance at my watch. He was wearing an impressive dark blue uniform with a number of gold stripes on the sleeve, and a white peaked cap—very appropriate for those who make their living high above the clouds. He had an unpleasant, pinched mouth and hard black eyes that took in everything and gave away nothing. He was carrying an elegant flat black leather case and he slapped Kross's hip with it before they shook hands.

"Raymond," said Kross. He pronounced it the French way, with accent on the second syllable.

"*Ca va?*" said Raymond. Kross grinned, inclined his head in my direction and said:

"This is my partner, Oscar Hansen."

"How do you do," I said, holding out my hand. It was ignored. All I got was an acknowledging nod, then Raymond faced Kross and said:

"I have to hurry. I'll see you again in a week on the way back, correct?"

"Correct," said Kross.

"Leave your coordinates with the airline office and make sure you're there when I arrive."

"Roger."

"See you then," said Raymond. He prodded Kross with the corner of his document case, nodded to me, and fucked off.

"Now what?" I said. Kross shrugged.

"Now we wait."

The plane Raymond piloted turned out to be an Air Afrique Boeing 707. It was slightly older than myself. A few pale rays of sunshine filtered through the clouds as we climbed onboard; they gave the dense rows of rivets that held the plane together a gleam of competence. It felt very much like a plane inside, the fuselage defining the shape of the walls curving around the barren, no-frills passenger cabin. The African stewardesses grinned wider and with more sincerity than the African American stewardesses I had seen in action, and that was when I felt for the first time I was about to enter a different world.

Raymond knew his stuff: the flying dinosaur seemed to leap into the air barely seconds into its takeoff run. I even fancied I detected a bit of extra dash solely for the purpose of impressing people. He certainly didn't need to bank the plane so sharply the moment the wheels were up—for a brief moment it was standing on its wingtip just a couple of thousand feet above a busy motorway. Once we cleared the clouds, it became very quiet inside: practically all the aircraft noise was restricted to the thick hiss of the ventilators.

I had secured the window seat but the view on display wasn't inspiring: pale, practically colourless sunshine dispersing on a sea of light grey fleece. I surprised Kross slightly by refusing a shot of the free booze dispensed along with the morning coffee. He got a double brandy for himself.

"It's a long flight," he told me. I said:

"That's all right. I had plenty of sleep. I intend to see the sights. Just tell me a few things. What's this hotel we're staying at?"

"Hotel Palais-Royal. Pride of Abidjan. It's practically a mini-city. It's got a casino, a cinema, a supermarket, swimming pools, tennis courts, and a fucking ice-skating rink specially put in for visiting Canadians."

"Must be expensive. I mean I do appreciate all the nice things in life, but maybe the travelling budget could've been a little smaller if – "

"I got us a special deal," Kross interrupted. "And I'll tell you this: when you're out to do important business, you stay at a good hotel. It buys you plenty of respect."

"Well, thanks for this insight," I said. Who the hell did he think he was talking to? In the golden eighties, we once even flew to fucking Australia to shoot a bunch of beer commercials: some accounting wizard had worked out this was the cheapest way to go. I said:

"What's the special deal? And how did you get it? Another pilot in the right place?"

"That's right. I know the manager. I know quite a few people in this part of the world."

"One wonders how you got to meet all these interesting people," I said. Kross wriggled on his seat, presumably to make himself more comfortable. He said:

"Well in this case, I set up the hotel security. It's probably the safest hotel in Africa, and they'll be very happy to have us as guests. You'll see." And he closed his eyes to indicate the interview over. It irritated me, so I said:

"I don't see why we have to stay there for a whole week when the actual business is to be done within three days."

"Raymond's flying back in a week," Kross said, eyes still shut. "Raymond's a fine pilot, and we stick with him. We do our stuff, then hang around and relax a little. Celebrate discreetly in one of the world-renowned hotel bars. Now shut up and let me sleep."

I tried to sleep too, but couldn't. My mind was too busy. First, I tried to work out the timetable. I got the idea I'd be making the actual trip on the third day. That left another three days till departure date. If Kross was going to pull a fast one on me, he would do it during those three days. He wouldn't do anything before we recovered the diamonds. It wouldn't make sense.

Following that, I tried to think of ways in which I could ensure my security during those three days. Every idea I came up with was flawed. Kross was clearly a talented and well-connected man. If he wanted to cheat me, it would be easier than taking candy from a child.

I worried about that until the view below changed. The clouds broke to reveal a red and brown sea of rocks. It stretched as far as my eye could reach, from its vantage point six miles above: a terrible stone plain, its only landmarks being the occasional boulder or cairn large enough to throw a noticeable shadow on the ground. If hell did exist, it would look like that: a desert as dead as Mars, baked reddish brown by a sun suspended in the endless sky.

But there was a terrible beauty in this desolation. I couldn't tear my eyes away and so didn't notice Kross had woken up. I was startled when he spoke.

"That's the Sahara," he informed me in a tone implying I belonged among the geographically disadvantaged. I said:

"Really? When I was a little kiddie, I thought it was a sea of sand."

"Now you know better."

"Yeah, I kind of worked it out by the time I graduated high school."

That shut him up. He leaned back and closed his eyes and either went back to sleep or at least pretended he did. It felt like a minor victory.

He woke up or pretended to wake up a couple of hours later, when the meal was served. It was delicious—I'd eaten worse in pricey restaurants. I commented on it and Kross shrugged and said 'French catering'. That was was the extent of our mealtime conversation.

When he'd finished eating, he instantly settled back in his seat and closed his eyes again and I said:

"You sure sleep a lot. Are you okay? I mean, do you feel all right?"

"I feel great," Kross said without opening his eyes. "I've got this healthy habit of sleeping when I can so that I manage without sleep when I can't."

"You think there's a possibility of us not getting a chance to sleep?"

"That possibility is always present. Can you shut up? Try to get some extra sleep, too."

I did try, and to my surprise I dozed off for a while; most likely, the meal helped, especially since I also drank one of those toy bottles of wine they serve on airplanes. I only realized that I'd fallen asleep when the duty free trolley arrived with a joyful clatter.

Kross insisted we purchase the all allowable booze and cigarettes ('I know you don't smoke, but they'll be useful as gifts.') He supervised the filling out of my immigration form. He informed me that he would be doing all the talking with the immigration ('Just hand your passport over when asked. Anyone gets curious, we're on the way to visit the Komoe national park. That's a game reserve in the northern part of the country.')

He also briefed me on the situation in Ghana. It was currently ruled by a former air force lieutenant who led two separate coups, and subsequently won the presidential election twice. His name was Jerry Rawlings, and earlier he'd caused an international uproar by executing a number of people for corruption. He disliked everything about the governments he'd overthrown earlier, and that included any foreign experts they'd employed.

"The reason why you can't enter the country," I said, and Kross nodded.

When I finally saw the sand dunes, they were already painted a burnt orange by the setting sun. The plane started losing altitude soon thereafter. By the time I spotted my first tree we were noticeably lower, and the ground was dark with the approaching night. There seemed to be a different quality to the air hissing in the ventilation. And then all of a sudden the sun disappeared, and the lights inside the plane went on.

There was a distant glare of lights faraway in front, but we landed in what appeared to be the middle of nowhere. Raymond strutted his stuff, landing so gently I wasn't aware we were on the ground until the engines reversed thrust. I was looking forward to flying with him again. Now and then I caught glimpses of forlorn-looking lights through the windows on the other side of the cabin.

Raymond drove the plane around the airport for what seemed a long time before parking it some distance away from the terminal. I was so eager to leave the plane that I stumbled while descending the boarding stairs. I didn't fall—I simply ran down a few steps fast and came to a stop against the broad and fleshy back of a suited, bespectacled, respectable African gentleman. He handled it very well—he hardly swayed at all—he looked over his shoulder, unsmiling, and commented in French. Kross instantly responded with something that made the African gentleman grin widely.

"Bienvenu à Abidjan," he told me.

"Yes, very much. Thank you," I said.

I walked down the remaining steps with the focus of an Olympic gymnast. Therefore it was a while before I realized that it was warm, so warm I felt as if I were wrapped in an invisible blanket. It was a while before everyone climbed aboard the bus that would take us to the terminal; I stood and waited while my jeans and shirt became moist and clingy.

By the time I got off the bus and into the air-conditioned terminal, I could feel rivulets of sweat beginning to flow between the hair on my head. Of course I had been to the tropics before: to be exact, twice, each time for a week of drunken debauch that is later referred to as a holiday. But this was something else. This was different. There was this smell, under an overlay of Pinesol or some other disinfectant: a faint but persistent tang of rotting vegetation. And needless to say, almost everyone was very black.

We collected the luggage first, then joined a line slowly snaking through a series of booths and desks. These were manned by officials that seemed to include a representative from the police, secret police (suit and sunglasses), and every branch of the armed forces, plus the token civilian in flowing white African robes. Each and every one of these gentlemen examined our passports. Kross always went first, and the procedure was always the same: a few words from him to the frowning official, and the passport would be slapped back into his hand with a delighted grin, mine would get a cursory glance, and we were through. It was impressive. It really inspired confidence in our venture.

My partner's performance reached new heights of excellence when we collected the luggage and hit the customs. While exchanging banter with our customs officer, he casually set down his duty-free bag on the inspection counter. The customs officer asked us to open all luggage: my conditioning took over and I helpfully unzipped my travel bag, but he didn't bother to look. He picked up the duty-free bag and put it down beside his leg while chalking green crosses on our luggage. And that was it; we were through.

Kross pointed a finger at a winking neon sign and said:

"Go there and cash a traveller's cheque for a hundred bucks, no more. We just need enough for the cab and tips. We'll get a better rate in town." I did as told and got many thousands of Central African francs, in floppy banknotes big enough to serve as bedsheets for millionaire dwarves.

In the meantime, Kross had secured the services of a taxi driver—a very respectable looking type with a razor-cut side parting in his hair and a gold-capped pen clipped to the white shirt pocket. He had a big gold watch on a bracelet that could have served as a choker for a small dog. He was short and wiry, and carried our luggage with an ease that suggested he wasn't a good guy to pick fights with.

The air outside the terminal building was like a soft blow: it felt twice as heavy as the conditioned variety, and it had a salty tang from the nearby ocean. Our cab turned out to be a white Peugeot 504 with fake zebra fur upholstery and a little lace curtain adorning the rear window. The interior smelled faintly of incense. It was air-conditioned, and the synthetic fur felt pleasantly dry and cool.

We motored out of the airport and onto a wide highway leading towards a patch of night sky bleached white by thousands of lights. I spent the first few minutes of the journey looking out of the window in an attempt to see something exotic and African. Unfortunately, the Africa on display consisted of vague shadows beyond the orangey, cosmopolitan glow of the fizzy sodium lights lining the four-lane road.

There wasn't much traffic, and all the cars seemed to be either French or Japanese; I spotted one old-fashioned Volkswagen station wagon. I saw many small Japanese minibuses, adorned with inscriptions in flowing, shadowed script, with canvas or plastic tarpaulins flapping atop the bundles strapped down to the roof. From time to time we passed an island of light belonging to a gas station. The gas stations looked like North American or European gas stations look, and many logos were familiar: Shell, Mobil, Total, Agip.

The bilingual Kross was engaged in a conversation with the driver. I fidgeted, sat still, fidgeted, sat still. Eventually I opened the window, stuck my face into the warm moist air, and breathed deeply. I immediately pulled back and cranked the window shut.

"You okay?" asked Kross, eyeing me warily over his shoulder.

""I'm fine. I just discovered it stinks out there. A cheesy smell, like old socks."

"It's probably raw cocoa beans," Kross said. "I daresay the port's not far away, and as a rule there's an inland breeze at night."

"Cocoa beans?"

"Main local export. Silos and silos full of the stuff. That's how it smells." He returned to his his fascinating conversation with the driver while I tried to reconcile the stink I'd felt with the rich, dark aroma of ready-to-eat chocolate. There was a lesson hidden within, I was sure. I couldn't nail it: it was like the dark vegetation we rushed past, a blurred form just beyond the reach of the motorway lights.

Slowly, the city crept out of the darkness. We passed a couple of solitary lights winking among ghostlike trees and bushes; then determined clumps of three or four buildings at a time began to appear; here and there, I saw a hand-painted store sign lit by a flickering fluorescent tube surrounded by a haze of insects. The traffic was thickening. Our driver swerved from lane to lane for a while, then gave up behind a truck whose tarp was flapping like a loose sail.

We passed an immense woman cooking something over an open fire next to the road. Three or four men waited patiently on a bench nearby, while the whippet-like dog at their feet snapped its jaws at the night air. This was followed by the first multi-level building since the airport: a three-storey cube of concrete with iron reinforcing rods still sticking out, the window openings covered by plastic sheets. Kross stopped talking with the driver and I seized this chance.

"So this is Abidjan," I said. He took this seriously. He said:

"Don't worry, that's not our hotel. These are just the suburbs on the rough side of the city."

"The rough side of the city?"

"You'll see."

Soon enough, I did. Most houses were variations on the concrete cube concept; the majority had pastel-coloured stucco in front, but the sides (and probably back) were raw concrete. Many retained the iron rods; maybe the rods were useful in some mysterious way, if only providing the inhabitants with a false sense of security. Numerous fires flickered along the sidewalks, and it took me a while to work out these were the kitchens of tiny outdoor eateries: they often featured a group of benches and tables nearby complete with a gaggle of hungry-looking characters. The high-speed motorway ceased to be a high-speed motorway and became a wide, clogged city street.

We slowed down to a crawl just in front of the entrance onto a bridge. I didn't mind the slowdown because of the view. The bridge ran for at least half a mile above a lagoon that sparkled with thousands of reflected lights. It led to a a different Abidjan: the skyline of the opposite bank featured a magnificent glittering shaft piercing the dark sky. I tapped Kross on the shoulder, pointed at this architectural wonder and said jokingly:

"I take it that's our hotel."

He grinned at me over his shoulder, and said:

"You're getting sharp, Oscar. That's correct."

CHAPTER ELEVEN

As the cab turned into the flower-bedded, fountained driveway leading to the hotel's front entrance, Kross slapped my hand with his passport and said:

"Take this and get our keys, they'll ask to see both passports. The reservation's in your name. We'll meet up by the rooms."

"The reservation's in my name, eh? What are the room numbers?"

"You'll find out, hopefully," said Kross. I bristled, but before I could think of a cutting answer the cab stopped, and I was ejected into the colonnaded hotel entrance. There were two admirals in full dress uniform flanking the huge automatic sliding doors. One of them saluted me as I went by.

The lobby was awe-inspiring, bigger than the main squares in many towns. The marble walls run up to a glass dome resembling a cathedral's. There were at least two fountains that added trickly sparkle to the multilingual noise of a hundred conversations. The air was spiced with the scent of exotic perfumes.

I had some difficulty zeroing in on the marble battlements of the reception counter; although it was the size of a small castle, it was dwarfed by the storefronts, the fountains, the neon signs. I crossed over to the reception, swimming through the sea of voices. I was feeling slightly intimidated, and consoled myself with the thought that the majority of all those exotic, important-sounding conversations ran along where-the-fuck-were-you-I-been-here-for-an-hour lines.

The room numbers were 1011 and 1012. While I waited for the elevator, I noted that most people in the hotel atrium were white. Black and shades of brown came next, and maybe ten per cent were of diverse different hues. One specimen in angry pink stood out in particular, and I reminded myself to stay out of the sun as much as possible. Kross had earlier told me a couple of stories about fresh arrivals having their brains boiled within a few hours of venturing outside.

As he'd promised, he was waiting by the rooms next to our luggage, somehow managing to appear impatient even when leaning against the wall. I handed him his key.

"Ten eleven all right?" I said.

"No, I want ten twelve." I raised an eyebrow while handing the key over, and said:

"Such a modern hotel, but they're still using keys, not cards."

"Power outages," Kross said.

"They don't have backup generators?"

Kross snorted.

"This place needs tons of juice just to run the ventilation and keep emergency lights on," he said. He put his key into the lock and added:

"I'll give you a shout in an hour or so."

"What for?"

"Dinner."

A couple of hours later I let my knife and fork clank down next to the gristly remains of my steak, and said:

"Now look here, I've got something to tell you. I understand you're the security expert. But maybe there's something you don't fully realize. I haven't spent all my life in crappy rooming houses. I've been in charge of up to thirty other people on ventures that cost ten thousand dollars per minute. I'm not a fucking snot-faced kid. So while I appreciate the need for discretion, this whole need-to-know business, I want to know the plan in detail. The exact setup. For example, I'd like to know how many hotel rooms around the world are reserved in my name."

Kross was smoking a cigarette and he blew smoke in my face when he said:

"Is that what you want to know—names?"

"No, no names," I said. "I don't need names. I need to know exactly how things will work. So let's drop all this smoke-and-mirrors business."

He considered this for a while. He looked round the half-empty, half-dark hotel restaurant (the cheapest of the three on offer; I'd insisted on it). Then he put out his cigarette, and said:

"Do I need to remind you what will happen if you talk about this to anyone else?"

"You don't."

"Fine." He leaned forward, putting his elbows on the table. He looked at my left eye and then at my right eye; he was probably trying to look inside my head. Then he said:

"Tomorrow, there's nothing for you to do but relax. We'll start early the next day. I want us out of the hotel by eight. We collect the car, which—note this—is reserved in your name. It's a white Peugeot 504, because it's the most common car around here. Manual gear shift, but you told me that's not a problem. We have to hit the border between eleven and noon at the latest. Noon is when my guy begins his shift."

"Your guy?"

"The guy in charge of the Ivory Coast customs post. We've done business before. And he in turn knows the guy in charge on the other, Ghanaian side. They've done business before too. It's that simple."

"And I just get waved through?"

"And you just get waved through. They'll stamp your passport. That's all."

"And you'll be waiting there the whole time?" He shrugged.

"It shouldn't take you more than six hours. It cannot take you more than seven hours. You have to get back before our guys go off duty."

"What if it takes me longer?"

"It won't take you longer. Most likely it's going to take around five hours. Two hours' relaxed drive each way, maximum one hour on the spot. That's it, and you're done."

I let out a long exhalation and waited while the red-jacketed waiter collected our plates. Kross ordered two more beers. We were drinking a local brand called Flag. It was good.

"That easy-peasy aspect is the part I have difficulty with," I said. "If this stuff is so easy to get at, how come it's still around after all those years? Almost two fucking centuries! And how do you know it's still there, anyway? You haven't checked lately, correct? There's only one way this stuff could be still around, just one way: it's hidden very well. And if it's hidden very well, then it's not easy to find."

"It's easy enough to find when you know where to look."

"The fuck it is. Jesus Christ. What do I have to do to make you tell me where it's hidden? You'll have to tell me anyway. For fuck's sake."

"Can't it wait till tomorrow?"

"No, it definitely can't wait till tomorrow." He thought about that for a while. Then he said:

"Okay. It's – "

"Kross!" exclaimed a melodious female voice close to my left ear. I jerked in my seat. Kross looked up and instantly switched on a big grin. He said:

"Mireille!" He got up from his seat and took a step forward and they started jabbering over my head in French.

I got up too and half turned and had to raise my hand to my mouth and pretend to cough. This was to hide the fact that my mouth had dropped open.

The woman I was looking at was stunning. She had dark shoulder-length hair with bangs and big dark eyes and a small slightly upturned nose and lips I wanted to kiss. She was wearing a grey canvas dress of a very utilitarian cut, which was just as well: a sexy outfit would have likely made me faint. When she looked at me and smiled I felt myself beginning to blush. I coughed again behind my raised hand and glanced at Kross.

"Oh I'm sorry," he said, switching to English. "This is a friend of mine. Oscar."

"Hello Oscar," said Mireille. We shook hands and it felt like touching God, or at any rate one of his favourite angels.

"Nice to meet you," I said, and sat down again. I had to.

"I'll get another chair," said the efficient Kross. "Here." He swung his chair around to the side of the table. Mireille sat down. She smiled at me, and I attempted to smile back. I had no idea what to say. Luckily Kross returned quickly accompanied by a grinning waiter who was carrying an extra chair. I heard Mireille order a Pernod and water. I kept trying to think of something to say to her, and failed.

In the meantime she was looking at Kross, and he was looking at her. It definitely was a reunion-of-old-pals type of scene. Maybe they were busy counting wrinkles.

"You haven't changed," she said in English.

"Neither have you," Kross said.

"How gallant." Then she looked at me and said:

"You two are here together or have you just met, too?"

It was an odd-sounding question and I didn't answer right away. Kross cut in saying something short in French in a don't-you-start-now tone. She frowned and began rooting through her handbag, a big flat shoulder-strapped pouch made from the brown scaly skin of an unidentified reptile. She pulled out a pack of cigarettes—I noticed she wasn't

156

wearing a wedding ring—tapped out a stubby cigarette and lit it. It was one of those dark-tobacco French brands that smell like cigars dipped in sauerkraut juice. However, she smoked with such style it made up for the stink. She began with an action that I applauded with all my heart—she took a deep drag and blew it out right into Kross's eyes.

"Don't screw around with me, Kross," she said. "Are you two together, and what are you doing here?" Kross held up his palms and grinned and I watched with a new interest: it was the first time I saw him look guilty.

"Oscar and I are here on a holiday," he said. "A week. It's his first time in Africa."

"So you two are together," she said. "On a vacation."

"That's right," I said easily. I could handle this, I thought. "We're going to the Komoe national park."

"The Komoe? You want to see if there are any elephants left, waiting to be photographed?" She turned to face Kross. "Is that the idea?"

"Hell yes," he said. "We already have a car rented." She snorted and said:

"An ordinary car? Or something with six wheels and a cannon? No," she raised her hand to silence Kross, who became somewhat agitated. "Don't tell me. I don't want to know. Just promise me one thing: that you're not here to cause trouble."

"We're not here to cause any mischief whatsoever," said Kross in ringing, clear tones. "And our car is a very ordinary Peugeot 504."

"You're going to the Komoe in a 504? You of all people know very well you need a four-wheel drive up there."

"We're going up to the Komoe," I said very firmly. She bent her head to look at me.

"If that's so you can visit me," she said. "I live nearby." I was speechless. Kross cut in:

"You're not based in Abidjan? Where are you?"

"Bondoukou. Right on the way into Komoe. I work at the hospital there. You can stop on your way in and on your way out. Check in, check out. That way," she said to Kross, "That way I'll know for sure."

"Hey," he said. "Of course. It will be our pleasure. Won't it, Oscar?" I quickly swallowed some Flag, and said:

"Sure. What do you do at the hospital, Mireille?" She looked me in the eye and said:

"I cut people open, remove this and that, and then I sew them up again." She glanced at her watch, and said to Kross:

"I have to go. I'm meeting someone here. See you in Bondoukou in a couple of days, *d'accord*?" She drained her glass, the ice cubes clinking, got up and turned to look at me and added:

"Goodbye."

The moment she was out of earshot, I hissed at Kross:

"Who the fuck is she?"

"Cool down, Oscar. She is who she says she is. A surgeon working here under a contract. Officially."

"And unofficially?"

"She might be doing a little work for SDECE. French intelligence service."

"She's a fucking spy!"

"She's not a fucking spy, and you're fucking stupid. Chances are she doesn't even know she's passing information to SDECE."

"What!?"

He clicked his tongue in an annoyed manner, as if I'd just soiled my diaper.

"It goes like this," he said, his tone implying he was talking to a retard. "You're shooting the shit over a beer with someone and you go oh, I drove down to Abidjan to get some shopping done, yeah, sure, got everything I wanted and I also ran into those two guys. Then this someone goes and writes a report mentioning the two new guys on the scene. Got it?"

"If she's so clueless, what was that crack about cars equipped with cannon?"

"She knows I've been an armoured car commander. And like most people, she doesn't like guns."

"But *you* like guns."

"Yes, I do. As someone put it, you can achieve a lot with a kind word, but you can achieve a hell of a lot more with a kind word and a gun."

"Fancy you quoting Al Capone," I said. "Well, well. Anyway, don't bullshit me, okay? She was way too suspicious of us. She's clearly thinking we're up to something. And that crack of hers—she didn't meet you while you were driving around in an armored car, did she?"

He let out an irritated snort, and said:

"Yes, that's exactly how we met. I actually got her out of really deep shit. She finds that difficult to forgive. But I understand. She views me as a mercenary soldier pure and simple, and she hates mercenaries. It's pretty irritating to have your ass saved by someone you don't like on principle."

"You saved her ass? Really?"

"Many years back. Look, we can go over everything later. We can spend all afternoon and evening tomorrow, if you like. But right now I've got to check on a couple of things, and make some final arrangements. All right?"

"What things? What arrangements?"

"I'll explain later. Got to go and see to them right now. Okay?"

I stared at Kross for a while. Then I said:

"Okay. But later means no later than tonight. Not tomorrow. Tomorrow I have the whole day to relax, right? Tonight."

"That's my boy," he said. He actually reached out and patted me on my arm before I could move it out of range. Then we paid our bill and split up, with myself going back to my room. I was feeling really tired. I wanted some rest. And the bed in my room promised to be very comfortable; I checked it out when I was done unpacking my stuff.

In fact, it was so comfortable I passed out almost right away. I had a shock when I woke up: I had no idea where I was, and what I was doing there. For a moment I thought I was still dreaming. My watch told me it was nearing ten, and since it was dark it had to be ten at night. I washed my face with cold water in the space-age bathroom—all steel and glass—but it still took me a while to get a grip on reality.

I was standing in front of the clock next to the door and resetting my watch to Abidjan time when I heard female voices in the corridor. They fell silent right outside my door. Then someone knocked on it, very sharply. It was a very unfeminine, commanding knock.

It was Kross, of course. He brought two women with him, two really good-looking prostitutes. They were both mulattas with long, snakelike braided hair: twenty-year-old modern Medusas skimpily dressed in vinyl. One wore white vinyl hot pants and a black vinyl vest. The other had a black vinyl miniskirt and a white vinyl bolero. It was impossible not to imagine them going down on each other. I said:

"Kross. What the fuck is this?"

"This," he said, "Is Angelique. And this is Monique. They both speak English. They've been around." He put his arms around them as he spoke, and they giggled appreciatively. I was pretty sure the three of them had been drinking. So these were the urgent arrangements, the things Kross had to see to right after our restaurant visit!

"Hello," the white hot pants said to me. She was very good-looking; she had a bright future ahead in her chosen profession. I said to Kross:

"I repeat. What the fuck is this?"

"I saw the way you looked at Mireille, and thought it was time for a little rest and recreation," Kross said. "We've worked so hard to get here. Besides, it's an essential part of getting acclimatized."

"Don't you fuck around with me."

"Oscar! *They* are the ones who want to fuck around with you."

"For fuck's sake. We were supposed to talk."

"We'll talk tomorrow."

"I thought you had something planned tomorrow. And I was supposed to relax."

"I just have to check out a couple of things on the web. There's an internet café downstairs. I'll definitely be done by noon. So why don't you start relaxing tonight? Which one do you like better? I like Angelique." He squeezed the hip of the black miniskirt and she let out a delighted yelp and bit him on the ear. He said something French to Monique, and opened the door.

"We'll talk first thing tomorrow. Crack of dawn—say, half past eleven. I'll give you a shout." He let the giggling Angelique pull him out into the corridor.

The door slammed shut. I looked at Monique. She looked back at me. I asked:

"Would you like a drink?"

She shook her head, grinning, and walked up to me. She stopped very close to me, and I moved a step back.

"My name is Monique," she said.

"I know. My name is Oscar."

"I know," she said, and stepped forward again. I stepped back. I said:

"Look, I don't know if I'm up to this."

Her grin didn't waver. She put a hand on her crotch and gave it a squeaky squeeze. She said:

"Then you can watch."

CHAPTER TWELVE

My first African morning found me in the bathroom, vigorously soaping my dick. True, Monique had repeatedly assured me she had a medical checkup every fortnight; she claimed she'd had one a couple of days earlier. True, she had brought a wide assortment of multi-coloured condoms (she'd told me *Pretty Woman* was her favourite movie). However, I'd seen my share of photos of emaciated AIDS victims, and now was hard at work with the hotel soap. As if it would, or could help.

I hadn't intended to have sex with Monique. But I did watch Monique for a while. Then I attempted to get a conversation going. I told her I was an art director by trade. She said she'd assumed I was in the movie business and I had to have a drink when I heard that. Things went on from there.

I'd just emerged from the bathroom when there was a soft knock on my door. I froze, then hastily strapped on my wristwatch—it was just past nine-thirty—and started looking for my pants. There was a harder knock on the door. I finally noticed a trouser leg coyly peeking out from under the bed. I bent down, but before I could retrieve my pants I heard the lock snap open and Kross rushed in.

163

He moved very fast. He closed and locked the door and crossed the room in the time I took to straighten up and gather the breath needed to tell him to go back to his basket. This was outrageous—and he'd taken my key! Then things got really outrageous. He hit me in the stomach. I couldn't breathe. All of a sudden I found myself curled up on the floor and wheezing like a leaky bicycle pump. It was clear that Kross was very good at hitting people. I wasn't in a hurry to get up, and let him do it again.

"Get up," said Kross, as if on cue. "You fucking useless cunt." He sounded as if he might apply a boot, so I got up. I felt so supremely ridiculous and defenseless in my underwear that I proceeded to pull my pants from under the bed and then onto myself, hopping awkwardly on one leg at one point. I hoped Kross wouldn't hit a guy who was busy putting on his pants.

He didn't. Instead, he said:

"You *cunt*. Who is that prick asking about Avery and the *Swallow* on the web? *Our* Avery and our *Swallow*. I know he's in Toronto, I know he and you are connected. If you lie to me now I'll fucking smash your face in."

I said very quickly:

"He's a very good friend of mine. I didn't tell anyone else. You've got nothing to worry about. He doesn't know why I asked him. And he's very discreet."

"*Discreet?!* Are you out of your fucking mind? He's broadcasting his interest to the entire fucking world!" He actually looked as if he might hit me again. I said quickly:

"He's only asking about the ship. Avery is supposed to have been a shipmate of one of my great-great-grandfathers. You must have noticed there's a Hansen mentioned too. That's all he knows. Nothing about the treasure."

Kross lost the desire to hit me; he deflated visibly. He shut his eyes and shook his head, looked at me, shook his head again, and lit a cigarette.

"I can't fucking believe it," he said. "You work in advertising. You're an intelligent man. If you had a body hidden in your closet, would you ask people to hang their coats inside? I can't fucking believe it." He stiffened again. "Who else did you tell?"

"No one. No one, I swear. And I didn't really tell Tad anything either. I told him a story about a naval ancestor. It clicked because he knows my old man is a retired naval officer." For some obscure reason, this last bit of information made Kross tense a little. He said:

"Oh, you people. You intelligent, beautiful, educated people. Walking around with heads stuck up your own asses. You never see anything. And you don't listen. You're just too fucking busy admiring your inner beauty."

"What the fuck – "

"Shut up. Shut up and listen for a change. There are very many people out there who actually use their eyes and ears. And when those people, people who do watch and listen see shit stirring, they want to know why. You fucking wally. I thought you claimed you weren't a snot-faced kid."

I couldn't think of a response to that. I silently stood there feeling guilty, and hating it.

"I wasn't sure," I said eventually. "I didn't see Greenbottle's book – "

"Oh, shut up. If you weren't sure, what the fuck are you doing here?"

After a while, I shrugged and said:

"I wanted to be here."

"Yes. You wanted to be here. And now you're here, and I wonder, really wonder, what the fuck I should do with you."

I felt icy dread. He'd said it in a very dispassionate way in spite of being angry, the way you'd ask a condemned man to watch his step while climbing the stairs to the scaffold.

"Do you mind if I put on a shirt?" I asked.

"I don't give a fuck. You can put on a dress if you want." He smoked in silence while I dressed. Then he said:

"All right. I'm not going to kill you over this, it would just cause more problems. But our original plan is blown. I don't trust you to go off by yourself. I don't trust you enough to tell you where the stuff is hidden. We'll have to do things the hard way. Fuck! You goddamn moron." He stared at me for a while. It was a very unpleasant stare. He said:

"So now, thanks to you I've got a very busy day. You can stay here, or go out—I don't care as long as you're back by nightfall. But if you open your mouth again to anyone at all about our business, no matter what you say or don't say I'll break your fucking neck."

"I'm sorry. I'm really sorry. If you'd brought Greenbottle's book with you like you'd promised, none of this would've happened."

"Don't you try to make it my fault."

"I'm not. I'm just explaining why I wanted to know a little bit more about the whole thing."

Kross was silent for a moment. Then he said:

"From now on, you keep your trap shut at all times. You don't even tell anyone the time of day without getting clearance from me first. What the fuck inspired you to tell Mireille we're going to the Komoe?"

"Well, that was to be the official excuse, right? And since she seemed suspicious—by the way, are we driving up there to see her?"

"I'm not telling you a goddamn thing about what we're going to do."

"Okay. I understand."

My meek attitude must have appeased Kross a little, because he said:

"I wasn't planning on driving up there. I'd have called her at the hospital to say we can't make it because you're shitting your brains out after eating from a street stall. Or whatever."

He ground his cigarette out with such force that it split, spilling half-burnt tobacco over the ashtray. I said:

"If I'm allowed to go out, can I have my key back?"

"I don't have your goddamn key. Maybe Monique took it." He walked to the door and opened it. He turned to give me an angry glare, and said:

"I still have my old master key from when I was working here. Make sure you're back by six." He shut the door very softly when he left, the way one shuts doors in a hospital or a morgue.

167

The moment he left, I collapsed into the armchair set next to the morning table, and buried my face in my hands. Fucking internet! And how did Kross find out Tad was in Toronto? The whole world-wide web phenomenon was something relatively new, and I really knew fuck-all about it.

The thing was, I'd never really taken to computers. In the school I went to, we were all forced to write with pens and ink; ballpoints were banned. The idea was to teach kids nice, legible handwriting because lots of important writing was done by hand back in the day. Anyway, I liked it. There was an element of artistry involved. And you had to get things right both the first time around and repeatedly thereafter, because there was no copy/paste, and paper was expensive.

But now, my old-fashioned preferences had caught up to bite me on the ass. All I could do was thank Providence for getting Tad so loaded Monday night that he required an ambulance the following morning. I'd intended to ask him him to run a search for Mark Kross, and I definitely didn't want to imagine the consequences once Kross found out about *that*.

What I wanted, first and foremost, was to find my hotel key. I eventually found it under my pillow. I had no idea why I put it there. So Kross had a master key, eh? Well, so he would if he'd really been in charge of setting up the hotel security. I felt suddenly hungry, and realized I had seven hours until six in the evening, a wad of big, floppy Central African franc banknotes, plus a wallet with plenty of traveller's cheques.

I pocketed the francs, and left. I thought that since I had plenty of time on my hands, I might just as well get a look at some of the attractions the hotel had to offer. I'd studied the brochure left in the room and apparently it had a lot, including a world-famous casino.

But in the end I didn't go to the world-famous hotel casino. I didn't visit the hotel's supermarket, either of its two swimming pools, or any of its three restaurants. I didn't even see the skating rink specially put in for visiting Canadians. As I was going down in the elevator, I had the recurring thought that Kross would dump me once we'd recovered the diamonds. It killed my appetite for tourist activities, and I returned to my room to spend a dreary and unpleasant afternoon. Its high point was something called a buffalo burger and a beer, brought in by room service.

Kross showed up just after six o'clock. He was very polite. He waited until I'd opened the door to let him in, and he didn't hit me. Instead, he said:

"Give me all the money you have. Well, you can leave yourself the francs and a a hundred bucks in traveller's cheques. Sign the rest, and give them to me along with your passport."

"Do you want my airline ticket too?" I asked.

"I haven't got time for this, fella. I've got a guy waiting. Move it."

I considered this and decided there was a slight but significant chance I might get punched in the stomach, so I moved. I left myself a couple of fifty dollar cheques—just tore them out and put them in my wallet. I signed the rest and handed them over the entire booklet to Kross: seventeen hundred US dollars. Somewhat grudgingly, he said:

"I need these for a vehicle. Don't worry, the guy's going to buy it back when we return. Treat it as an expensive rental."

"What are you getting for seventeen hundred? A motorbike?" He allowed himself a small smile.

"You'll see later. Be here at nine." And he fucked off. He seemed to be in a real hurry.

I got myself a Coke from the mini-bar and spent the next hour trying to work out why Kross wanted almost all my money. He had twice as much as me, to start with. After taking my money, he'd have at least eight thousand dollars. But five thousand had been originally earmarked for bribes. And he needed to keep at least a grand for unexpected expenses.

Then it hit me that Kross might have taken almost all my money to make sure I didn't run. He knew I was broke and couldn't afford to return to Toronto with a hundred dollars in my pocket. And then I thought that maybe he took my money as the first step prior to dumping me. My imagination started throwing up various scenarios of how that could happen and I spent the next couple of hours going round in fucking circles, figuratively and literally. I got so tired from all this walking I eventually had to lie down.

At five to nine, the phone in my room chirped seductively. I stared at it for a while, afraid to pick it up and wondering who might be calling.

It was Kross, naturally. He told me to meet him in the restaurant we'd been to the previous night.

"We'll have to talk about everything over dinner," he told me. "I want to turn in early. I'll take the same table as last night or another nearby, so that you don't get lost trying to find me."

On the way down I wondered why he hadn't said that *we* needed to turn in early. Was he about to tell me I was out? Yes, and that was why he'd taken almost all my money! He was going to discard me. I felt a lump growing in my throat as I left the elevator, and made my way to the restaurant. I squared my shoulders and promised myself a stiff drink before I ate, maybe more than one. Kross would be the one paying, by default. I decided I'd choose an expensive Scotch.

As advertised, he was seated at our table from the previous evening. He'd already ordered a beer for me, upsetting my plan. He looked tired and dusty. I sat down across from him, and said:

"I hope everything went well."

He nodded.

"We need to talk," he said.

"Yes, I know," I said, reaching for my glass. The beer tasted good, though not as good as a whisky would. Kross took out a cigarette, and rolled it between his fingers for a while before he lit it. He said:

"I don't really need you any more. I have to go in person anyway, so I might as well do it alone. You could still be helpful if you stuck to doing what I tell you to do, and when I tell you to do it. Otherwise you're just a pain."

He paused, likely expecting me to start promising I'll lick his boots if he agreed to take me along. I didn't say anything. I drank more beer. Eventually Kross said:

"You've invested money in our little enterprise, and I know raising that money hasn't been easy. So, you're entitled to one last chance. One very last chance. You can come with me if you stay hundred per cent disciplined at all times. Or you can catch the next plane home. Your ticket can be rebooked to another flight. And one last thing: if you decide to come, you'll be getting a quarter, not a third. You're not as important any more. It's still a generous cut in the circumstances."

"A quarter," I said, and found that I'd run out of beer.

"Yes."

"Or a flight home."

"Yes."

"So how much would a quarter amount to?"

"Between a hundred and two fifty. Certainly not less than a hundred thousand American."

"Can I think about it?"

"Two minutes."

"Can I have a whisky while I think about it?"

"No."

It was a no-brainer. I wasn't going back with a hundred dollars when I could be going back with a hundred thousand dollars. The unpleasant events that took place earlier had finally, completely convinced me that Avery's treasure was real. Kross wouldn't have been so angry with me, otherwise.

And the fact that he gave me a choice to come along or leave—surely that meant he wasn't going to dump me, or do me any harm.

"I'm in as long as we don't get shot at," I said. "Will we get shot at?"

He considered this carefully, much too carefully for my liking.

"Not if we do everything my way," he said. So there it was. There could be trouble, after all.

I could hear blood pounding in my head when I said:

"In for a third, in for a quarter. Okay."

CHAPTER THIRTEEN

Kross outlined his new plan to me over the post-meal beers. He was careful to reveal as few details as possible. I was informed that we would be crossing into Ghana illegally; he knew the perfect spot. It was located several hours' driving north of Abidjan.

I was unpleasantly shocked. I asked Kross if he was sure we could get away with an illegal entry plus many hours of driving around, visa-less, in a country that had declared a Kross embargo. He said yes, he was goddamn sure, that's why he wanted to do it that way. That was it, end of broadcast. Further instalments would be forthcoming as necessity arose.

Kross did tell me at least one lie that evening. He said that I needed to be ready to leave at eight am; the vehicle he'd bought, a four-wheel-drive Toyota, was 'being fixed' and wouldn't be ready before the morning. But I was woken up by the chirping phone by my bed just before dawn: the inky darkness in my room was beginning to turn grey.

"Get your ass out of bed, Oscar," said Kross softly. "Be ready to leave in half an hour. Pack lightly. Leave your luggage, just take an overnight bag."

"Okay. I – "

He hung up. I replaced the receiver, and checked my watch: it showed five forty six. I picked the phone up again, ordered breakfast, and went to wash.

We met in front of the elevators at exactly six thirty one. He was carrying a big, sausage-shaped black nylon bag that I hadn't seen earlier. I asked him about the luggage we were leaving in our rooms and he revealed that the rooms were ours for the week, and that they were free of charge. Well, not *entirely* free of charge; in accordance with the local custom he'd been obliged to present a thank-you gift: a thousand American. This in turn led to another thank-you gift: two hotel hookers, personally selected by the hotel manager.

The Toyota four-wheel-drive Kross had acquired was a small pickup truck. It had been freshly painted khaki: it still smelled strongly of paint. I stood by the truck and inhaled its chemical aroma while Kross settled things with a tired-looking, elderly African gentleman in a white shirt and sharply creased tan slacks. The Toyota's engine was running: it emitted a steady, reassuring rumble.

The passenger door was unlocked, and when I opened it I saw that the truck had been metallic blue until very recently: that was the colour of the metal interior. The truck seemed to be in good shape; the dials on the dashboard sparkled eagerly. It had two gear shift sticks—one higher than the other—and they both shook in unison with the throbbing engine. I put my bag behind the passenger seat. There were a couple of cigarette burns on the upholstery, but it looked comfortable enough. The odometer showed the truck had travelled just over a hundred and twenty-five thousand kilometres, but that could be misleading. Odometers didn't show the most important thing: the mileage that was still left.

The driver's door squeaked open and Kross climbed in. He was wearing a pair of teardrop aviator sunglasses of the kind favoured by motorcycle cops. I hadn't seen him wearing them ever before, and he looked strange. He swung his bag inside, got into his seat, and fucked around adjusting it for the better part of a minute. I nearly laughed when he pulled on a pair of string driving gloves; it appeared he took driving very, very seriously.

"No safety belt?" I asked.

"No. But you can strap yourself in if you like."

"I told myself I'll be following your example."

He glanced at me sharply, saw I wasn't smiling, and said:

"Seat belts can be awkward when you want to get out in a hurry."

I said nothing, just nodded, and we drove off.

There was a big advantage to setting out so early: there was hardly any traffic. We drove down a broad two-lane road for maybe a minute, then turned into a six-lane avenue decorated with billboards advertising Flag beer, Nido chocolate drink, and several brands of exotic cigarettes. They weren't very creative: basically big product shots. Most had a big dark hand holding out the product as if it was the torch of liberty.

The architecture beyond the billboards was similarly uninspired. The majority of buildings consisted of variations on the concrete cube theme. We did pass a group of ambitious high-rises, white paint blistered and peeling from the walls as if they too suffered from sunburn; and at one point the road ran along what appeared to be a golf course that featured palms and enormous agaves.

Eventually the six lanes narrowed down to four, and then to two: by that time the city had dwindled to rows of shacks with rust-streaked, corrugated iron roofs. The gaps between the buildings began to grow; the vacant lots became increasingly overgrown; and suddenly there were no more houses at all, just tall, savage-looking yellowish grass that swayed triumphantly. Here and there, a lucky seedling had sprouted into a full-grown bush or tree; and occasionally there would be a cone-shaped tower of red mud erected by termites. A couple I saw were higher than me, with long spindly minarets rising from the sides. But otherwise it was a sea of grass, waist-deep in some places and shoulder-high in others.

We didn't talk. The Toyota had no air-conditioning, so the windows were wide open and the roar of air at over a hundred kilometres per hour precluded any conversation. In spite of all the ventilation, it started getting hot around nine. By that time, the traffic had thickened. There always were two or three other vehicles in view: Japanese-made minibuses, Peugeot 504 taxis, juggernaut trucks, and plenty of light motorcycles: Suzukis, Yamahas, Kawasakis, a few Hondas. Their helmet-less drivers all kept to the edge of the road, so they weren't a problem; but all other traffic tended to bunch up behind the trucks, and overtaking always meant passing more than one vehicle.

Before very long I was clutching the dashboard grab rail and wishing I'd strapped myself in after all. There was one particularly hairy moment when Kross was overtaking a couple of minibuses behind a long tanker truck. The tanker was spewing black smoke from the exhaust and trailing a grounding chain that struck dangerous-looking sparks as it bounced and twisted on the road. And when we drew level with the tanker's rear wheels, its driver accelerated.

Kross swore and floored the gas pedal. We hit a pothole and the Toyota skittered like a startled horse. My face was so close to one of the huge wheels that I could smell the hot rubber. Another truck appeared from behind the curve ahead, close enough for me to make out the three-point Mercedes logo on the radiator grille. Kross flicked the lights on and put his elbow on the horn and the driver of the Merc slowed down enough to let us cut across the tanker's snout: it protested with a deafening blare from its horn. I let go of the dashboard grip and rubbed the fresh sweat from my face.

"That was exciting," I said. Kross reached to get a cigarette from the pack he'd put on the dashboard. He punched the knob of the cigarette lighter in the dashboard and said:

"Fucking asshole." He pulled out the lighter and lit his cigarette and that was the extent of our conversation for the next couple of hours.

Before long, the exotic countryside ceased to be entertaining. I amused myself by watching all the motorcycle tightrope artists. The first prize went to a guy driving a Suzuki one-handed while holding onto a full crate of Fanta Orange balanced on his head. Well, he couldn't really put it anywhere else: his wife rode right behind him with an infant strapped to her back, and he had another kid sitting before him, astride the gas tank.

Around eleven o'clock, we stopped at a Shell station to refuel both the car and our own selves. I wanted to use the lavatory, but Kross told me:

"Don't go there. We'll be eating lunch soon, and it will be the last proper meal you'll have in the next twenty-four hours. You don't want to lose your appetite."

"I still need to take a piss."

"Go behind the buildings. Everyone does. I'll pretend I need to top up the radiator so that we can rinse our hands."

"You were right," I told Kross a few minutes later, shaking my hands dry as he replaced the water hose. "Everyone *does* piss behind the buildings. I think I lost some of my appetite. Could I ask you about a few things?"

"You can always ask."

"I think something's going wrong with my eyesight. Everything seems to have a reddish hue, even the sun."

"There's nothing wrong with your eyesight. That's harmattan. Wind from the desert, loaded with dust. We're not far from the end of the dry season, so actually it's pretty mild."

"Red dust?"

"Yes, dust. Finer than talcum powder, but very abrasive. Remember those rocks we flew over? Well, you'll remember them for a long time. This dust gets everywhere and stays there. You'll be finding it a year from now in your stuff."

"Good to know," I said. "Thank you. By the way, do you think you can tell me a little about what happens next? Just a little? I mean I don't even have anyone else to talk to. Just you."

He hesitated briefly, then nodded.

"Okay," he said. "We can talk about that in the car."

"We'll be driving through Bondoukou shortly," he told me, once we'd gotten moving again.

"Really? We're going to see Mireille?"

He laughed, and said:

"Fuck no. No way. We don't want anyone to note our presence here. We are keeping our heads down and driving straight through to a village just a stone's throw from the border. Then we'll take a dirt track to the spot I know. We'll be in Ghana less than an hour from now."

But as it turned out, Kross was wrong. A minute later, we had to pull to a stop and wait as a couple of teenaged boys drove a herd of cattle across the road, savagely whipping the animals' flanks with thorny branches. The cattle were huge, white, and skinny, with ribs showing plainly under the short white fur; they also had big curved horns that would've made me afraid to hit them with anything short of an assault rifle. But the boys slapped and whipped them with impunity, maybe because the cows seemed immune to pain; they trotted across unhurriedly, ignoring the blows.

I turned to Kross and saw that he was staring at one of the dials on the dashboard. He frowned, and tapped it with his finger.

"Invisibility meter all right?" I asked. He didn't answer. The last two cows moseyed across the road, one of them squirting a burst of liquid shit right in front of the Toyota.

"I hope this means good luck," I said.

It didn't. It started well: when we entered Bondoukou, Kross impressed me by expertly threading the Toyota through the traffic: other vehicles, small herds of goats, and plenty of pedestrians. But before long, we got caught in a traffic jam caused by yet another tanker truck.

It was wedged in between a flimsy wooden stall on one side of the road and the big open gutter on the other. The driver was trying to turn it around, and it definitely wasn't a three-point turn: it was a fifty-point turn as the huge vehicle shuddered back and forth, gaining a few degrees at a time. An audience had gathered, and four or five driving experts shouted and waved at the tanker pilot, issuing what was most likely conflicting advice. It would have taken much less time to take the wooden stall apart and reassemble it elsewhere; it consisted of a folding table under a thatched roof supported by four gnarled poles.

I glanced at Kross and saw that he was tense. He tapped the invisibility meter again.

"Fuck," he said.

"They're all watching that guy there," I said. "We're invisible." Kross snorted.

"Battery's nearly flat," he said. "Should be fully charged after a drive like that. Fuck! Those guys, they just aren't happy if they don't find a way to pull a fast one somewhere."

"So what now? We buy a new battery?" He shook his head. He said:

"It's not as simple as that. It's not charging. We probably need a new alternator. I'll make sure he pays for it when we get back."

"You mean your guy?"

"No, the Pope." That brought the conversation to a close.

It was another minute or so before the tanker pilot completed his dance and rolled past, shifting up every couple of seconds—his truck seemed to have an infinite number of gears. It was another five minutes or so before we could move; the vehicles in front got going one by one as their drivers and passengers completed assorted roadside deals, finished important conversations, and so on. We travelled at walking speed for a few minutes, then had to halt for a gaggle of goats that had urgent business on the other side of the road. It was worse than rush hour in a big city. My sweat and the dust had combined into a greasy paste, and I left rusty prints on everything I touched.

I looked at my watch when Kross pointed out a Total service station sign that hove into view maybe two hundred yards away. I looked at it again when we finally got there, and found that the journey had taken nearly three minutes. Throughout that time we were besieged by a horde of teenaged hawkers of newspapers, soft drinks, fruit, chewing gum, cigarettes—I just sat and stared stonily ahead while Kross spat out the appropriate French phrase at those that got too aggressive.

There was a long, loose lineup at the gas pumps; it blocked access to the service area and Kross hit the horn, then poked his head through the window and shouted at a meditating minibus driver. The minibus moved to let us pass; a local matron seated inside gave us a look of utter contempt.

Kross stopped the Toyota by the service bay and got out. I watched him walk up to a tall African smoking a cigarette next to a small red Kawasaki motorbike missing its front wheel. Kross asked something, the guy nodded, and they disappeared together inside the service bay.

I was set for a long wait but Kross reappeared almost instantly. He was accompanied by a worried-looking guy liberally covered in grease and oil. He pointed out the Toyota to him and handed over the keys, followed by an eloquent little bunch of banknotes. The guy stopped looking worried, and nodded decisively.

Kross walked back to the Toyota, mouth set in a grim line. He opened the door and announced:

"It's gonna take a couple of hours. Let's go have that lunch now. There's a place down the road."

"What about our bags?"

"Leave them. No one will touch them."

I wasn't so sure of that. But I got out and followed him down the station lot and across the road, weaving between the crawling cars. He stopped by a tree sparsely shading the entrance to a biggish building with blotchy red stucco.

I came to a halt beside him and looked at the sign over the dark doorway. It was executed in a fancy, flowing white script. I said:

"The Trocadero. Where Bondoukou highlife congregates. I like the size of their air conditioner."

Kross didn't react. He seemed to be in some sort of trance. Later on, I decided that it was probably his professional sixth sense setting off a tiny alarm in his head.

But I didn't have that professional sixth sense. So I stepped forward, and entered the Trocadero.

I stopped as soon as I entered to get my bearings: it seemed very dark inside. Kross squeezed past me and stopped too. And then a familiar female voice said:

"How wonderful. So you decided to visit me after all."

Mireille was sitting at a table right to the side of the entrance, almost literally under my nose, which of course was why I hadn't noticed her. She was holding a half-empty bottle of Fanta with a striped straw sticking out. She was wearing a white T-shirt with big, floppy sleeves and a grin, the grin of a kid who has played a successful prank. She'd pulled her hair into a ponytail, and she was more beautiful than ever.

"He insisted," Kross said.

Mireille's grin turned into a thoughtful smile. She said:

"How charming. Would you like to sit down?"

The moment we did, she said:

"You must have started out really early to make it here by lunchtime. You're driving up to the game reserve, correct? Are you stopping here for the night?"

"No," Kross said. I was silent, mindful of his earlier instructions.

"You've made reservations at the lodge? They're often full up."

"We haven't. But I'm sure we'll find something."

She shook her head, smiling.

"Captain Kross," she said. "Always confident everything will work out."

I twitched in my seat when I heard Kross called a captain. Mireille noticed. She didn't miss much. She said:

"Oscar. Something on your mind? You're very quiet."

"Yes," I said. "I was wondering how to ask about the lavatory in French."

"You go through that door there," she said, pointing. "Then you walk to the end of a short hallway and turn right, no, left. Right is for ladies."

"Thank you," I said, and got up. As I walked away, I heard Kross break into rapid French.

CHAPTER FOURTEEN

I spent a couple of minutes standing at the end of the advertised hallway. It was incredible, walking into Mireille—just like that!—for the second time in three days. Could it really be just a coincidence? The odds against it were astronomical. I liked her so much that it made me stupid, and I was increasingly beginning to fancy some sort of divine intervention—she and I, we were simply meant for each other—when I remembered what Kross had said about her passing information to French intelligence, wittingly or not.

I was 100% on my guard when I rejoined Kross and Mireille at our table. But I was still unprepared for what I learned next.

It ran thusly: Mireille had been out shopping, and her car was full of bags and cartons. We were the designated porters. After driving to her place and unpacking, we'd receive our reward: a meal at the canteen. Mireille was living in a housing complex that she called a camp. It was inhabited by the higher-ranking hospital staff, and consisted of a number of small bungalows plus a combined canteen/café and bar/recreation centre. We could play a game of table tennis if we liked.

"The food's no worse than here," Mireille said. "And at least you can be sure what you eat won't start eating you in return. Parasites," she added, seeing the blank look on my face. She turned to Kross, and added:

"Later, I will drive you back so you can collect your car."

I very much liked the idea of spending some time in Mireille's company. But I was surprised Kross had let her talk him into something like that. My chance to ask why came when Mireille went into the store next door to the Trocadero to collect some of her shopping.

"What the fuck is this?" I asked Kross as soon as she disappeared. It felt nice, this role reversal—usually it was Kross that used that tone. "I thought you wanted to stay invisible. I thought you wanted to keep a low profile."

"She thinks something's up," he said.

"Something as in us being up to no good?"

"Yes."

"Smart woman."

"Which is why we have to play along," said Kross. "Act exactly as we would on a pleasure trip. Help her with her shopping, eat together, play tourists happy to meet an old friend."

"And?"

"Her shift starts at four in the afternoon, and the car's supposed to be ready by three thirty. She'll drop us off there before starting work."

"Perfect."

"As long as you don't open your big mouth."

"My big mouth? Sorry. One gets that way in advertising. All right, all right! I won't say a word."

Mireille's car turned out be a dusty white Renault sedan. I kept resolutely quiet all the way to Mireille's house. She and Kross conducted a lively conversation throughout the drive, talking in English for my benefit. Of course, I listened hungrily for anything that might reveal something about her.

I was disappointed. They discussed exciting topics such as inflation and the availability of selected goods and services, and the impact this availability had on the quality of life: for example, Mireille said the hospital and the adjoining camp had their own generators, which made her immune to the consequences of frequent power cuts. Kross remarked it was nice to know there always was a cold beer in the fridge.

The 'camp' turned out to be a compound of maybe thirty small square bungalows arranged in a scattered circle around the advertised canteen. There were many trees, carefully pruned, and the houses were surrounded by decorative shrubs and bushes, mostly hibiscus. The whole scene would have been downright cozy had it not been for the merciless sun and the immense, equally merciless sky, tinged red by the desert dust: the kind of sky that said it was a long way home.

Mireille proposed that we wash up at her place after unpacking the shopping. Kross agreed; after that we rode in silence, except for the gravel crunching under our wheels, until she stopped in front of her bungalow. It was fairly isolated from the other houses, its back pushing into a small grove of banana palms that grew in the far corner of the compound.

It turned out there really was a lot of shopping. The Renault's trunk was packed solid with crates and cartons: a lot of water, soft drinks, and beer. I commented on that, and Kross said:

"This is Africa. You need to drink a lot of liquids." He took every chance he could to make me feel the village idiot. I said:

"I was just wondering how she'd have dealt with all that if we weren't around."

"She'd just carry everything inside by herself. She's a tough cookie."

I grabbed a crate of Fanta and put my free arm around a carton of beer. Mireille's bungalow was painted white, like all the other buildings in the compound. A few steps led up to small, semi-enclosed verandah, from which a tough-looking French window opened into the living room. The dark wooden furniture—sofa set, dining set, a couple of bookcases—looked locally made; the green vinyl tile floor gave off a faint antiseptic smell. Everything looked very clean, and very empty: it was almost as if no one lived inside the house.

It took us three trips each to move Mireille's shopping inside. Mireille went to take a shower, while Kross and I carried everything into the kitchen. Usually, a woman's kitchen offers reliable hints as to her personality; but it wasn't so this time.

It was a very African kitchen. It was cool and dark, the broad ribbed leaves of the banana palms blocking most of the light that came through the insect screen in the window. The kitchen counter was a slab of concrete painted a glossy white. A huge refrigerator hummed expensively in one corner; in the other, a classroom-style chair stood next to a big rough-looking table which featured a short row of three empty bottles lined up neatly against the wall: one Flag, one mineral water, one Fanta. There was nothing else on show, not even a plate or cup left to dry in the wire dryer next to the sink.

"Can I ask you something?" I said to Kross. He shrugged in answer.

"What is the deal with her? Doesn't she have a family?"

"She's a widow. No children."

"Seems pretty young for a widow."

"Shit happens. Shut up now, I think she's coming."

She was. When she appeared, I saw that she'd changed into the familiar grey canvas dress. She glanced around the kitchen, taking in the crates, cartons, and bags that I'd artfully arranged into an eye-pleasing display, and said:

"Wonderful. You guys are free to use the bathroom now."

"You go first," I said to Kross, before he could say the same thing.

"I won't be a minute," he said, turning to leave. It was probably meant as a warning for me: an instruction to say as little as possible.

"Nice place you've got," I said to Mireille. She ignored it, and said:

"You and Kross. You're good friends?"

"Good enough to take a trip together. He really knows his way around here."

"You don't look like someone who gets lost easily," she said.

"You'd be surprised." Her lips curled in a sceptic smile, and she asked:

"Are you in the same line of work?"

"As him? No." She was looking at me expectantly, so I uttered a silly self-conscious giggle and said:

"I'm an art director. I work in advertising. I took a couple of weeks' vacation. This is just a pleasure trip."

"How come you're travelling with Kross?"

"We're, uh, neighbours back in Toronto. Really. Next door neighbours, as a matter of fact. That's how I came to know him. When I told him I was planning a holiday in Africa, he said he'd come along. He said once you've got Africa in your blood, you just have to return, again and again. Is it true?"

"That's a good question," she said.

"What do you mean?"

She gave me a long, silent, appraising look.

"Be careful," she said. "Be very careful. And now excuse me, I have to get my cigarettes."

She was gone for quite a while. I moved to the living room, and looked around. It was really bare. There were a couple of colourful French magazines on the coffee table and a transistor radio on a dark wood credenza. There also was a bookcase made of the same dark wood as the rest of the furniture, but all it contained were several fat volumes that turned out to be medical literature in French. It was a place inhabited by someone who only came home to sleep.

I heard footsteps approaching and Kross entered the room, hair wet and freshly combed.

"Your turn, Oscar," he said. "Don't take too long."

Mireille's bathroom was as unrevealing as the kitchen and the living room. It contained a large wall-hung cabinet which likely hid her stuff. I didn't look inside.

I washed hastily, sluicing water over my arms and face and leaving rusty smudges on the clean side of the yellow towel hanging next to the hand basin; Kross had left his marks on the other. When I returned to the living room, Kross and Mireille were already standing on the little verandah. They were eager to get going. We didn't talk at all while we walked to the canteen. The cheerful tourists-visiting-friend vibe was definitely missing.

There were other people in the canteen, and our meal—slightly bitter beef and rice with hot red sauce and green beans —quickly turned into a social event. I had the feeling this kind of thing happened whenever new faces showed up. The big tables could easily seat a dozen people, and ours was almost full before five minutes were up.

I was engaged in a lengthy conversation by an ophthalmologist from Pakistan. He had very sad eyes. I was on alert for tricky questions, but he didn't ask any. He wasn't that interested in me; he told me a lot about himself instead. He said his contract was almost up and that he was due to return home in a few months. Did I know anything about the current requirements for immigrating to Canada? I explained that having been born in Canada, I took no interest in immigration regulations. So he told me what *he* knew, and it was a fucking lot. It was pretty clear he'd begun researching the subject the moment he arrived in Africa.

It was a big relief when Mireille got up and told everyone that we had to go. Kross and I followed her out of the canteen and to her house. She left us waiting by the car while she went inside to get her work things, as she put it. The moment she was out of earshot I said to Kross:

"Well, so much for keeping a low profile."

He said nothing. I tried again:

"Any changes to the plan?"

"Yes, one. We'll have to move really fast now."

"How fast?"

"We'll be spending the next twenty-four hours in the car."

After a pause, I asked:

"How long have you known Mireille?"

"Six years. Haven't seen her for five."

"She's been a widow for five years?"

"Six. Shut up. She's coming."

During our drive to the garage repairing the Toyota, I quietly sat in the back of the car and listened to Mireille talk. She told us a work story, about an old geezer who refused to take the prescribed laxative. He was very fond of enemas. He enjoyed young female nurses touching intimate parts of his body. The nurses, in turn, made sure there was plenty of laxative dissolved in the water they used. The suffering people were willing to endure for a bit of sex, said Mireille, making both of us laugh a little unconvincingly.

Mireille didn't just drop us off at the service station and drive away. She insisted on staying until we made sure the Toyota had been repaired. It had, and after Kross drove it out into the open she inspected it pretty thoroughly.

"Good choice for going into the game reserve," she said. "What happened to the Peugeot you said you'd rented?"

"We took your advice about getting a four-wheel-drive," Kross said. "We were forced to, actually. The car we were going to get broke down. That's what we were told, anyway. I asked around and got this instead." He was really good at lying. He sounded convincing. I thought Mireille bought his explanation. But maybe she didn't, because she said:

"It's funny that you aren't carrying any cameras."

"They're in the bag," I said. I turned to Kross.

"You did pack them, didn't you?" I said. I threw him a lifeline there: he could have said no, he forgot to. But he said:

"Yes, of course."

"That's wonderful," said Mireille. "Why don't you dig one out and take a picture? I'd like to have a picture with you. A souvenir."

"It's getting late, Mireille," Kross said. "How about we visit you on the way back? Then we can take as many pictures as you like."

"How long are you going to stay there?"

"Depends how much we like it there," grinned Kross. "Might be a couple of days."

"So I'll see you Sunday-Monday?"

"You will."

"*Au revoir*," she said, and left. We watched her drive away. Kross said:

"And now, it's our turn to do some shopping."

"For what? Cameras? We haven't brought any, right?"

"For food and drink."

The road to Ghana was a narrow dirt track. It ran straight as an arrow, bordered on both sides by waist-high yellow grass and clusters of trees. We passed a small airfield with a single laterite runway and a solitary white building in need of fresh paint. There was no other traffic and we made good speed, but then had to slow down to a crawl while driving through a village. It was a tiny village, but it seemed like all of its goats chose that moment to hold a social event in the middle of the road.

Kross didn't accelerate after we left the goats and the buildings behind. I was about to ask him why when he turned into another dirt track that suddenly appeared on our right. It was even narrower, and blades of tall grass whipped the sides of the Toyota. We passed by a few flat, sprawling buildings resembling warehouses some distance away, then the track turned 90 degrees left and we were driving through wild country. The trees first became denser, then disappeared entirely to reveal a series of crop fields, barren except for a scattering of what looked like weeds. Beyond the fields to the left, a line of trees snaked roughly parallel to our track. Kross noticed me staring and said:

"That's the river marking the border with Ghana. Though 'river' might be overstating it a little. It's the dry season, so it won't be more than a shallow creek. We'll be driving across it shortly."

"And then? What's the plan?"

"We'll drive cross-country until we find a good spot to stay the night. It will be dark soon, and there's no point in driving after sunset. People travelling at night often get pulled over at checkpoints. We'll get going again in the morning, hit the spot and do the business, and drive back. That's the plan."

"I haven't seen any road blocks so far."

"That's because Ivory Coast hasn't ever had a military coup. So far, anyway. Ghana's had a few."

I had more questions for him—I had a *lot* of questions for him—but suddenly another red mouth yawned at us from the yellow grass, and Kross swung the wheel over without touching the brake.

I was thrown against my door as the rear of the truck slewed sideways and the fucking door opened. I screamed and caught hold of the dashboard grip at the last possible moment. A couple of small branches whipped my head and the door smashed into my shoulder. I put everything I had, my whole being into my left arm and heaved and felt the dashboard grip loosen just a little as I flung myself back into my seat. I caught the swinging door, slammed it shut and locked it and finally looked at Kross. He was grinning at me, bug-like in his big sunglasses.

"Nice work!" he shouted. "You should do it for money!"

"Keep your fucking eyes on the road!" I shouted back. I grabbed the seatbelt and strapped myself in, finally.

The track ended abruptly after another minute or so, and the Toyota started bouncing over hard dried soil. The thuds, bangs, and squeals of stressed metal must have carried for miles. I sensed every ear in the bush tuning into us. I anticipated someone or something showing up to stop us. But that didn't happen, and a few minutes later we reached the advertised river.

Kross had been right in his prediction. It was more of a riverbed than a river: a band of shale and muddy sand maybe thirty paces wide, with a ribbon of milky brown water flowing sluggishly down the middle. I saw a clear tire imprint right next to the water, and said:

"Someone's been here not so long ago."

"It's a popular spot," Kross said. He turned off the engine and listened for a while. I listened with him but all I heard was a thousand crickets rubbing their hind legs or whatever they do to make noise.

"Popular with whom?" I asked eventually.

"Smugglers. Like I told you, the other shore's Ghana."

"If it's a popular spot with smugglers, it's bound to be popular with the border guards or local cops or whatever."

"It is. They're paid well to stay away."

"We're going to be paying them?"

"We don't have any bribe money left," he said. "But they always set up shop about half a mile down the track, at the entrance to the village there. More comfortable, convenient for refreshments. That's why we'll be driving cross country for a little while."

And with these encouraging words, he slipped the Toyota into gear and gave it just enough gas to get it going. He let the truck roll down to the water and inched it across on half-clutch. The water barely covered the hubcaps, but a couple of times the the crankcase shield screeched horribly as we dragged it over a protruding stone. The creek was so narrow the Toyota could almost straddle it; the back wheels splashed into the water and just a heartbeat later the front wheels hit the other bank, the suspension letting out a delighted whinny.

Kross motored up the slight incline at walking speed; I noticed a relatively fresh crumpled cigarette pack lying next to the track and was hit by a wave of paranoia—I could swear someone was watching us. Kross must have felt something similar too: he stopped and killed the engine at the top of the rise and we both sat silently for a while, radars on, sonars pinging. A faraway bird shrieked mockingly. The crickets chirped and hissed and zinged; the setting sun dappled the landscape with flickering shadows.

"All right," Kross said eventually. "Time to look for a place to spend the night."

CHAPTER FIFTEEN

For the next half hour, we drove at walking speed through the bush, heading roughly south. The vegetation around us steadily grew thicker, and we had to make many detours around dense clumps of trees. About halfway through that drive, I saw a dirt track about fifty yards ahead. So did Kross, and he stopped and switched off the engine and we sat there for a minute, ears flapping. Nothing stirred, and the only noise was the irritated screeching of an invisible bird.

Kross got the Toyota going again, and accelerated to drive across the track before dropping back to our customary walking speed. I estimated we'd gone well over a mile when he stopped and said:

"Looks like the right spot for tonight."

The right spot was a shallow hollow in the ground behind the father of all baobabs: a monster tree whose enormous trunk was scarred by at least a couple of centuries of existence. Some distance away, shrubs and trees converged to block the view from all angles. Kross parked the Toyota in the hollow, switched off the engine and said:

"Okay. We've got at most half an hour of light left, so let's get cracking." He got up, twisting to reach behind the seats. He pulled out our bags and dropped them in my surprised lap. Then he pulled out another bag that I'd failed to notice: a dirty canvas hold-all whose clanking, shifting contents suggested tools. He sat down again, zipped the bag open, and rummaged in it for a while making mysterious tinkling noises.

"Here," he said, handing me a monkey wrench. I briefly considered braining him with it—purely abstract, as when you look up at a plane in the sky and wonder what it would be like to be the pilot. Then Kross brained *me,* in a manner of speaking: he tossed a vehicle registration plate into my overloaded lap.

"Put this on the front," he said. I saw that he was holding a registration plate, too. I also noted he had equipped himself with a professional flat spanner—a much better tool than my monkey wrench. I said:

"What the fuck is this?"

"It's a Ghanaian registration plate. Vehicles with foreign registration plates always get stopped and checked."

"You have the papers to go with this?"

"Don't be fucking silly." He dumped the tinkling bag on the floor and added:

"Come on. The light's going." He opened his door and jumped out.

I got out of the Toyota the way people get out of funeral cars: slow and dignified. I walked to the front of the truck, dropped into a squat, and stared at the registration plate fixed to the front bumper. This was crazy.

Kross's spanner clanged against the rear of the truck and I heard him muffle a curse. I got down to work, impeded by the fact that the nuts holding the front registration plate had been welded on with baked dirt. The wrench was loose; its jaw kept slipping. The new plate was white on black, three letters and four digits; the old plate was black on white, two letters and five digits. There definitely was a striking difference, and I could see Kross's point.

I had managed to get one nut off and was working on the other when I heard Kross approach. I didn't look at him. He watched me struggling for a few heartbeats, then said:

"Oh for fuck's sake. Move over." I did, and watched him while he changed plates and fastened the nuts with the swiftness of a regular grease monkey. He got up, took the monkey wrench from me, and said:

"Go wash your hands. I left a rag soaked with gas for you in the back, and some water."

"Are we going to have dinner?"

"Move." His tone reminded me of the time he punched me in the stomach, and I didn't tarry. The rag hung from the tailboard as advertised. I wiped my hands, then rinsed them with water. My hands were far from clean, but hopefully the gasoline had killed all the microbes. I collected the rag and the empty bottle and joined Kross, who was fucking around with our luggage yet again.

He got out his bag and put it down on the ground and zipped it open. I was half-expecting him to take out a camera—surprise, surprise!—and ask me to take a picture. But he extracted a couple of mangled squares of folded clothing instead, and thrust them at me without a word. I unfolded the clothes and my lip sagged so sharply it practically hit the ground.

The clothes consisted of an olive green T-shirt with a small breast pocket, and a pair of camouflage pants. It was unmistakably military gear. I said:

"You want me to wear this?"

"How did you guess?"

He turned away, pulling off his shirt and I saw his scar for the first time. It was an ugly, ragged sickle running from his waist to just below his left tit, an inch-wide band of glistening mashed-banana skin. He glanced at me, saw me staring, and said:

"Barbed wire. Now get going, for fuck's sake." He pulled his T-shirt over his head, turned round and started unbuttoning his pants, so I turned round too and changed my clothes. The T-shirt was brand new: it still smelled of the chemicals used to fix the colour. The pants had double straps on each side to adjust the waist, and buttoned cuffs at the bottom. They fit well. I turned around and looked at Kross, who was busy digging in his bag again. I said:

"New socks?"

"New boots." He pulled them out of the bag, and handed them to me: visibly used, heavy brown leather military boots with straps on the high ankle cuffs.

"Look," I said, "Is all this really necessary?"

"Just put them on. We'll talk about it while we eat."

"So that's how you guys dress for dinner," I said. I put on the boots, laced them up, tightened and buckled the ankle straps. My heart was thudding crazily in my head by the time I straightened up and took a couple of cautious steps. My new footwear was a perfect fit! I said:

"They're a perfect fit." I couldn't quite keep the surprise out of my voice, and Kross sounded pleased with himself when he said:

"They should. You and I wear the same size. They actually used to be mine. Well broken in, so you'll find them pretty comfortable."

I stared at him, wondering how the fuck he'd found out my shoe size. He tuned into my thoughts, grinned, and said:

"You keep forgetting it's my job to notice things."

Although Kross had brought along plastic cutlery and napkins—yet another proof of his superior foresight and planning—our twilight feast was far from a gourmet meal. The French bread was very African in character: it tasted as if the dough was equal parts flour and powdered milk. The warm, mushy corned beef and tepid water added up to a very filling combination.

I maintained a slightly resentful silence while I ate. When I was done, I said:

"Now can you tell me what these costumes are about?"

Kross wiped his mouth and let out a discreet yet manly belch. He said:

"There are around a hundred foreign military instructors and advisors in this country at any given time. Most of them are white, and all have demigod status regardless of actual rank. They answer to the current chief and no one else. And they don't get stopped at checkpoints."

"But you told me the current chief hates foreign military advisors."

"The guys the previous government hired, yes. Not the ones *he's* hired."

"You think we're going to run into a checkpoint?"

Kross shrugged.

"We have to take the highway to the coast," he said. "There are always checkpoints on a highway."

"And we'll get waved through?"

"Yes."

"And if we don't? What if they ask to see our documents?"

"I'll deal with it. Don't worry, you won't have to show anything to anyone. You won't even have to speak. All you'll have to do is sit there looking pissed off and important. You have a natural talent for that."

"I've got a talent for looking pissed off and important? What the fuck are you talking about?"

He hissed with exasperation.

"Look," he said. "I'm not a fucking shrink and this isn't the time. Or place. Just act naturally even though you're shitting your pants. You can do it."

"I'm touched by your faith."

"Try to get some sleep, okay? We've got a very long day tomorrow and I don't want to be riding with a red-eyed zombie. I need you alert."

"I'll be more than alert. I'll be fizzing with nerves."

"You'll get bored after the first hour."

I didn't contradict him. I could think of nothing to say without sounding neurotic. He let out a soft sigh and was asleep, just like that. And then, all of a sudden, it was night. It was as if someone had flicked a cosmic switch, thrown a heavy black blanket over everything. For a while I just sat there in my new clothes, and worried about things. It was very dark—no moon—and I couldn't even tell the time on my watch: there wasn't enough light to make its hands glow.

While Kross snored softly by my side, I began to panic. What the fuck was I doing? And it was nothing compared to what I would be doing next. I would be impersonating a foreign military advisor while being in Ghana illegally in the first place. Wouldn't that make me a spy? Spies got thrown in jail, at best; in Africa, spies likely were shot or hanged. And that would be a merciful ending to all the tortures they'd put me through to extract information I didn't have.

I went on like this for a long time and it fucking wore me out, thinking about this stuff. So eventually, I fell asleep.

When I woke up, the night was just beginning to lift: there was a faint glow above the horizon. It was cool—I had goosebumps on my bare arms—and the air smelled clean and fresh. Something chattered abruptly up in the baobab branches, out of sight, and I felt Kross's hand slip from my shoulder and realized that he'd tugged me awake.

"Was that a monkey?" I said.

"A bird. Here, take this water." I became aware of a strong smell of aftershave. I looked at him and saw he had combed his hair, too. He looked very bright-eyed and bushy-tailed, even though it was still night, technically. I took the big plastic Volvic bottle he was prodding me with and he said:

"Get yourself looking good. Don't forget your neck. Use up the whole bottle if that's what it takes, we've got plenty more."

I was being told to wash my neck like a fucking kid. I got my toiletries from my bag, got out of the cab and washed silently, then shaved by touch. Dawn was breaking with the rapidity of something happening too late and trying to make up for lost time. I was in Africa, deep in the fucking bush, sluicing water over my face and neck, combing my wet hair. There was no denying all this was happening to *me*.

It got light quickly even though the sun was still below the horizon. Its approach was heralded by a band of sky coloured pink grapefruit. I ate a stale African baguette with another tin of mushy corned beef. After that Kross disappeared into the bush to have a manly bowel movement, advising me to do the same. I couldn't. I just dripped some pale piss on a thin, straggly column of ants behind a nearby bush. They were big brutes; the unexpected rain made them briefly anxious; then they reformed ranks and carried on. I decided to model my behaviour on those ants.

Kross returned to the Toyota in high spirits, just like a dog bouncing back from its morning crap. He gave my neck an appraising look after he'd seated himself. He inserted the key in the ignition and asked:

"You all set?"

I said:

"What's the deal with the back of my neck? You keep looking at it. Selecting the right spot for the karate chop?"

He laughed very easily at that; a little too easily, I thought. I was sure breaking my neck had passed through his mind at least once.

"You have a bit of sunburn there. It's getting better."

He really was good at making me feel like a fucking kid. I said through clenched teeth:

"I'm all set. Let's go."

This time, we headed straight into the rising sun. When we set out it was still invisible; when we turned south again a minute later, its rim had risen above the horizon. It continued to rise so quickly it was almost possible to see it moving. But of course the sun didn't move: we were the ones doing the moving, the entire planet. All those efforts, all this activity, all that travelling back and forth—and all the time we were going round in fucking circles. That was the reality of it, the cosmic joke.

It got hot fast. We had both windows fully open, but were going too slowly to generate even a light breeze. Kross kept taking his foot off the gas every few seconds. This snail-like pace made me apprehensive: I began imagining patrols or land mines or whatever lying in wait. Kross wasn't the kind of guy who drove slowly when he could drive fast. Eventually I decided he probably wanted to hear other traffic before the traffic heard him.

As it happened, we didn't hear or see any other traffic for quite a while. We crawled through the bush for over half an hour, making frequent detours around assorted obstacles. The sun often made it impossible to see where we were going with any clarity. Soon enough it had climbed above the horizon in all its glory and whenever we turned east my eyes hurt, no matter how hard I squinted. The omniscient Kross said:

"I've been meaning to ask you about something. Why the hell don't you have sunglasses?"

"I don't like wearing sunglasses," I said. "Tinted lens distort colours. I like seeing things exactly as they are." Kross snorted with amusement.

"Good for you," he said. "Suffering for the sake of art."

I didn't answer, and after a short while I let my head drop down and closed my eyes. They itched, and my fists itched to rub them, but I didn't: it would make me look like a weeping kiddie. Kross was beginning to give me an inferiority complex. Everything was conspiring to give me a serious inferiority complex: getting fired and staying unemployed, living in a fucking rooming house, my impending divorce. It kind of made sense an African jail would be next.

Suddenly the Toyota came to a very abrupt stop, and I hit my bowed head on the grip mounted on the dashboard even though we'd been going really slow. Kross turned off the engine. Squinting through the windshield, I saw that we had come to a track through the bush. It was actually broad enough to be called a dirt road.

Kross started up again and crept up to the track. Then he turned right and sped up to sixty and for the first time I thought: we can actually do this, and felt a small burst of elation. After a couple of minutes I said:

"No traffic? Is that normal?"

"It will get busy very soon."

The first traffic we encountered consisted of an African riding a bicycle whose back carrier was piled head-high with suspicious-looking little bundles wrapped in black plastic. He was travelling in the opposite direction and exactly down the middle of the road. We flew out at him from around a curve, and in his haste to get out of the way he fell off his bicycle and the bundles went flying everywhere. I turned round in my seat but all I saw was red dust kicked up by our wheels. The next piece of oncoming traffic consisted of an ancient Bedford truck, and we were forced to pull to the side to let it through.

We hit the highway to the coast a couple of minutes later: an uneven band of shiny black asphalt, ragged at the edges. It was a tired road, a road that had been pounded by the wheels of innumerable vehicles, all bearing their own special cargo of hope. Travel revives hope the way water revives a wilting plant. At least that's how it works for me. As Kross accelerated, I hoped many things.

Naturally my strongest hope was that we wouldn't be stopped, and for quite a while we weren't. We motored briskly; the road dipped, bobbed, and weaved like an exhausted fighter trying to survive until the final bell, and the Toyota squealed and whinnied as Kross chivvied it along. When I glanced at the speedometer, its red needle was hovering just past 120.

It didn't last. Other traffic began to appear, and it was different from traffic in Ivory Coast in two respects. It featured mostly Japanese-made vehicles instead of French, and the flowing inscriptions decorating the minibuses were in English. Some bore names such as the Sampa Express and Sunyani Lightning; others advised that Jesus Saves, and God Protects His Flock. They were probably meant to reassure the passengers: most of the minibuses were driven at breakneck speed.

There was also a number of juggernaut trucks of different makes, and predictably it was these that slowed us down the most. We were stuck behind one, a Fiat heavily loaded with cartons that purported to contain Star beer, when we came across our first checkpoint. I only saw it when the truck in front began to brake.

Kross didn't stop. He flicked the turn indicator on and changed lanes to pass the halting truck. In front, I saw fat, flaming metal barrels on both sides of the road and camouflage-smocked, green-bereted soldiers carrying assault rifles. One of them stood between the barrels with an imperiously raised hand. Kross smacked the horn button with his palm and flashed his lights, and the corporal—he had a double chevron on his sleeve—stepped aside, his arm jerking up in a sloppy salute. Kross actually saluted him back, with a dismissive all right at ease now wave when he brought his hand back down on the wheel. He had done this before. I said:

"You've done this hundreds of times. Haven't you."

"Yes."

After a pause, I said:

"You don't sound pleased. Was my performance okay?"

Kross snorted, and said:

"No, you did great. Just right for a senior desk wallah pissed off at having to shake his ass in a truck early in the morning."

"Senior," I said wonderingly.

"You're the passenger."

"How much longer to get there?"

"Four or five hours. Depends on the traffic."

I settled back in my seat, and watched the countryside go by. After a short while the back of my T-shirt was wet through; I had to sit up again to let it dry. The air blasting through the window was getting warmer by the minute.

We hit the next checkpoint just over an hour later. There were no other vehicles in front of us this time, and I saw the familiar flaming barrels a good way off.

Kross blipped the horn and flashed his lights when we were about a hundred yards away, and the soldier standing in the road stepped aside with visible reluctance. There were no salutes this time: the five or six assembled representatives of the Ghanaian military stared at us sullenly as we sped past. But I was reassured because I finally noticed that the camo pants and boots Kross and I wore were identical with the local army issue. They probably *were* Ghanaian army issue. Kross would have made sure of that.

Right after that second checkpoint we entered hilly country, and I finally got to see the jungle. It was slightly startling. One moment we were climbing the incline of a gentle hill, surrounded by grass and isolated clumps of trees; we went over the top and instantly there was a solid wall of green on either side of the road. Occasionally, we passed a man-made clearing: a patch of ground burnt out of the jungle, the blackened, limbless corpses of trees sticking out of the quilt of ashes. Just once, I saw a man working in one of the black fields; he was chopping away at a pile of half-burnt debris with a big cutlass.

It wasn't all jungle. We also passed through a few villages and small towns. We stopped for gas in a small town called Berekum; it was just past eight in the morning. It turned out Kross was well-supplied with cedis, the local currency. He paid for the gas and four cold Cokes with that. He also bought a couple of big packs of soda crackers. He gave me one of those saying:

"That will kill the sour taste after drinking this shit."

"Why did you buy that shit, then?"

"Because it's good for people with a busy lifestyle. Plenty of calories plus caffeine in one attractive package. And we're going to be fucking busy for the next twenty hours."

"How long until we reach Dixcove?"

"Six to eight hours. Depends on the traffic."

"So we won't be able to make it back by nightfall. And you said, no driving after nightfall. Are we going to spend the night here, I mean in Ghana?"

"Probably. We'll see. We'll play it by ear."

"You mean you'll play it by ear with me coming along like a retard following the Pied Piper."

"Something like that."

This ended our conversation, and we resumed our journey in silence.

We got stopped at a checkpoint maybe half an hour later. It was hidden around a curve, and we were going fast because there was no minibus or truck in front, for a change. Kross had to brake sharply when the soldier in the middle of the road refused to budge following the horn and lights routine. There was a group of soldiers by one of the barrels, and a big army tent pitched under a tree a short distance off the road. A couple of military guys sat at a camping table in front of the tent. They appeared to be drinking beer; they had to be the officers in charge. A couple of green Land Rovers were parked nearby.

The soldier that had forced us to stop walked up to Kross's window. Kross looked right past him, and barked:

"Sergeant!"

One of the guys by the barrel detached himself and walked up to the Toyota. I stared straight ahead, doing my best to look pissed off; but when Kross shifted to take something out of his back pocket I glanced sideways. He was handing a narrow green booklet to the sergeant, a big man with a big head and angry bloodshot eyes. The teenaged private who had stopped us seemed apprehensive.

"Sorry to bodah you, major," said the sergeant, returning the booklet. Kross nodded, and said:

"What's all this about?"

"Plenty Indian hemp kamin true dis way," said the sergeant. Kross nodded again.

"Best of luck, boys," he said. He turned back to the wheel and then added:

"What's the name of your CO, sergeant?"

"Captain Sankey. Sah." And we drove away. I watched the side rear view mirror, saw the sergeant staring after us, watched him break into a trot towards the camping table.

"Trouble," I said. I was expecting Kross to laugh it off, but he shocked me. He said:

"Yes. I know Sankey and he knows me. From a long time ago, and we were both lieutenants at the time. It will take him a while to connect the dots, and by that time we should be well on our way back."

"You think we'll make it?"

"I'm sure we can make it."

"I'm glad that things are in your competent hands. Major." Kross allowed himself a small smile. He said:

"Maybe I'll finally start getting some respect around here."

CHAPTER SIXTEEN

We ran into two more checkpoints. The first came three-quarters of an hour later, right after our road joined another: wider, busier, and with more potholes even though the road surface—gravel-studded asphalt—looked newer than on the road we'd just left.

I fully anticipated being stopped again, with more trouble developing—this time around, they'd ask to see *my* documents. But Kross went ahead with his horn-and-lights routine, and it worked: we were waved through.

The countryside had changed from hills to a gently undulating plain, but the road kept twisting this way and that, almost each curve concealing a surprise. Many were nasty—trucks belching black smoke, swaying minibuses that were too slow for Kross's taste but too fast to overtake safely, mad motorcyclists. I saw one that had his entire family with him: the wife behind him with an infant strapped to her back, a kid sitting on the carrier rack over the back wheel, and another halfway up the fuel tank, thin black legs dangling dangerously close to the finned cylinder of an engine that was sure to be overheating.

But there were also nice surprises. One of these was a convoy of women on bicycles going the other way. They all had huge bowls or buckets atop their heads, cushioned by thick wads of fabric. Just two of them were holding up a hand to stabilize the load. They were riding along the dirt siding, and it couldn't have been a smooth ride. We passed by too fast for me to work out how that magic was possible.

After close to an hour we came to a fork. The road we'd been on continued to the right, but Kross turned left, onto a ribbon of ragged blacktop. In places, the road consisted almost equally of potholes and pothole patches, sometimes stacked three or four high. But this was probably the reason for the silver lining: there wasn't much traffic on that road.

Kross exploited that to the fullest. We were doing over a hundred most of the time, the Toyota shuddering and shaking and complaining. When we stopped to take yet another piss—we were drinking water constantly, it was starting to get really hot again—I complained, too.

"It's better to go fast over a road like that," Kross told me. "Then you fly over the potholes. And we still have a long way to go."

"How long?"

"Anything between four and six hours."

"Six hours of this? Christ."

"Well, that's why we'll try to cut it down to four."

We hit another checkpoint just a few minutes later. Kross's patented routine worked again, and I began to feel fresh confidence. We were in hilly country again, and the air was noticeably cooler. Every quarter hour or so we passed through a village or a little town; then it was every ten minutes or so, then five, and then traffic got thicker and it was back to ten. The jungle grew sparser, melted away leaving isolated clumps of trees; the hills turned into hillocks.

Around three in the afternoon, we stopped for gas and ate: corned beef and soda crackers, Cokes. When we'd finished, Kross said:

"We're getting close. We'll turn into a dirt road soon, and drive for a few minutes. Then we'll park and I'll go get what we came for. You'll stay with the car. OK?"

"How long will you be gone?"

"Not long."

"What do I do if you don't come back?"

"I'll be back."

"But – "

"I said I'll be back."

"Good," I said. "I just wouldn't know what to do without you." He grinned at me, and said:

"You'd work something out. You're a smart guy. But there'll be no need for that. Let's go."

And we went, and it went exactly as prophesied by Kross. We drove for maybe ten minutes, passing through a couple of hamlets and narrowly missing a demented yellow dog that stood howling in the middle of the road.

The jungle made a strong comeback. At times it formed an impenetrable wall of green. I was really happy that Kross would be the one to dive into that wall. I couldn't imagine doing that myself, as we'd initially planned. I'd probably get either stuck or lost after twenty steps.

Kross had slowed down to around twenty, and it was obvious he was looking for the right spot to park the pickup. He found it quickly: the dirt road bent in a curve that widened to a lay-by.

Kross parked the Toyota in the lay-by and switched off the engine and I said:

"So this is it?"

"Looks like it, doesn't it," he said, draping himself over the back rest of his seat to get at the bags.

"I wouldn't know," I said. "I mean, I don't even know whether you're a captain or a major. According to Mireille, you're a captain."

"I got promoted in the meantime."

"By who?"

"By my employer."

"But you didn't set her straight."

"Why should I?"

I tried to think of a reason, and failed. I watched him pull the dirty hold-all with the tools from behind the seats. Then he jumped out of the cab and went round to the Toyota's front and raised the bonnet.

I got out too and edged around the side of the truck: the ground dropped off abruptly beyond the lay-by. I joined Kross just as he was lifting a plastic cap clear of the engine. It had wires feeding into spindly nipples, and Kross began to disconnect them. I said:

"That's the distributor cap, right? Why are you disconnecting it? You afraid I'll make myself scarce?"

He laughed at that, a little too easily for my taste.

"Don't be silly," he said. "If someone takes a close interest in you while I'm gone, you'll explain the distributor cap went kaput and your companion has taken it to a garage to get it fixed."

"What do I say when someone asks my name? Or asks for my papers?"

"Just tell anyone who stops to move on."

"And if they don't?"

"Then you'll just have to use your brains to get them going. You look like a military advisor. Act like one. I'll be back soon, an hour to two hours tops."

He went to climb back into the cab. I stood still, mind buzzing with ugly possibilities. He re-emerged carrying a small shovel. I said:

"What if some cops happen to come by? Or soldiers?"

"Act the part. Tell them to fuck off. You don't have to talk to them. You don't have to talk to anyone who isn't at least a colonel, and there won't be any colonels coming along in the next couple of hours. Trust me."

"That's just another way of saying fuck you."

Kross laughed again. He was in a jolly mood. He said:

"See you soon." He turned round and half-ran down the steep slope and plunged into jungle. It was sparser than it was back in the hills—I could actually see gaps in the vegetation—but all the same he disappeared from sight instantly. Only a swaying branch confirmed that he'd really been here and said what he'd said to me. Then it stopped swaying, and I was truly alone.

I climbed back inside the cab and had a drink of water. I intended to stay there—I calculated it made me less approachable—but it was just too hot inside. I got out, and took up a stance behind the Toyota. Everything was very still and very quiet. It felt ominous, in a way.

I paced back and forth behind the pickup, stopping and listening each time I turned around. At first I was both anxious and excited, but before twenty minutes were up I began to feel bored. It was the heat that did it. I could almost feel its weight on my shoulders. It squeezed out any energy I had left and shredded my thoughts into disconnected ramblings. I tried to revive myself with a Coke but it was warm and frothy and left a bad taste in my mouth.

By the time a full hour had passed, all I wanted to do was take a nap. The only traffic I saw in all that time was an old man on a bicycle, with blue plastic buckets dangling from the handlebar. He nodded to me as he went by. I didn't nod back, just stared at him in silence as he rode away. He probably thought it was a hostile stare. Eventually I stopped pacing back and forth and stood facing the jungle, willing Kross to reappear.

When I heard a vehicle approaching, I didn't even bother to look that way. I assumed that since it was coming from the opposite direction, it couldn't have anything to do with us and our little show at the checkpoint commanded by captain Sankey. I only glanced at the approaching vehicle when I heard it slow down and stop—too late to dive into the vegetation.

It was a dark blue Land Rover and a very big man was in already in the process of climbing out of the driver's seat. He wore a dark blue tunic with shorts and a peaked cap. He looked like a cop in uniform and most likely *was* a cop in uniform. He was joined by a bald guy in civvies: white short-sleeved shirt and tan slacks. They crossed the road together and I saw that the guy in civvies was pretty old, with a disarming saint-like semi-circle of white hair running around his head.

But as he got closer, lightly touching the Toyota's hood in passing, I saw that he was pissed off in a very unsaintly manner. The uniformed copper deferentially followed a few steps behind; I was dealing with someone senior here. This wasn't good.

The old guy came to a stop uncomfortably close to me and for a while we looked at each other in silence, with me doing my best to appear pissed off and important. Then he said:

"I'm superintendent George Boswell. And who are you?"

"Nice to meet you, superintendent," I said. I hit the tone I used when someone was pestering me, and it didn't come off too badly. But it was a mistake: it made him angry. He said:

"I asked who you are. Name?"

"Major Peter Haslam." It came out just like that—the name of my former boss at Shit, Bullshit, and Balls. It sounded natural, it sounded like the truth. This was good.

"I'd like to see some identification, major."

My passport and wallet were hidden in my bag, inside the car. I didn't know whether this was good or bad. I said:

"How about you show me yours first, superintendent."

We stared at each other, and he looked as if he had just bitten into something very bitter. He said:

"I have to ask you to come with me... major. Since you refuse to identify yourself, we'll have to clear things up back at the station." He moved a couple of steps, obviously clearing the way for the uniformed brute to get at me. I said:

"You have no jurisdiction over me, superintendent. You want me to go anywhere, come back with a military police officer. It could mean more trouble than you think."

"You're threatening me."

"I'm advising you."

"Well let me advise you of this. Major. If you don't come along, the constable here will make you." I looked at the advertised constable. He'd struck me as a big guy as soon as he'd climbed out of the Land Rover. Up close, he was even bigger. He probably passed the time uprooting trees and breaking them into matchwood. I sighed, and said:

"He seems like a nice lad. I wouldn't want him to get hurt. But you're making a very bad mistake."

Then I turned away from him and walked around the Toyota, shutting the windows and locking the doors. The superintendent and his gorilla watched me in silence, remaining patient even though I dragged it out in the silly hope that Kross would pop out of the trees, and sort everything out in a jiffy. But of course he didn't, and eventually I followed the superintendent to the Land Rover across the road. I really wished I was wearing sunglasses, like anyone with half a brain did in Africa. I could feel my face beginning to show fear. Boswell would need just one look at my panicked peepers to pull out the handcuffs.

He sat with me in the back; the constable drove. It took a supreme effort of will to resist looking over my shoulder at the Toyota. I focused on sitting upright in what I imagined was a military manner, on rearranging my face into irritated disgust, and on the constable's broad neck. It featured a couple of interesting warts, which let me brood a little on how this magnificent specimen of the human race could be felled by a single out-of-order cell. Life was full of surprises, and it seemed most of those were bad. I thought: African jail, here I come.

It wasn't a long drive. The jungle thinned and dispersed and I caught glimpses of the ocean, less than half a mile away. We passed a signpost that said Fort Metal Cross 1/2 mile and I realized this had to be the fort at which Avery showed up after abandoning his ship and getting rid of Connacher, one way or another. Then we went round yet another curve and suddenly Dixcove lay revealed in front and below: a small, rusty brown town squeezed into a clearing at the base of a small bay.

Beyond the town, the fort's white walls rose atop a large cliff overgrown with grass and shrubs; I could see the black snouts of the cannon poking out of the embrasures. There was a tiny island with two slender palm trees right in the middle of the bay, maybe two hundred yards from the shore. Small waves splashed against the half-submerged rocks that ringed the island, dappling the water with foam.

The constable drove down the incline and into the town, and predictably had to slow down sharply. I got a good look at everything. I saw a few white tourists, all with the quietly alert air of satisfied predators on the prowl. Then the Land

Rover turned into a side street adjoining the town market—most of the wooden stalls were empty, it was getting late for business—and stopped behind another Land Rover just like ours. It was parked in front of a low white building with the word POLICE painted over the entrance in very big blue capitals, in a font that had to be a local invention. It looked like Helvetica with serifs.

A policeman lounged about on a small wooden bench to the side of the entrance; he sprang up and saluted very smartly when we got out of the car. Mr. Boswell had real clout with his men. He had clout with me too. He scared me, saintly white hair notwithstanding. So I gathered my panicked thoughts together and said:

"I don't know what you hope to achieve by bringing me here. I'm not going to answer any of your questions because you don't have the right to ask me any. In fact, you'd do well to just drive me back to my vehicle right now before things get really complicated."

"We'll see," said Boswell. He said something very quietly in the local lingo, and both constables said 'yassa' and hurriedly stepped behind me, one on each side. I meekly followed Boswell inside the police station and found myself in a large whitewashed room. There were a couple of benches against the entrance wall, and three desks set in a line across the floor marked the boundary of the public section.

There was a typewriter on one desk and an computer on the other. It wasn't switched on, but that wasn't comforting. I tried to calculate the chance that this particular police station was connected to the internet. The third desk featured a telephone, so it was likely. A quick web search for Peter Haslam would yield surprising results. There was a photo of him on the SB&B page.

I followed Boswell past the desks and to a massive wooden door. Boswell opened it to reveal a corridor. I followed him, and saw entrances to a couple of rooms on the left and a heavily barred window on the right, and through that window the top of a whitewashed wall studded with broken glass. There was an exceptionally massive door at the far end of the corridor. It had to lead to the jail; it was sheathed in metal and had a small square window crisscrossed with a couple of metal bars.

Superintendent Boswell entered the first room, beckoning me to follow without looking back. It featured a desk with two chairs on either side. There was another computer and a phone on that desk. If everything was in working order, all Boswell had to do was plug in the modem and I'd be totally fucked inside five minutes. I had no idea what to do. I couldn't count on Kross. He'd likely return to the Toyota, see that I was missing, shrug, and drive away keeping my cut for himself. It only made sense.

I sat down in the chair fronting the desk without waiting for an invitation, leaned back, and crossed my legs. A frowning superintendent Boswell made his way around the desk, and settled into his chair with a sigh. He looked at me with something like new appreciation and I gave him the most unpleasant stare I could produce. It had no effect. He was likely well-used to getting I'll-kill-you glares from the criminals he met. I said:

"Could I get something to drink?"

He nodded, and said something in the native lingo to the doorway—he'd left the door open. He didn't raise his voice, yet seconds later two constables came bustling in. They were carrying rifles, and I was frightened for the second it took me to realize they didn't mean to use them on me, at least not yet. The guns were fairly ancient, bolt-action pieces with oddly blunt business ends. I remembered seeing rifles like that in World War Two movies. I even remembered what they were called: Lee Enfield.

The superintendent issued instructions *sotto voce*, and the constables nodded while stuffing clips of cartridges into the tops of their thick knee-high socks. This suggested they were planning to use those rifles in the near future, hopefully not on me. Then they both left; one returned with ice tinkling inside a pitcher of water, and two big glasses.

He stood waiting while the superintendent unlocked a drawer and took out a large military walkie-talkie—its metal case was painted olive green. He handed it to the constable and I realized that I hadn't seen a radio in the Land Rover or inside the building. A moment later I heard a vehicle being started up.

I felt sure the two constables were going to guard the Toyota. Kross would emerge from the jungle to see two rifles pointed at him. But maybe he wouldn't. He'd likely dealt with situations like that many times in his career. Maybe he'd even find a way to save my ass, if he cared to. That was a big if.

Superintendent Boswell was busy pouring water. He carefully measured out a single cube of ice into each glass, and pushed one a couple of inches my way. I nodded a thanks and picked it up. I decided I'd let him kick off the conversation.

I sipped the water, and turned slightly in my chair to look through the barred window to my left. I could see the fort. Its gleaming white walls seemed too new, as if the slaves had just finished building it yesterday instead of centuries earlier. I could feel Boswell's eyes on me. I kept sipping the water and looking at the view until my glass was empty. I put it back on the desk and saw that Boswell's glass was empty too.

He didn't pour us more water. He opened another drawer, made mysterious rustling noises, and eventually pulled out a big, folded paper sheet. It was yellowed with age. He unfolded it and slid it over the desk in my direction without saying anything. Then he leaned back in his chair in a way that suggested satisfaction from a job well done.

It was a Wanted poster. It featured eight male mug shots arranged in two rows: five white, two black, one dusky East Indian. The headline, set in proper Helvetica, said that the owners of the featured faces were WANTED FOR TREASON, ARMED ROBBERY, AND MURDER. Kross was in the top row, second from left. He was wearing a uniform.

There was a fat paragraph of text under the two rows of rogues. The print swam crazily when I tried to read, but I got the gist. A group of expatriate military instructors seriously breached their contracts with the government by robbing the headquarters of the Paramount Mining Corporation. A security guard was shot dead. Anyone with any information on the suspects was to immediately report it to the authorities and so on and so forth. I began to gag. I managed to convert it into a water-logged belch as I pushed the poster back at the superintendent. I said:

"Whoops. Excuse me. Could I have some more of that excellent iced water, superintendent?" He poured it while looking at me. I took a sip. I said:

"I don't see myself or my name there. So could you explain why your brought me here? Then I think it would be best if you drove me back to my vehicle. It's my responsibility."

"It's well looked after," he said. "Do you recognize any of the faces in those photographs?"

"No."

After a short silence, he said:

"I am formally requesting that you produce your identification. Right now."

I smiled, and cleared my throat. Then I said:

"I'm formally telling you that you have no authority whatsoever to ask me for identification, and I request that you take me back to my vehicle. Immediately."

He jerked as if I'd slapped him. He said:

"You racist dog. Sergeant." For a moment I thought he was speaking to me and wondered why I'd been demoted. Then I heard a chair scrape in the other room, hurried footsteps, and the advertised sergeant joined us.

He was smaller than the constable who'd driven us earlier by maybe an inch, no more, but he had wider shoulders. Most importantly, he held a submachine gun which was aimed vaguely in my direction. It had a fat perforated barrel and a curved magazine jutting from its side. I found all my attention focusing on that barrel. It had shiny patches where the dark finish had worn off and a fine web of scratches, and this well-used look made it more frightening.

"You still think you're gods," said the superintendent. "You still think we aren't any better than children. Nothing's changed. That's what you think. I'll give you a new thought or two. There haven't been any white mercenaries in this country for over a year. It's obvious you haven't been here for more than a few days. Your superior white skin just gave you away. Sergeant."

A drawer banged open while I looked at the sergeant. The sergeant motioned me to stand up with the muzzle of his gun. I stood up. He approached me, plucking up the pair of handcuffs the superintendent had placed on the desk. He stuck the muzzle of the gun in my neck and tapped my right arm.

It was no contest. While he cuffed my arms behind my back, the superintendent fished out a flat automatic pistol from his desk and worked its slide: I heard the cartridge snap into place. Everything was happening so fast I didn't really have the time to get properly scared. I had no idea what would happen next.

What happened next was that there was a loud squawk. It seemed to come from the superintendent's desk. He opened a drawer and took out another walkie-talkie and raised it to his head.

"Boswell," he said. Then he listened. He opened his mouth to say something, closed it, listened more. And more. He began to frown, and said:

"I've lost you. Come in please. Can you hear me?"

Even if someone did, they weren't saying. Eventually he pressed a switch on the walkie-talkie and held it loosely by his side. He glanced at his watch and looked at the window, at the fort. Then he looked at me and said:

"You're coming with us. Sergeant." The sergeant encouraged me to move with a prod of the barrel. I led the way out of the room, but not before I noticed the superintendent slipping the flat automatic into the side pocket of his pants.

Propelled by frequent prods of the sergeant's gun, I exited the station and climbed into the back of the remaining Land Rover. We didn't draw any attention; a group of women clad in bright-patterned swathes of fabric, from armpit to ankle, were talking by one of the empty market stalls across the street; one of them threw a glance and then, it seemed to me, they purposefully avoided looking in our direction. I was prodded to get inside the car and found that it was very uncomfortable to sit with hands cuffed behind my back.

This Land Rover wasn't the one I'd rode in earlier; there was a coarsely stitched tear in the right rear seat. The superintendent got in the back with me. Once seated, he took out his pistol and held it in his lap, while the sergeant carefully placed his submachine gun on the front passenger seat before starting the engine. This particular Land Rover *had* a radio mounted in the centre of the dashboard, and its right front fender featured a long whip-like antenna that trembled and swayed as we drove. But the radio didn't come alight when the sergeant switched the ignition on; it seemed communications were restricted to the walkie-talkies. I finally understood that the call Boswell had received must have come from one of the constables sent to guard the Toyota.

I didn't exactly follow the countryside during the drive to the Toyota. I had to focus on not shitting myself with fright. I only regained situational awareness when we began to slow down. Through the front window I saw the other Land Rover, parked on the lay-by with its snout almost touching the Toyota's. There was no one around.

The sergeant pulled to the side of the road and stopped a few paces from the other vehicles. He left the engine running. For a while, we all sat silently in the Land Rover. Then Boswell said something exotic to the sergeant, who yassaed softly.

He picked up the submachine gun and got out of the car. Then he walked up to the abandoned cars holding the gun as if it was a two-handed sword, the barrel pointing upward. He disappeared behind the Land Rover; after a while, he emerged from behind the Toyota. He looked at us and shook his head. The superintendent raised his free hand and pointed at the jungle; I noticed his gun hand wasn't lying relaxed in his lap any more. His pistol was pointed at me.

My eyes followed the direction indicated by the superintendent, and I saw a broken branch drooping towards the ground: a teardrop of pale wood gleamed on the wounded trunk. The sergeant made his way towards the tree in a purposeful crouch. This time, the gun barrel was pointing straight ahead. He stopped by the tree and examined it briefly; then he slid into the vegetation.

We sat still. I watched the dashboard clock for a while before realizing it wasn't working; its hands were stuck at five to three. Unfortunately, I couldn't check mine. The handcuffs were really beginning to bite and I thought oh mother, what have I done.

Time passed, urged on by the uneven rumblings of the engine; the windshield shuddered in unison; the road blurred, came into focus, blurred again. There was no other traffic. I closed my eyes; beside me, the superintendent stirred and let out a soft moan. Kross's voice said:

"Freeze or I'll blow your fucking head off. Good. Now hand that pistol to me very, very slowly."

CHAPTER SEVENTEEN

I turned my head very, very slowly, just as instructed, and looked to my right. Boswell sat very still. His head was oddly tilted and when I bent forward I saw that Kross was pressing the muzzle of the submachine gun I'd seen earlier into the superintendent's cheek.

I glanced at the gun in Boswell's lap and saw that he was turning it around to grip it by the barrel. Then he offered it to Kross, butt first, and Kross snatched it out of his hand as swiftly as a striking snake.

"Now unlock his cuffs," he said to the superintendent. I turned around in my seat to make things easier, and felt the superintendent put his hand around my wrist as he fitted the key into the lock. He had rough, sandpapery skin and bone-hard calluses. The lock snapped, and suddenly I was able to breathe properly again. It just hadn't been possible with hands cuffed behind my back.

"Grab those cuffs and put them on him, then switch off that damn engine," Kross said. It took me a while to understand that he was addressing me. It took me another to learn how to handle the handcuffs. I'd never been into bondage or any of the S&M stuff. Obviously that had been a mistake.

Boswell was very cooperative. Without being asked, he turned in his seat and put his wrists behind his back. After two fumbled failures I finally managed to get the handcuffs on.

"Get out, both of you," Kross said. It was awkward for Boswell to comply with his hands cuffed behind his back, or maybe he was playing for time. I'd managed to switch the Land Rover's engine off, get out, and walk around the car just in time to see Kross grip Boswell's arm and haul him out of his seat. His other hand held the submachine gun by his side, barrel pointing at the ground. He glanced down the road, and so did I.

I saw a a man on a bicycle maybe a hundred paces away. He'd stopped, one leg extended to the ground, and it was obvious that he was staring at us. The moment I looked at him he threw the bicycle around and rode away, pedalling hard. Kross raised his gun again and stuck it into Boswell's belly and said:

"Check his pockets."

Once again, I was slow to work out he meant me. I felt really uncomfortable thrusting my hand into each of Boswell's pockets. This was the first time I'd ever done something like that to anybody.

The keys to the Toyota were in Boswell's left side trouser pocket, together with what had to be his house keys. The right back pocket yielded an old, dog-eared black wallet, and the right side pocket—a small notebook, with a short metal ballpoint pen clipped to the front cover.

I stepped around Boswell and gave everything to Kross, including the keys to the handcuffs. He dropped the lot into the side pocket of his camo pants, and suddenly Boswell said:

"Major Haslam."

I saw Kross's lips twitch, and he threw me an amused glance. He prodded Boswell with the barrel of his gun and said:

"Go on. Say your piece to major Haslam. But quickly because you and I, we're going for a walk."

Boswell was staring at me with such intensity his eyes were bulging out of their sockets. He said:

"Major Haslam. This man is a murderer and a thief. A war criminal, just like his Nazi father. You must not help him. You must help *me*."

"That's enough," said Kross. He grabbed Boswell's arm and and half-swung, half-pushed him down the sloped siding. Boswell staggered down a few steps and very nearly fell down. He stopped to regain his balance and looked back at us with great hate.

"Take this," said Kross. I looked at him: he was holding out Boswell's pistol. I took it with some reluctance, and put it in my pocket.

"I'll be back in ten," Kross said. "Stay here and wait. Got it?"

"What if someone tries to arrest me again?"

"Play for time. You've got a gun now, haven't you?"

And with that he turned away and trotted down to Boswell. Then they went off together, Boswell leading, Kross following close behind. He gave the superintendent an encouraging prod with the barrel as they got near the tree with the broken branch. Then they disappeared into the jungle.

I looked left: nothing and no one to see. I looked right: ditto. I wondered whether the man on the bicycle would raise an alarm and decided that he wouldn't. It was unlikely there was a phone line connected to any of the two hamlets we'd passed, and there was no chance of a cellular phone network. Also, anyone with a brain would be uneasy about contacting the police about anything that already involved the police. And the bicycle guy was sure to know who owned those two dark blue Land Rovers.

I wondered if the Dixcove police station had more than two running vehicles and decided they probably did. Then I wondered about the chances of another Land Rover or whatever showing up. I seriously doubted my ability to threaten anyone with Boswell's pistol.

I took it out of my pocket and examined it. It was a small flat automatic with an antiquated look. Its black finish was very worn and the handgrips were scratched and pitted. It felt really odd in my hand. This was the first time ever that I held a handgun other than an air gun.

Of course I had an idea of how to work Boswell's gun: I'd seen my share of movies that featured loving closeups of guns of all kinds, including automatics. And so I knew that there was some sort of safety switch somewhere. But I couldn't see anything that could be a safety switch on Boswell's gun, and anyway the idea of firing it at anyone scared me shitless. I put the pistol back in my pocket.

I glanced at my watch: two minutes gone. I had less than eight minutes to decide what to do next. Boswell claimed Kross was a murderer and a thief. He had a Wanted poster that confirmed it.

The wisest, safest course of action was to grab my bag from the Toyota, jump into the Land Rover I'd arrived in, and drive away: I'd left the keys in the ignition when I turned off its engine. But what next? Where could I go, driving a stolen police vehicle?

If I turned myself in, I'd end up in jail anyway. Illegal entry, aiding and abetting a criminal, lying about my identity—why the hell did I invent that Haslam bullshit? I could have said that I was just a tourist. Many male tourists wore military gear. It was comfortable, and broadcast a don't-fuck-with-me message. I should have told Boswell the truth about myself when he'd challenged me.

But I knew why I didn't. At best, I'd have ended up being deported, with a hundred dollars in my pocket. And when I was waiting for Kross by the Toyota, I felt sure he'd return with the diamonds. I'd already begun to congratulate myself.

Unfortunately, it was likely the diamonds came from a much more recent robbery than I'd been told. That whole Greenbottle/Avery story was bullshit, and Kross went to Vancouver to poke a girl he knew a few times before leaving for Africa, not to fetch some imaginary book.

But this didn't really change my present situation. My present situation dictated a clear priority: get the fuck out of Ghana as quickly as possible. And this just wasn't possible without Kross: I was sure to screw up on my own. Kross was

239

Mr. Competence. He'd already dealt with two constables armed with rifles, another with a submachine gun, and Boswell. I had no doubt he'd find a way to get us out.

I had to play along. I had to continue playing Major Haslam. If I didn't, Kross might well decide to dump me in the bush somewhere, hopefully without a hole in the head. Which raised the question of what he'd actually done with all those cops. If he'd killed any of them –

I was fizzing with tension and sweating like a pig by the time Kross showed up. He was a minute late, and he was carrying a small arsenal: a rifle slung from each shoulder, and the submachine gun.

I worked hard on my major Haslam act as Kross approached. When he joined me, I said:

"Where are the bags of diamonds? I was expecting to see a couple."

Kross liked that. He threw his head back and barked with laughter.

"No bags," he said. "Just a couple of big handfuls. But there are some nice stones in there, easily over fifty grand each. Overall it's better than I expected. Could be over a couple of million dollars' worth in total. On the black market, that is."

"You really found them? Avery's diamonds?"

"Yes."

"Can I see them?"

"Later," he said. "Let me put away all this stuff, then let's get going. We need to move fast."

I helped him, passing over the rifles as he hid them under our bags. I noted that he made the submachine gun easily accessible, with the grip between the seats and the side-mounted magazine pointing upwards. He only needed to reach down to whip it out in one swift movement. It made me apprehensive.

"Do you think you might have to use that thing?" I asked, pointing. He didn't answer. He just looked at me the way people look at open-mouthed morons.

I stood and waited while he replaced the Toyota's distributor cap and took same from the two Land Rovers. He threw them into into the bush, aiming carefully so that they landed close to the wounded tree. As soon as we were both seated in the Toyota, I said:

"What did you do to those cops? Where did you take them?"

"I left them hugging palm trees within shouting distance of the beach. Someone will pass close enough sooner or later."

"Hugging palm trees?"

"They were all carrying handcuffs. Very convenient. It might be a while before someone frees them, but they can chat with each other to pass the time."

"How humane."

"No need to be cruel without a reason," Kross said, and started the engine. It fired right away with a reassuring rumble. He backed up a little to get clear of the Land Rover in front, and as he did so he added:

241

"I've even taken care to throw those distributor caps where they can be easily found. Getting them replaced would cost a lot of trouble and money, relatively speaking. Probably eat up their incidental expenses budget for the whole year."

It sounded as if he hadn't killed any of the cops. It sounded as if he was thinking about starting a fundraiser on their behalf. I said:

"You amaze me."

"It's the little things that matter," Kross told me. "Besides, I really like Ghanaians. They're good people. The nicest Africans I've ever met, and I've met plenty. Hell, they're nicer than most whites." He winked at me and swung the Toyota around in a tight turn, and we were off.

I was tense and silent until we'd passed through both of the hamlets on the dirt road. I didn't notice anyone paying us any more attention than we'd received previously; if anything, we got a bit less. It made me bold enough to ask:

"So what's the plan now? The sun's starting to set."

"We'll have to keep going through the night."

"But you said everyone gets stopped at night."

"We won't run into a checkpoint for a few hours."

"Why?"

Kross didn't answer and when I glanced at him, I saw that he was grinning triumphantly. He said:

"I deployed a bit of misinformation. Told the superintendent and his men to take it easy because we'll be out of the country within a couple of hours, well before anyone can do anything about it. Of course they *will* try to do something about it. They'll put everyone they've got on the coastal road going west to the border with Ivory Coast. And we're going north."

"They could still send out a general alert. There was a radio in one of the Land Rovers. And they had two walkie-talkies."

"They still have them, but I took out the batteries. And that radio you're talking about is a relay station for the walkie-talkies, nothing more."

"You sure?"

"I'm sure."

"Well as long as you're sure," I said.

We didn't speak for the next couple of hours. Kross was busy driving as fast as he could, which was enough to make me speechless all by itself. But in addition to that, I was busy digesting what I'd just heard.

So, Kross hadn't hurt the cops. This didn't mean he hadn't killed anyone before. He very likely did, and Boswell had grounds for calling him a murderer. I didn't care about that, what concerned me was that Boswell had also called Kross a thief. And the Wanted poster confirmed the theft of diamonds from a mining operation.

I went around in fucking circles trying to think of a way to broach that subject without getting myself shot and dumped in the bush. I viewed and reviewed every bit of data submitted by my buzzing brain. It would be a very, very sensitive subject with Kross, no two words about it. It called for great diplomacy.

Eventually I said:

"Hey, Kross."

"What?"

"I saw a Wanted poster at the police station. It had your mug on it, along with others."

"Yeah, you would. I told you I can't enter Ghana, right?"

"But why?"

"I told you that. Okay, I'll explain again. I signed a contract with the government that was overthrown. I couldn't just switch sides after the coup. So I buggered off, and that made me a deserter."

"That poster also said you stole some diamonds while you were deserting."

"It's not true. Yeah, some diamonds did get stolen during that coup, but not by me."

"Oh yes? By whom?"

"By the manager of the diamond mining operation. He'd been stealing for years, most likely, and got scared that with the coup and subsequent inspections and so on he could get caught. A couple of the guys—I mean instructors like me, same situation—were passing through on their way to the border, and he asked them for a lift. There was a coup underway, so they were happy to assist a fellow European."

"How do you know?"

"They told me."

"So why are they blaming you and your friends?"

"Later on, that asshole spread the story that he was forced to open the safe at gunpoint, and kidnapped. So everyone blamed the mercenary dogs, and we all got hit with the charge, not just the two guys involved. And they didn't steal anything, either. But this way, that asshole got to keep the diamonds while everyone looked elsewhere."

"That poster said a security guard was killed."

"Not by them. They really had no reason to kill anyone."

"I think I understand," I said.

Kross glanced at me sharply. After a while, he said:

"You're thinking that's where our diamonds came from, don't you. Well, what are you going to do about it?"

"Nothing," I said. "I don't give a fuck. All I care is that we get out of this fucking country and I get my share."

"That's the right attitude," Kross said. Then he went back to concentrating on his driving, and I went back to digesting information. It was beginning to give me heartburn.

I gradually became aware that there was something odd in Boswell's accusations. Calling Kross a murderer and a thief was fine, only to be expected in those circumstances. However, that bit about the Nazi father—that just didn't fit. It seemed odd and contrived. And precisely because it seemed odd, it could be true.

But even if Kross's father had really been a Nazi war criminal—so what? My old man was a sailor, and by the time I was fourteen I swore to never follow in his footsteps.

And suddenly, I remembered a novel I'd read around that time, when I was fourteen. It was a wartime adventure story. Its hero was a valiant captain in the Royal Navy. He was hunting down German U-boots lurking off the coast of Africa, lying in ambush for ships carrying supplies to the beleaguered British Isles. Of course the valiant captain tracked down and sank a number of the evil submarines, and one of these was carrying diamonds taken from a steamship it had intercepted earlier. I even remembered the name of that steamship: *SS Glasgow Castle*. It had stuck in my memory because I knew there was no castle in Glasgow. There was a castle in Edinburgh, but not in Glasgow.

It was insane to link this to my present situation, but I did it anyway. I began to imagine various related scenarios. Kross's father rowing ashore in a dinghy, hiding the diamonds for future reference. Lying on his deathbed and revealing the secret to his son—maybe there even was a hand-drawn map held out by a trembling, withered hand. And Kross could easily be a German name.

Naturally he'd invent a coverup story. Helping yourself to diamonds left nearly two centuries earlier by a disaffected sailor was one thing. It was another if they'd been British government property just over forty years ago. And having a father who sank civilian ships, and maybe machine-gunned any floating survivors... It wasn't the kind of thing you'd want to share with people.

We stopped for gas at dusk. There was a small store at the station and Kross gave me a thin wad of cedi notes to buy water and Cokes and food, if any was available. I got two loaves of sliced white bread in plastic bags and six cans of corned beef—what else. They did have the advantage of not requiring a can opener.

When I got back, the Toyota had been refueled and we were ready to go. I watched Kross pay the attendant and tell him to keep the change. He really fancied himself as a considerate kind of guy. He probably felt the need to counterbalance all those people he'd killed. Everyone liked to think well of themselves.

The moment we drove out of the station, Kross said:

"It's going to be completely dark in twenty minutes. So we'll be taking a different road, one that doesn't cross the state boundary for a while. It means an extra half an hour, but it will take us where we need to go."

"What state boundary?"

"A boundary between states, as in the United States of America. Only over here they're called regions. There's pretty much always a checkpoint where the road crosses into the next region."

"But we'll hit a checkpoint sooner or later, won't we? What happens if there's no way we can drive around it? Because of the jungle or whatever?"

"We'll bluff our way through. Just like we did before."

"What about that captain that knows you? You know, the commander of that checkpoint we stopped at?"

"Sankey? He won't report anything until the evening. And army clerks are just like regular clerks: they're never in a hurry. It will take time for the news to spread around. We're good at least until tomorrow afternoon. And by that time we'll be over the border."

"So basically we're perfectly safe," I said, with maximum sarcasm.

"Yeah. More or less."

There wasn't anything I could say to that which couldn't be interpreted as cowardly whining, so I shut up and focused on making myself feel safe instead of frightened. It wasn't possible. It was very dark and we were driving very fast through hilly jungle, which was spooky. Luckily there was virtually no other traffic. When I commented, Kross told me Africans didn't like to drive at night.

"That sounds very sensible to me," I said.

We drove on, almost alone on the road, for a good two hours. From time to time a bunch of lights would appear in front and each time, I half-expected a checkpoint. We didn't encounter any. We passed through sleepy villages and tiny towns completely unimpeded. Even the goats were asleep. Eventually I said:

"Can I ask you something?"

"Sure."

"The diamonds. Where were they hidden, exactly?"

"Right where the bush met the beach."

"You told me they were hidden in a special place."

"They were in a juju cave."

"A what?"

"A kind of sacred cave."

"You're shitting me!"

"I'm not! It's a group of rocks clumped together to form a sort of a cave inside."

"What makes it a juju cave?"

"Those rocks have a special feature. Any kind of wind or breeze and they begin to make those moaning sounds. It's just air passing through the slits, but the locals think the rocks are inhabited by evil spirits."

"Will you show them to me? The diamonds?"

"Sure. On our very next stop, if you like. Be prepared they don't look very exciting."

"You said some are large."

"They're still rough diamonds. They all look like glassy gravel."

After a pause, I said:

"Okay, let's assume we made it across the border. What comes next?"

"We'll visit the Komoe just like we told everyone we would. Maybe even visit Mireille on the way back to Abidjan. Might be useful if anyone asks any questions later. Then we relax at the hotel for a day, and fly back to Paris with Raymond."

"And we walk onto the plane carrying the diamonds, just like that?"

"Raymond will take care of that business. We're old friends. Saved his skin more than once."

I didn't want to find out what was involved in saving Raymond's skin. It seemed saving people's skins was Kross's specialty. I didn't want to find out more; I'd had all the excitement I could handle. So we kept quiet for the next half an hour or so, until Kross said:

"Okay. We're getting close to a junction right on the state line. Chances are there'll be a checkpoint set up. So we'll stop now to eat and take a leak. If something goes wrong, we won't be stopping for a while."

"Fine by me."

The sliced white bread turned out to be very sweet. But it went well with the inevitable corned beef: I ate more than half of my loaf, and Kross actually finished his. Disabling four cops probably burned up plenty of calories.

When we'd finished eating and taken the advertised leak, Kross said:

"Want to see the diamonds?"

"Sure."

We got back into the Toyota's cab and Kross switched the courtesy light on. Then he unbuttoned his other leg pocket, the one that didn't contain Boswell's gear, and pulled out a blue pouch of the kind used for cosmetics. He unzipped it and spread its jaws wide and held it out to me.

"Can I take out a few?" I asked.

"Sure."

I reached inside the pouch and took a large pinch of what felt like tiny pebbles. I put them in my palm and held them up to the light. Kross had been right, as usual: they didn't look exciting. Crumbs of reddish yellow glass, nothing more. And all very small. Kross said:

"The bigger ones are at the bottom. You know something, this is as good a time as any to divvy up the loot. If we get separated, you'll have your share in your pocket."

"You think we'll get separated?"

"I hope not. But life likes surprises."

"You can say that again," I said with fervour. "Okay, let's do it."

Kross cut the plastic bag his bread came in and turned into a sheet, an action that revealed he kept a knife hidden in the cuff of his boot. Then he spread the sheet over his lap and emptied the pouch over it.

They made a nice little mound, the diamonds—more than enough to fill my cupped hands. I counted several big boys which fell out last, being at the bottom of the pouch. I saw one that seemed as big as a peanut.

Kross divided the pile into two halves with his knife. Then he asked:

"Which pile do you like better?"

"Better?"

"Larger. Which pile is larger."

I stared hard and said:

"The one closer to me. On your right."

"Okay," he said. He swept the smaller pile back into the pouch, and repeated the process of dividing what remained into two piles. He even took the trouble of picking out the bigger diamonds and distributing them equally. Then he said:

"Our final agreement was you get a quarter. So, which pile is yours?"

I knew it would be a very difficult choice, so without looking I said:

"Same as before, the one that's closer. On your right."

Kross pursed his lips. Then he took a large pinch of diamonds from the other pile, and dropped it on mine. He said:

"A small bonus. You didn't do too badly overall, major Haslam. By the way, who the fuck is Haslam?"

"My former boss."

"Should've chosen a different name. Something unconnected."

"Major Haslam sounds good," I said.

"You advertising guys," he said, shaking his head.

He cut a square out of the plastic and packed my diamonds into a flat package the size of my palm.

"Best put it in your boot," he told me, when he was handing it over. "Slide it under the cuff and behind your ankle bone. You have a spare pair of socks?"

"I do."

"Then wrap it in a sock first."

He lit a cigarette and watched me carry out his instructions. It was irritating. I said:

"What about you?"

"Oh, I'll carry mine in my pocket. I won't let anyone pat me down. By the way, do you still have that pistol?"

"Yes. I'm not sure how it works. Never handled a pistol before."

"You familiar with any kind of firearm at all?"

"Just a rifle. A bolt-action twenty-two. Shot a few cans and bottles. I was actually quite good at that."

"Fine. If the shit hits the fan, you'll take one of the Enfields. They're both in decent shape. Same action as your twenty-two, but with a five-round magazine."

"I don't intend to do any shooting whatsoever," I said.

"You'll change your mind when someone starts to shoot at you. You ready?"

"I am."

"Let's go."

CHAPTER EIGHTEEN

We ran into a checkpoint less than five minutes later. We'd just shot out from around a curve and it was less than a hundred metres away, much too close to stop and retreat. What Kross called a mammy lorry—a truck converted to carry passengers—was parked on the other side of the road, lights doused. For some reason—no fuel?—the flames dancing atop the inevitable barrels were very low, too feeble to cast a warning glow into the sky. We were driving with high beams on and in their light I saw a bunch of people huddled around the mammy lorry and a soldier walking to to the centre of the road, his hand raised and signalling us to stop.

Kross didn't. He accelerated instead, flicking the switch between high and low beams repeatedly and adding a blast on the horn. The soldier jumped out of the way at the last moment.

"Fuck!" I shouted.

Kross didn't react. He just kept going and within a moment our headlights lit up another curve. It took us at most twenty seconds to reach that curve, but they were the longest twenty seconds of my life: I was waiting to hear shots and bullets striking the Toyota. I discovered I'd been holding my breath only once we'd gotten round that bend.

A hundred questions were milling around in my head. I glanced at Kross. He was fully focused on his driving. He needed to. The speedo needle was hovering well past 100, which was suicidal speed at night on that particular road. It was a bad time to strike up a conversation with the driver.

So I attempted to answer some of those questions myself, and quickly found out it made no sense. I knew the answers already. We were roughly halfway to the spot where we'd crossed the border on our way in. Dawn would be breaking by the time we got there. There was a long night ahead of me.

There was an oil-stained map with scotch-taped folds that came with the Toyota, and I'd had a look at it earlier. I'd have given a lot to take another look, but there was no question of turning a light on or indeed making any kind of move that would distract Kross from his driving. We went through a series of hills and it was extra scary because Kross switched the lights off for a couple of seconds when motoring up a slope. I quickly learned why: on our second hill, the lights of a vehicle climbing up the other side lit up the sky.

It was a Land Rover. Like us, it was going fast and we shot past each other right on the summit of the hill. It was hogging the road and if Kross hadn't edged to the side the moment he saw its headlamps lighting up the sky, there'd have been a collision. My respect for Kross reached new heights. He was truly a major. It was a mystery really how he'd ended up in a rooming house. Someone with his skills and qualifications –

Someone with his skills and qualifications would only move to a rooming house in order to hide. I'd already seen him on one Wanted poster. There probably were others. Associating with Kross was a good way to make sure my mug appeared on a Wanted poster, too. I was lucky not to have been photographed or fingerprinted at the police station. I was lucky to be rescued by Kross shortly thereafter. All I could do was hope that my run of luck—*our* run of luck—would continue.

It did for several hours, during which I accumulated several questions for Kross. My chance came when he stopped to clean the front windshield: it was getting hard to see anything through it because of all the splattered insect corpses.

I offered to help but was dismissed with a curt 'it's fine'. I got out of the cab to stretch my legs while Kross worked with grim determination on the windshield.

"I really could help," I offered after a while.

"I'm almost done."

After a pause, I asked:

"Do you think there could be any consequences caused by us running through that checkpoint?"

"There could be."

That froze me. I'd been expecting to hear the usual 'everything's fine' bullshit. I cleared my throat and said:

"Could you give me an inkling of what could happen? I mean it's obviously better if I'm prepared before it does."

"We could run into a checkpoint with a roadblock."

"I, um, what are the chances of that happening?"

"Fifty-fifty. I didn't like that Land Rover we passed right after the checkpoint. It was an army vehicle. It probably contained the commander of that checkpoint, returning to his post after a pleasant time in town."

"So?"

"He'll be eager to cover up his absence, and demonstrate that he's on the ball. So after his guys tell him what happened, he'll get on the blower to broadcast a warning. Especially since he saw us go past. I'm sure he or his driver noticed we're whites."

That shut me up for a while. Once we were back inside the cab, I asked:

"Is there anything we can do about it? I don't mean the roadblock. I mean the whole fucking situation."

Kross lit a cigarette and inhaled with obvious enjoyment—it was his first in a while. Puffing smoke, he said:

"We'll head straight for the border, and get off the road as soon as possible."

"I'll keep my fingers crossed," I said. Kross threw me a funny look, and blew some smoke my way. Then he switched on the engine, and we resumed our breakneck drive.

It got really bad after the next junction. Kross turned left onto a road that led directly west. But as soon as we'd left the little town clustered around the crossroads, the road got so bad flying over the potholes wasn't an option: the road basically consisted of potholes ringed with asphalt. Kross had to slow down to fifty-sixty, and I was repeatedly thrown around as the Toyota weaved and lurched.

Just after three in the morning when we came to another junction buried inside a village with aspirations to become a town: there was a flickering neon sign above a closed BP station. The road we were on continued west; but to my surprise, Kross turned right, which meant north.

"I thought we were going straight to the border," I said.

"But not on a road that actually crosses into Ivory Coast. It will have checkpoints for sure, more than one. This road we're on doesn't go across. Further on the border bends east and the road bends west and they run parallel for a while. Close enough so that if it comes to worst, we can walk over to the other side."

"You really seem to know your way around the roads here."

Kross snorted, and said:

"I spent two years teaching Ghanaian soldiers how to operate an armoured car. We did a lot of driving around. I've been on this very road at least twice. It and the border almost meet no more than an hour's drive from here. Trouble is, I can't remember the lay of the land too well. There is a river, not the one we'd crossed, another one. I'm not sure we can cross it in this heap."

"No fords?"

"None that I remember. What I do remember is that rivers here feature crocodiles. Anyway, we'll cross that bridge when we come to it," Kross said, and grinned.

I didn't see anything to grin about. The perspective of swimming across a jungle river infested with crocodiles failed to amuse me. And hiking cross-country, at night—the country in question was presently very hilly. Some of the hills were so steep the road had to sweep up the slope in serpentines.

Fortunately, things improved right after we'd driven over a particularly steep hill that was just short of becoming a full-fledged mountain. The road sashayed down to a rolling plain, and began to run straight for long stretches. Numerous clearings began to appear in the jungle, and we passed through a succession of small towns. After one of these the blacktop suddenly gave way to red laterite and it got very noisy with all the pebbles and gravel hitting the metal underside of the Toyota.

"Not far now!" Kross shouted. "Twenty minutes! At least there are no potholes!" And he stepped on the gas.

There were no potholes any more, that much was true. But the road surface was very uneven, at times resembling a washing board, and it ran over numerous small hillocks and other gentle rises that weren't quite so gentle at high speed. We were being shaken so hard that I bit my tongue.

"Slow down!" I shouted. "Five minutes more won't make a difference."

"It's going to start getting light soon!" Kross shouted back. "I want us over the border before dawn!"

The Toyota's dashboard clock wasn't working, and reading the time on my watch was next to impossible: it was dark and I was being constantly tossed around. I got the impression that it was around four and saw confirmation when I looked out of my side window: I could see a band of not-quite-so-dark sky just above the horizon.

We came to another tiny town, and I could have a drink of water without splashing it all over myself. We were driving through at no more than forty and it was good we did because it prevented us from running into a couple of sleeping cows, hidden behind the only bend in the road in the whole fucking town.

Kross stopped the Toyota and cursed and so did I: deep open gutters on both sides of the road meant going around those fucking cows was impossible. Then Kross got out and walked up to the cows. He stopped and stooped and reached down to his boot, got out his knife and stuck it into the cow's ass.

It bellowed so loudly that I cringed in my seat, but it refused to move. Kross gave it a kick and said something I didn't catch. The cow got up slowly, complaining again when Kross prodded it with the knife. He kept repeating a phrase I couldn't understand and which sounded really strange, maybe because it was a magic spell: the cow finally consented to move a couple of paces, leaving a gap wide enough to squeeze the Toyota through.

'What did you say to that cow? What were the magic words?' I asked the moment Kross was back inside the cab.

"I told it to move ass in Twi."

"In what?"

"In Twi. Local language. Picked up a few useful phrases listening to officers and non-coms shouting at the soldiers."

Less than a minute later, we left the town behind and Kross accelerated hard. I hung on for dear life to the dashboard grip with one hand and to my seat with the other. I didn't dare look at the speedometer. When I glanced out

259

of my side window, I saw that the band of lighter sky above the horizon had broadened appreciably. The jungle was gone, pushed away from the road as if by a magic hand: only small, frightened clumps of trees remained. All was explained when we slowed down to drive through another townlet and saw an arrow-shaped sign to turn left for Adwuofua Lumber.

A few minutes later, after we'd raced through a tiny hamlet, I looked at Kross and shouted:

"How much longer?"

He didn't answer, maybe because there was a sharp curve coming up. I decided I'd ask again once we'd gone through but I never got to ask that question.

When we rounded that curve, our headlights illuminated a big army truck parked right across the road: its nose was buried in the bush on the left side. The right side featured six or seven soldiers standing next to the tailboard. One of them, a tall bereted type with a pistol holster, took a step forward and raised his hand.

Kross slowed down. I thought we were going to stop. I thought he would try to bullshit his way through. Then he emitted a maniacal giggle and flipped the turn indicator on, just as if he'd been about to park on a busy city street. I knew then what he was up to and clutched my seat as if I was trying to rip it off the floor. He changed down and shouted:

"Sit low and hang on!" And he immediately swung the wheel to the right and floored the gas pedal, catapulting us into the bush. I heard a shout, there was a jarring crunch—all I could do was hold onto my seat. Staying seated took all my strength. My head hit the dashboard and I literally saw a couple of green stars. We tore into the bush, engine screaming, the Toyota banging, groaning, and whinnying. Then I heard this: *pop-pop pop-pop-pop.*

I looked up from the swaying floor just in time to see the side mirror explode. There was a loud crack and it simply disappeared. I was thrown against the door as Kross wrenched the Land Rover to the left. Then we were back on the dirt road and he was slamming through the gears, accelerating hard and hopefully raising a cloud of dust thick enough to hide us from the soldiers.

I felt my face start to sting, put a hand up and touched a piece of glass embedded right next to the corner of my eye. I managed to squeeze it out—no mean achievement in the lurching, shaking cab—and began applying the same technique to the shard stuck in my cheek. Suddenly, the Land Rover slewed crazily; Kross had to fight hard to bring it back under control. I heard a thumping noise coming from the back of the car, a noise that I'd heard before, in my other life.

"They got the tires!" I screamed at Kross. He nodded grimly. I glanced at the the speedo: it showed sixty, then fifty, then forty.

"Hang on!" shouted Kross. He shifted down, switched the lights off and cut across the road, driving into the bush on the other side. There was already enough light to make out shapes at short range: the night was ending. But almost immediately the right front wheel dropped into a hidden hole with a sickening crunch, and a moment later a loud grinding noise began. It seemed to be coming from the front axle.

Kross slowed down until we were crawling along just above walking speed. Before long, the Toyota started to squeal like a stuck pig. Kross maneuvered it carefully behind a clump of trees, stopped, and switched off the engine.

"Right," he said. "Let's get the fuck out of here." He threw himself around in his seat and started pulling stuff out from the back.

"I'll get rid of this glass in my face, first," I said. I hadn't been hoping for cries of concern, but it irked me that Kross didn't react at all. I squeezed out the shard buried in my cheek, and then the one in my temple. By the time I was done, Kross had taken all of our belongings out of the Toyota. He was standing with his back turned to me, fucking around with one of the rifles.

I got out of the cab and listened hard. I couldn't hear any vehicles. We were maybe half a mile from the road, no more, and it was very quiet. The soldiers who'd shot at us weren't chasing us in their truck. It was only good sense. They wouldn't know if they hit the tires or anything else for that matter. It was dark and everything was happening fast and then we were gone, a fact that likely made them think they'd missed.

I walked around the front of the Toyota and joined Kross. He'd turned his attention to the submachine gun. He'd taken the ammo clip out and was snapping the lock back and forth.

"Fucking piece of shit," he said. I assumed he was referring to the gun. When he'd slapped the magazine back in place, I asked:

"What's the plan?"

"We're going to get the fuck away from here. What else? Pack your bag, and take one of the Enfields. Be careful, I put one up the spout in both of them. There's another five in the clip."

"Pack my bag?"

"Take half the water and the food. You still have that pistol?"

"Yes."

"You better give it to me. It's likely another piece of junk."

"You're welcome to it," I said as I handed him the pistol. "I couldn't even find the safety switch."

Kross looked at the pistol and grinned.

"It's got an in-built safety mechanism," he said. "See the trigger? It's a solid block of metal. Pulling it back releases the safety. Now go and pack and choose a rifle, they're both okay. And do it fast. We've gotta move out of here."

My half of the food and the water came to two one-litre bottles of Volvic, a few floppy slices of bread, some soda crackers, and two cans of corned beef. I could probably survive a day on that, but it wouldn't be a pleasant day. I squeezed everything into my bag and examined the rifles. One of them had the initials 'AG' cut into the wooden butt, the cuts darkened with age, and that was the one I chose.

I rejoined Kross with my bag slung from one shoulder and the rifle from the other. He'd slung his bag across his back, the strap across his chest. The submachine gun hung from his neck, and he'd also helped himself to a rifle. With

Boswell's pistol in his pocket and a knife in his boot, he was a small walking arsenal. I guessed people in his line of work were into that kind of thing. I said:

"How far are we from the border?"

"A couple of hours' walk. Maybe less."

"That's not too far."

"It depends."

"On what?"

"On us being spotted. It will be day in half an hour. That's when the fun will start. You ready?"

I wasn't ready. I was completely unprepared for that whole guns in the bush business. But this wasn't the right time to remind Kross that all I'd initially agreed to was drive a car for a few hours, and pick up the diamonds. So I said:

"Sure I'm ready."

"Good. Follow me a few steps back, all right? And keep your eyes and ears open. Okay. Let's go."

It was already light enough to walk at a brisk pace. We were on a rolling plain, with steeper slopes here and there. Thickets of trees often grew on these gentle rises; otherwise it was mostly bushes and shrubs and yellowed grass—sometimes higher than my waist, and sometimes barely reaching the ankles.

Sunrise was heralded by an angry screech from a hidden creature that probably disapproved of our presence. Within moments, everything was bathed in reddish light. I was amazed to see a long, wiggling shape precede me as I walked. It took me a while to realize I was watching my own shadow. It didn't say much about my mental state.

I heard the buzz of a faraway engine: it sounded like one of those innumerable light motorbikes and scooters that we'd encountered on the road. Kross heard it too. He stopped to listen, looked at me and said:

"It's nothing to worry about, just a bike."

"I know," I said. "How about a drink?"

"Good idea. But just a couple of mouthfuls, okay?"

"Was that sound coming from the road we were on?" I asked, when I was putting the water bottle back into my bag.

"No. It's from the track I wanted to take before our journey was so rudely interrupted. It runs straight west to a village that's right next to the border. Home to local smugglers. I remember my boys suddenly smoking French cigarettes after we'd paid a visit."

"Maybe we should head away from that road."

"We can't afford the time to make a detour big enough to count. And anyway it's better to hear danger before it shows up."

His words turned out to be unpleasantly prophetic. Around twenty minutes after we'd resumed walking, I heard a hum in the air. This time, Kross didn't stop to listen. He began walking faster instead, kept going fast even when the hum faded away. I broke into a trot and caught up with him and said:

"What was that?"

"A helicopter."

"They, their army has helicopters?"

"Sure they have. From now on we're keeping close to some trees at all times, okay?"

"Fine by me."

It turned out to be less than fine. It made numerous little detours necessary. There were also large treeless areas which we crossed at double speed.

I heard a couple more motorcycles pass by on the invisible track, then a larger engine that made Kross stop and listen with a hand cupped to his ear. When the sound faded away, he said:

"That was a truck. I don't like that. It could be that it belongs to a successful smuggler, but—whatever. We've got to speed up a little."

He began going almost twice as fast, breaking into a trot whenever we had to cross a treeless patch. Before long, I was completely wet with sweat, and my breath was coming in ragged gasps. I was totally out of shape. I couldn't imagine going on like that for more than an hour, tops. I consoled myself with the thought that according to our calculations, we'd be over the border by then.

A few minutes later we were trotting across open ground when I heard a faraway shout. Kross heard it too—he threw a glance sideways—but he continued without changing direction or pace. Suddenly there was a loud smack followed by a whistling sound and Kross was shouting "Go, go, go!", turning right and breaking into a huddled run.

I ran after him. He was heading for a rocky knoll that had to be at least a two hundred yards away. Halfway there, my heart and lungs began to feel as if they would burst. I couldn't go on and I stopped, bent over gasping for breath and grasping my knees, and looked over my shoulder.

I saw ant-like people strung out in a line. They were coming from the direction of the track and they had to be soldiers.

"Move, dumbass!" Kross shouted. I saw he was already close to the knoll and heard a couple of faint, faraway claps and something smacked into the ground just a few steps from my feet.

That was the encouragement I needed. I was suddenly full of energy and ran so fast I felt a breeze on my face. I reached the top of the rise and wrongfooted it and tumbled down the gentle slope, my photographer's bag kicking me in a kidney with a metal-reinforced corner before falling off my shoulder.

I got myself together and saw that Kross was lying on the slope, his rifle extended over the ridge, the submachine gun and his bag lying on the ground by his side. He was looking at me and he said:

"You all right?"

"I'm fine."

He nodded, and said:

"We have to split up. They need a scare. You go on and I'll give them one."

"What the fuck do you mean?"

"I'll be better off without having you to worry about."

I was silent. He raised his arm and pointed and said:

"See that baobab there? The big fat guy all on his own? Keep going in that direction until you've left it a few hundred paces behind. Then turn left and head west again until you reach the border. It can't be more than a mile away. You'll see it from a distance. There'll be trees growing along the river."

"The river you were talking about earlier?"

"Yes. That's the border. Get across, and you're safe. Watch out for crocodiles. One swipe of the tail and you've got no legs. If you see one don't shoot, it won't feel a thing unless you nail it in the right spot. Just run like hell. They are fast but they run out of steam very quickly."

"Got it."

"Good. Once you're across, dump the gun and change your clothes. Get to a road and get a ride to Bondoukou. Go to Mireille's and tell her our car fucked up and I'm getting it fixed. I'll join you within twenty four hours. If I don't, go back to Abidjan, to the hotel. If I still don't show up, leave as scheduled. We'll meet at home."

"Home," I said, and nearly laughed.

"Go to the Air Afrique office in the hotel and leave a message for Raymond Best. He'll help with everything. *Capitaine* Raymond Best. Got it?"

"Got it," I mumbled. "But what do I tell him? So that he knows everything's kosher?"

Kross frowned and it was then that we heard the shouts. They sounded like an order followed by several affirmatives and they were uncomfortably close.

"Tell him that Giselle was right," said Kross. "Tell him I'll see him soon. Giselle. Got it?"

"Giselle," I repeated.

"Okay. Fuck off now. I'll keep them busy for a while. And take this, you have no money."

He tossed a rubber-banded roll of banknotes in my direction. It hit me in the chest.

I picked it up and hesitated: I had the feeling I'll never see him again. I said:

"Kross. Just one thing. Why did you choose me? Spare me the bullshit that there was no one else. Why me?"

He smiled tightly and said:

"Because I like you."

CHAPTER NINETEEN

I got going, the rising sun on my right. I walked crouched at first; then I straightened up a little and broke into a trot, heading for the baobab.

I hadn't taken fifty steps when I heard a couple of shouts and a whip-like crack immediately followed by a horrible scream. I knew it was Kross shooting and that he'd scored a hit. I broke into a full-speed run. I didn't look back until I reached the baobab.

I stopped behind its fat trunk and peeked out. I couldn't see Kross anywhere. The screaming went on and on; it didn't sound human, it sounded like an animal in extreme pain—when I was a kid I heard a run-over dog make a noise like that.

I started running again, my eyes fixed on a copse whose trees grew thickly enough to provide good cover. I had to slow down to a walk fairly quickly. My heart was thumping like a bass drum and there was a high-pitched whistling in my ears. I was very thirsty and unexpectedly, also very hungry. I slowed down still more and tried to wipe the sweat, or rather the salty mud off my face and succeeded in rubbing some grit into the corner of my eye. The cuts from the glass stung and burned. I started calculating the chances of getting infected by an exotic, deadly parasite.

Then suddenly, *crrack*. And another bloodcurdling scream.

I was instantly running again. The copse I'd chosen seemed to retreat instead of getting closer. When I finally got to the trees, I was wheezing and trembling like an ancient steam engine. I got out the Volvic, got my breath under control, and drank. I couldn't get enough. It took a real effort to stop.

I tried to estimate how far away I'd gotten and it had to be less than half a mile. It was too early to turn west. But the border was supposedly just a mile away. I decided I'd check out the lay of the land in that direction.

My bag felt very heavy when I slung it back onto my shoulder, even though really it was lighter by the water I'd drunk. And that fucking rifle was a hefty piece of solid wood and metal—I was shocked to realize I'd sooner ditch the bag than the rifle. It had already started to make me feel stronger, safer, better. It was working its gun magic on me.

I raised my head to check for silent helicopters and saw a big bird circling high up in the sky, gliding on outstretched wings with serrated tips. It was a vulture, and it was probably evaluating me as a future meal, trying to decide whether it was worthwhile to hang around. I'd have given a lot to know what went on in that bird's brain. I had the feeling it knew the score.

Suddenly I heard a deep, growling grunt in the trees a few steps away. Then the grass swishing and rustling as something fairly big rushed towards me.

I was off like a fucking Olympic sprinter. I ran as fast as I could and then even faster when I heard a throaty snarl right behind me. It couldn't go on forever and it didn't. I tripped and fell just as I was about to run out of breath.

Nothing attacked me. I lay still and got my breathing back under control. Then I slowly raised my head. Something tickled my hand. I looked and saw a big red ant on the first joint of my forefinger. It waggled its antennae inquiringly. I shook it off and raised myself into a crouch, then straightened up with the rifle held ready.

I saw the wild pig that had attacked me just before it disappeared between the trees. It couldn't have been higher than my knee. He or she was a brave little bastard, to charge an animal four times bigger. Maybe there was a litter that needed defending? I told myself to model my behavior on that pig.

I couldn't hear any shooting going on, and no one was screaming at the moment. I looked around. Trees and the undulating ground limited the view to half a mile, tops. No one would be able to see me from the dirt road, not even if they stood on the roof of a truck and had binoculars. I decided I would head straight for the border.

This time, I hung my bag sideways and across my back, with the strap cutting into my neck—I wanted to keep my arms free for the rifle. I walked steadily for a few minutes: peace all around, no shots, screams, or homicidal wild pigs. My heartbeat and breath were back to normal, but I felt fucking tired, as if I'd been walking all night. My legs ached whenever I had to climb yet another gentle slope.

After twenty minutes had passed, I began to feel newly apprehensive. At my pace, twenty minutes meant I'd covered a mile or more. I could see a knoll of respectable height slightly to the right. I adjusted my course and a few minutes later I was standing on its summit.

I immediately saw a line of trees in front, running roughly north to south. They were at most a quarter mile away and the tree line bent and twisted this way and that, exactly as it would when following a stream or a river. I almost whooped with joy, and immediately resumed walking. I didn't feel tired any more. I even repeatedly broke into a run, sprinting between bushes with surprising style. As I got closer, I remembered Kross's warning about crocodiles and slowed down and started paying really good attention where I was going.

The tree line wasn't dense, but half a dozen crocs could easily lay concealed in the thick undergrowth. I held the rifle ready to fire, with a finger on the trigger. Every few steps I stopped to listen. All sorts of life were making their presence known with an assortment of chirps, hisses, clicks, and whistles. I couldn't hear anything indicating there might be crocodiles around, but who knew—maybe they whistled and chirped in their sleep.

I raised my foot and stamped hard on the ground a few times. Some insects in the vicinity shut up briefly; otherwise there was no reaction. I stepped forward, brushing tall grass aside with the barrel of the rifle, and I finally saw the river.

It was well hidden because it was a small, narrow river—narrow enough to qualify as a stream, except there wasn't any current showing. A running leap would get me across, especially since I was standing on an overhang at least five feet higher than the water. Had I taken just two more steps, I'd have tumbled down.

I had a drink of water and pondered my options. The overhang was at the apex of a steep curve in the river, and the finger of land directly across was very thickly overgrown. It looked like a perfect relaxation spot for crocodiles and other reptiles. I didn't want to land there, following a running leap.

I backed out of the trees and began walking along the river. I saw what promised to be good spot less than a minute later. The vegetation wasn't as dense, allowing an unimpeded run before jumping. When I got to the riverbank, I saw that this was indeed the perfect place. There was a similar gap in the trees on the other side and the river seemed to be narrower than earlier, maybe because it was running straight. And there even was an oblong rock in the middle of the water, its top just below the surface. I could use it as a stepping stone.

I looked at that rock more closely and it became obvious that I was looking at a crocodile. It was perfectly still in the weak current, its jaw pointing upstream—it was likely waiting for food to float its way. I made out the eyes and the nostrils protruding just above the water surface. It wasn't a big crocodile, no longer than my leg.

I raised the rifle to my shoulder and aimed between and behind the eyes. I felt fairly confident I could hit it right in the middle of its stupid, reptile brain. I'd been able to hit a standard-sized can right in the middle at double the distance from a .22. I once wowed a couple of friends by shattering bottles we'd lined up fifty long strides away, one shot per bottle. And if I missed this time, I could easily run away—it would take the croc time to get out of the water and onto the steep bank. If it even bothered to do that, because it seemed to be a very lazy crocodile. It had noticed me, I was sure, but it just totally ignored me.

I was about to shoot when I realized that the shot would probably be heard for miles around. That did it. I couldn't shoot that croc. I stared at it with real loathing. Then I had the thought there might be other crocs around which might be less lazy, and hastily left the bank and resumed walking along the river, still going north.

It took me almost half an hour to find the perfect spot to get across the river. It was perfect because there was a path running right up to the water, and continuing on the other side. The river in that spot was so shallow I could actually see the bottom.

I walked a dozen steps down the track, turned around, counted down from three to zero, and launched myself like a fucking rocket. I reached such good speed that I almost toppled over upon landing on the other bank. I ran up the short slope and stopped and listened and heard a hum, the same hum that I'd heard earlier, the hum of a faraway helicopter.

There was a huge acacia growing a short distance away from the river. Telling myself that I had nothing to fear—technically I was in Ivory Coast already—I trotted to hide behind its trunk. I ran a check for animal life in the immediate vicinity, and put my bag and the rifle on the ground. Then I slid my head around the trunk like an ultra-cautious snake.

For quite a while I couldn't see the helicopter at all: it was flying at me straight out of the sun, as recommended by Richthofen. It was fairly close by the time it finally took shape: a big black blob suddenly detached itself from the sun and filled out with colour as it turned to hover over the river, less than a hundred yards from where I crouched.

It made a deafening racket. It was painted green-brown like a Battle of Britain Hurricane, and it looked similarly antiquated. The cockpit windows were arranged like a jetliner's, in a narrow arc above a bulbous nose. The main rotor was mounted atop a big hump perforated with numerous ventilation slits. The side door was slid back and the opening featured two soldiers, squatting and looking around. I could see the green straps of their security harnesses, and that one of them was holding an assault rifle. The other held a pair of binoculars and he chose that very moment to raise them to his face and I swiftly retracted my mug behind the tree trunk.

A few very long seconds ticked by. The helicopter kept whop-whop-whopping in the same spot and I was beginning to get worried when there was a sudden change in engine tone. I risked a peek. It was flying away, going south.

"Fuck," I said. *Fuck!* I allowed myself a moment for self-congratulation. Then I set about a change of costume.

I pulled out a white T-shirt and a pair of khaki chinos out of my bag. Both were very badly creased, which could appear suspicious to anyone with eyes and a brain. It was very obvious they'd been pulled out of a bag a moment earlier, and who would go for a change of wardrobe in the middle of the bush? But then I realized that once I began walking again, they'd be wet with sweat within minutes and the wrinkles would dissolve.

My suede desert boots felt very flimsy on my feet after the military boots. I didn't know what to do with the diamonds. I definitely didn't want to put them in my bag. So eventually, I just shoved them into my side pocket. The bulge showed when I looked down, as if I'd suddenly grown a tumour on my thigh, and I hit it with my fist a couple of times to flatten it out.

I also didn't know what to do with all the military gear: the clothes, the boots, the rifle. I couldn't see a spot that made a good hiding place. If someone found this shit right next to the border following a firefight nearby, eyebrows would be raised and questions asked even though all the shooting took place on the other side, in Ghana.

I ended up packing the clothes and the boots in my bag, wrapping the boots in the dirty T-shirt. It was a tight fit and when I'd finished doing that I realized my wallet and my passport were in the zipped inside pocket, so I had to take everything out again to get them.

My brain simply wasn't working properly, and this was confirmed when I tried to find out how much money I had. There was the roll of CFA franc banknotes Kross had thrown at me and they were big notes, 10,000 each. There were more in my wallet, mostly 1,000 and 500 notes. My malfunctioning brain forced me to count everything I had three times before I finally concluded that I had nearly a quarter million CFA francs. At the current exchange rate, that worked out to around four hundred American dollars.

I also had two traveller's cheques worth fifty American each, for a total of five hundred. And then there was my credit card. I'd been making the minimum payments and it was maybe five bucks under the limit. I could likely use it just once before the money police got wise.

It would be a tight squeeze if Kross didn't show up. He'd told me to wait for twenty-four hours, so I had to pay for single night's accommodation in Bondoukou anyway. But then I'd have to pay my way to Abidjan, and stay at the hotel before my flight back. It was a very expensive hotel and I could only hope that the arrangement Kross had made with the manager would also apply to me on my own. Maybe if worst came to worst I could bullshit the manager I'd been involved in setting up the hotel security too, in a remote consultant capacity or something like that.

I put the passport/wallet money combo into my other side pocket and wondered what to do with the rifle. It crossed my mind it would be good to wipe it clean of fingerprints. I was actually about to do that when I realized I would be carrying it with me and leaving fresh prints all over. I couldn't leave it right next to the border, and that fucking river was too shallow to drop it in.

In the end I slung my bag from one shoulder, the rifle from the other, and walked up to the dirt path intersected by the river. It curved out of sight a couple of hundred paces away and I definitely wanted to be out of sight. So I walked quickly, scanning the roadside for a good spot to dump the rifle, and cursing myself for not dropping it into the river after all. But I knew why I hadn't done that. It wasn't about the water being too shallow to hide the gun. I just never wanted to get close to that river ever again. I also couldn't see myself revisiting Africa in my lifetime. Well, maybe Morocco or Egypt. But that would be that.

I walked into the curve still carrying that fucking rifle. I noticed a couple of dried cowpats beside the track, but no good spots to dump the gun. Then I was past the curve and the track ran straight for a stretch and I saw two tiny silhouettes at the end of that stretch, one even tinier than the other. It seemed they were coming my way. I slipped the rifle off my shoulder and slung it as far as I could into the bush, giving the butt a good push. It flew straight as an arrow and mercifully landed in a patch of taller grass.

I resumed walking, the silhouettes in front rapidly growing larger. They turned into a crippled man accompanied by a young boy, both dressed in tattered shorts and T-shirts. The cripple had a wooden crutch stuck under his arm on his legless side. He was actually lucky, to have a working arm on his legless side. The other arm ended in a rounded, calloused stump that rested on the boy's shoulder.

In spite of all this, he seemed to be happy. He seemed to be grinning. When we drew closer still, I saw he didn't have a nose or upper lip: his teeth were exposed in a permanent grinning snarl. The little boy said something in French and they stopped. I stopped too and the boy held up a battered metal bowl that contained a single coin: his good-luck piece. I looked at the leper and he seemed to resent that—his snarl became ferocious. Then I understood he was trying to smile.

I needed all the cash I had so there was only one thing to do. I half-turned round and got the sock out of my pocket and untied it. I didn't bother with the knot, just squeezed out a stone piercing a hole in the plastic. It was bigger than average, the size and shape of a watermelon seed, a tear squeezed out of mother Earth.

I turned and reached to put it into the bowl and just then the light caught it and it glowed briefly with hot pink fire. I dropped it into the bowl—*pink!*—and looked at the leper's face again and saw that he'd recognized the stone for what it was. He looked frightened, and so did the boy. So I did the best thing I could do: I walked away.

After a few steps I looked over my shoulder and saw that they were hurrying towards the river, the frantically worked crutch kicking up angry puffs of red dust. Did they intend to cross the border too? Was leprosy a passport on this continent? I hoped he wouldn't get into trouble because of that diamond. I hoped he'd find a buyer he could trust.

I walked on, to the end of that straight stretch and round another curve. The track seemed to get wider after that second curve and there more cowpats to be seen. But there was a noticeable shortage of cows and cowherds and indeed anything resembling civilization. I still had one bottle of water left, and I wasn't hungry any more. I had over five hundred dollars in cash and traveller's cheques, and over half a million in diamonds. Kross had said the whole haul was better than expected, over two million, and he'd ended up giving me more than a quarter. Things really weren't all that bad.

And then suddenly they got a whole lot better because after rounding another curve I saw buildings, a whole village, not even a quarter mile away. As I got closer, things got better still: there was a minibus parked on the track. A couple of men were busy tying a blue plastic tarp over the bundles on its roof rack. Other people were already seated inside.

Numerous eyes watched me approach. It didn't matter. I walked to the front of the bus, digging out my wallet along the way—it was finally glorious, civilized money time, a time when I could pay for getting something done instead of doing it myself. The driver's door was open and I stopped and looked up at the driver's expectant black face.

"Bondoukou?" I croaked. He smiled and nodded and said something which ended with 'francs'. He called me a monsieur. I wanted to hug and kiss him. I said:

"That's okay. I have plenty of money."

CHAPTER TWENTY

Just a couple of hours later, I was getting out of a cab in front of the entrance to the Bondoukou hospital's residential compound.

I was feeling considerably better, having slept on the bus. My travelling companions consisted mainly of women—some were extremely fat—burdened with many baskets, plastic buckets, and bowls of vegetables, fruit, and other produce. There were several bunches of chicken suffering silently, tied two and three apiece by the ankles and hung upside down. I also heard at least one intermittently bleating goat.

I felt right at home and slept like a baby and was woken up by the driver after everyone else had decamped. I was completely ghosted out: he kept shaking my arm and I kept shaking my head just so I could get it to work. I stumbled out of the bus still spaced out. I saw everything as if I were watching a movie while high on bad drugs. But the fact was that I was standing at the edge of the familiar Total gas station in Bondoukou. I could even see the Trocadero across the road.

I went to the Trocadero and had four cold Cokes: I was afraid beer would make me pass out. I also had the local take on a shish kebab, big blackened cubes of beef sprinkled with a yellowish powdered spice and served with chopped purple onion. I had another Coke and bought three to go, plus a mickey of cognac. I also bought a couple of raisin buns from a passing vendor as I waited to wave down a cab, and wolfed them down on the drive to Mireille's place.

Things were looking up, no two words about it. I enthusiastically greeted the watchman lounging around on a straw mat in front of the compound entrance, a whacking big cutlass lying next to him. I walked down the gravelled path leading to Mireille's bungalow with a springing step. Sugar and caffeine were a marvelous combination.

She wasn't home. I tapped then knocked increasingly loudly on the glass panels of the verandah's French windows. Her absence wasn't surprising: it was around eleven in the morning, an hour when most people were at work. But this didn't make it any less disappointing.

I sat down on the verandah steps and refreshed myself with a not-so-cold-anymore Coke. After a while, I pulled out the cognac. It claimed to be Courvoisier and it definitely had been expensive enough. But it was probably counterfeit Courvoisier, cheap brandy flavoured with various additives. The Trocadero clientele weren't exactly cognac connoisseurs. I had to check it out.

The first sip established that whatever it was, it was excellent firewater. The second convinced me I was drinking the genuine article. I had a third to make sure and put the bottle away and leaned against the top step. I stared at the quiet bungalows, the hibiscus bushes, the weaving gravelled paths. Everything was so peaceful and well-ordered. It was fucking paradise, and all that bliss just knocked me out.

Mireille woke me up when she got back from work. She told me later that she'd received reports of an unidentified white male camping on her front steps, but thought it might be an amorous and somewhat alcoholic Swedish obstetrician that had been pursuing her recently. She kept saying Oscar Oscar Oscar like a stuck record, and I remember wishing she'd go away and let me sleep. My eyelids were gummed together and I felt the slime stretching when I forced them open. I began to rub my eyes and Mireille slapped my hand. She said:

"Stop that. There's dirt and blood all over your face. What happened? Why are you here? Where's Kross?"

I had the answers to those questions well-rehearsed. I said:

"Well, we had a little misfortune. Truck broke down in the bush. He's getting it fixed. Told me to wait here."

Mireille didn't look pleased. I added:

"He said he'll turn up within twenty-four hours, and that he'll come to your place first. So please tell him I made it all right and that I'm waiting for him at, at the—can you recommend a motel or some kind of rented accommodation around here? Just for a single night."

She pondered that for a little while. Then she said:

"What you need before anything else is a wash. Come." She went up the stairs and unlocked the door and went inside without another word.

I picked up my two bags—I had acquired a plastic carrier bag with my shopping—and went inside Mireille's house. I put down my bags next to the door, to facilitate a quick exit if desired. I heard water running in the kitchen. Then Mireille called out:

"Oscar? Come here."

She'd been busy in the meantime. She had the kettle going and a chair and bowl of water ready: she was shaking drops of yellow liquid into it from a dangerous-looking bottle when I entered. I was told to sit down and she proceeded to clean my face with a cloth. I protested that she was too kind, that I could do that myself. She frowned and told me to wait and exited the kitchen. She returned with a pair of tweezers. Pinching my cheek, she plucked something with the tweezers and said:

"You've got glass in your face. Broken windscreen? You had an accident and that's why the truck broke down?"

"Oh no. This? No. I was walking along the road for a long time and had all sorts of road shit thrown in my face by the traffic. Pebbles and glass and so on."

It sounded pretty lame. Mireille continued to work on my face in what's popularly known as a disbelieving silence. I could feel her breath on my forehead and she was one hell of an attractive woman. I did my best to nip related thoughts in the bud and behave like a patient treated by a doctor. When she'd finished, I said:

"Thank you very much. I'm sorry to show up like that and put you to all this trouble. I – "

She cut me short with a spare-me-the-bullshit wave.

"No trouble," she said, tipping the bowl into the sink. When the water stopped gurgling down the drain she said:

"It's me who... I have to apologize. You gave me a shock. I was expecting – " And that was when she told me about the Swedish obstetrician. Apparently he'd camped on the verandah steps a couple of times in a beer-induced stupor. Seeing me instead wasn't a nice surprise: I looked a mess, and smelled of alcohol.

Then she said:

"You probably wouldn't mind a shower. You can use the towel you did last time you were here—I didn't have time to do the laundry. And I'll go and talk to Jean-Pierre. The administrator. A couple of the bungalows are empty and I'll ask him if you can stay a single night."

"That's really very kind of you."

"He was just going into the canteen when I left. If I catch him right after his dinner he'll be very agreeable. You're not allowed to give him money—that would be a bribe—but you can buy him a carton of Flag. You can get it at the canteen. Better price than in town."

"You know everything," I said. She smiled when she heard that. She looked right into my eyes and said:

"You'd better believe it. When did you say you expect Kross to show up?"

Hearing him brought into the conversation was grating. After a short silence, I said:

"Within twenty four hours. His exact words."

"Good. In the meantime you can tell me about your little adventure in the bush."

For the briefest moment it did feel as if she knew everything, but I recovered quickly and quite skillfully. I said:

"I'd much rather talk about you."

"You don't want to talk about Kross? I'm not sure you know him as well as I do."

"Sure," I said bitterly. "We can talk about Kross."

"Ah. Don't worry. We'll talk plenty about me too. Give me your passport. I'll have to show it to Jean-Pierre. Don't worry, I'll give it back."

She said that because she noticed I became slightly dismayed at the idea of handing my passport over. So I made a show of presenting it to her with effusive thanks and escorted her to the door. When she'd left, I extracted the pouch with my bathroom gear from my bag along with the towel I'd brought and hadn't used so far. Then I hit the bathroom and took a long, luxurious shower.

The towel Kross and I had used just a couple of days earlier was thrown atop a tall wickerwork hamper in the corner of the bathroom. I used it to clean the mirror—a mist had formed even though I'd taken a cold shower. It was really hard to believe I'd used that towel fifty hours earlier. It felt like fifty days, no, fifty weeks.

I brushed my teeth and shaved and combed my hair. But I still looked like shit in spite of the nice tan I'd acquired in the meantime. My face was decorated by at least a dozen cuts, nicks, and scratches, and there was a bruise on my right cheekbone. My eyes were sunk in deep brown holes and they weren't happy. I kept hearing the whip-like crack of the rifle, followed by the scream.

But I had a handful of diamonds in my pocket. Nothing in life came free of charge. I'd paid for those diamonds already and I'd pay plenty more, every time I remembered that scream, right until I fucking died. I didn't care where the diamonds had come from. They were my diamonds now.

I took my two cans of now-warm Coke and I put them in Mireille's fridge, appropriating a cold bottle of Fanta in exchange. I went to drink it on the verandah, scaring away a pair of fist-sized orange-throated black birds that had been gabbing on the top step. As I leaned on the balustrade and sipped the Fanta, I wondered about Kross. I'd taken a good long look once I'd reached that baobab and I hadn't seen him even though I could even make out details like the spot where I'd fallen down earlier, crushing a few plants.

Since Kross was so good at disappearing, there was a big chance he would show up in the very near future. Maybe he was about to step through the entrance to the compound. I repeatedly glanced in that direction as I drank the Fanta. I only noticed Mireille returning from the canteen when she was a short distance away.

I knew something was wrong instantly. She approached with her eyes fixed on the ground, didn't look at me until she'd joined me on the verandah. She said:

"You fucking son of a bitch. I heard it all on the radio in the canteen. Three people killed. You son of a bitch. Get the fuck out of my house before I change my mind and report you. Get out now."

She was holding my passport and she slapped my face with it and dropped it on the floor. She walked to the verandah steps and stopped and said:

289

"I'm coming back in ten minutes. You'd better not be here." She ran down the steps and walked away.

I picked up my passport and forced myself to finish the Fanta. Then I started running.

I had an extraordinary stroke of luck when I ran out of the compound and onto the road: I managed to halt a cab whose driver spoke some English. I immediately asked if he could drive me to Abidjan. He couldn't, but it was possible a friend of his could. I asked him to take me to his friend right away and promised him a bonus if the friend agreed to take me to Abidjan.

He parked his cab across from the familiar Total station, steps away from the Trocadero. There just had to be a strong supernatural bond between the Total station, the Trocadero, and myself. My cab driver asked me to wait and walked away. I was expecting him to enter the Trocadero but he didn't, he disappeared into an alleyway further on. I sat sweating and promising myself to never ever again set foot in Africa, not even Egypt or Morocco. I'd set out to see the Pyramids and end up in front of the fucking Trocadero in Bondoukou, for sure.

My driver returned ten minutes later, accompanied by the advertised friend: dreadlocks, shades, Bob Marley T-shirt, jeans, and an extremely long, curved fingernail on the little finger of his left hand. All this was topped off by a wide-brimmed hat of the kind favoured by cowboys. Things didn't look good.

But appearances could be deceiving, and I was told the clawed cowboy had a cab of his own, and knew English—it was obvious he was perfect for the job. What was more, he was willing to take me to Abidjan. There was just one hitch: he wanted to leave in the morning.

I didn't want to stay in Bondoukou even a minute longer. Every passing minute increased the chance Mireille would change her mind. Maybe she was planning to report me later anyway, just to keep her conscience clean. I explained my plane was leaving the next day and that my car had broken down. The clawed cowboy said it was bad to drive at night, and my cab driver agreed. I told them that they were wrong, it was good to drive at night because there was no traffic and it paid better.

After some haggling the cowboy agreed to set out instantly, and take me to Abidjan for two hundred thousand francs, half up front. I gave my cab driver twenty thousand for the cab fare plus the promised bonus. That left me with four thousand CFA francs—a single frugal meal at the hotel restaurant—and the hundred American in traveller's cheques.

I was told to wait by the Trocadero's entrance while my new driver fetched his car. I didn't like that much. I spent most of my waiting time calculating the odds he'd actually show up—he'd already collected a hundred thousand from the white retard who wanted to drive all night to Abidjan. But the dear boy did show up less than twenty minutes later. He had a white Peugeot 504 with red plush seats. They were very comfortable and I went to sleep the moment we left Bondoukou.

When I woke up the driver was gone and the car was parked right in front of the fucking Trocadero. I was so groggy and ghosted out it took me a while to realize this was a different bar, different place. It was called Tropicana to start with but there was a Shell station right across the road, which suggested some sort of parallel reality. The Peugeot's dashboard clock showed twelve past three in the morning.

I was beginning to get properly paranoid by the time the clawed cowboy emerged from the Tropicana. He was carrying a brown paper bag blotted with grease. He walked up to the car and opened my door and held the bag out to me.

"*Pour toi,*" he said. "*Deux milles francs.* Two thousand."

The bag contained a can of Coke and a hamburger. One of the signs decorating the Tropicana's entrance advertised this combo as costing a thousand, so I guessed I was paying for the driver's meal too. I wouldn't have minded at all, except that it left me with exactly 2500 CFA francs.

"We go when you eat," my driver told me. He didn't want people spilling stuff on the plush upholstery: it would be hell to clean. So I got out of the car and ate standing next to him and we chatted a little. We would reach Abidjan inside an hour, he told me. Where should he drop me off? I told him Hotel Palais-Royal and this got him agitated, because it meant driving through the whole city twice. Eventually I gave him another 500 francs.

Following this he slid into the driver's seat whistling something cheerful, and we set off. When we entered the city, I began feeling newly apprehensive. The border shootout had made the news. Maybe there was a nationwide alert posted for a Mark Kross and Oscar Hansen, international criminals and ruthless killers. I couldn't totally rule out the unpleasant possibility I'd be arrested the moment I showed up at the hotel.

But everything ended wonderfully well. The admirals on door duty—somewhat relaxed at this late/early hour—didn't pounce on me, and there weren't any cops around. Getting my room key from the sleepy receptionist went very smoothly. A few minutes later I was back in my old room, room ten eleven. It felt like home, and I felt close to tears.

I had a very long shower and then helped myself to a scotch from the mini-bar and belatedly thought I might be asked to pay for it when I was leaving. It was best to leave without checking out. I was a criminal anyway. In for a penny, in for a pound.

I alternately paced around my room and lay on the bed, plotting my escape from the hotel, until the Air Afrique office opened. I went there the moment it did, to leave a message for *capitaine* Raymond Best. It was *très urgent*, I told them. *Capitaine* Best was waiting for it, was expecting to receive it as soon as he landed his plane tomorrow. I invested my remaining 2000 francs and was rewarded with the assurance my message would be waiting at the airport.

I went to a 24-hour currency exchange counter next and cashed one of my traveller's checks. I didn't get a good rate but still got thirty thousand francs. I went around to the familiar restaurant—it was the cheapest in the complex—and studied the prices on the menu displayed on a stand by the entrance. Then I went back to my room and ordered a big dinner from room service. I didn't want to spend any more cash, and I was a criminal anyway.

It occurred to me that Mireille knew Kross and I had been staying at the Palais-Royal. I wondered whether she did report me in the end, and if she did—whether she'd included this detail. But I had to stay in my room anyway. I had nowhere else to go. And in approximately thirty hours' time, Raymond Best would be trying to contact me at this hotel, in this room. At least I hoped so. I'd be completely fucked if he didn't get in touch.

Sure, I could always return home without the diamonds. Taking the risk to smuggle them in made little sense. They were uncut, and I couldn't sell them without arousing suspicion. Attempting to get them cut would raise eyebrows, too.

Diamonds or not, I was going to experience a hard landing upon returning home. To my rented room, without enough money to pay the rent. Of course there was always welfare. I could go to their office and beg them to bail me out. They probably would, this was their mission after all. I would be able to live a few months longer until I committed suicide after my fiftieth failed job interview.

They were bad thoughts to have while sitting in the luxurious room of a five-star hotel. I had difficulty falling asleep that night despite depleting the contents of the mini-bar. Morning wasn't much better. I wasted as much time as I could in the bathroom. At least some of the nicks and scratches on my face had healed.

After treating myself to a gigantic brunch from the room service, I just sat and tried to keep myself from looking at the phone every ten seconds. I remembered meeting Mireille a week earlier and how much I liked her, right away. Now she thought I was a piece of shit and I would never see her again. I wondered whether I'd ever see Kross, and had the feeling I wouldn't.

To pass the time, I decided I'd repack my belongings and discovered I still had that fucking military gear: T-shirt, camo pants, boots. I couldn't leave it at the hotel: it was too incriminating. But I couldn't see myself cruising the neighbourhood looking for trash containers big enough to hide all that stuff. I decided I'd dump it at the airport. I put the military gear in a plastic bag and packed it last for easy access later; then it was back to staring at the telephone.

It finally rang a few minutes after sunset. I was so nervous I nearly dropped the receiver when I picked it up. When I heard 'C'est Raymond', my knees changed into jelly and I had to sit down on the bed. He cut me short when I began to explain what and why, and told me to expect him in an hour.

That particular hour was eighty three minutes long. When he finally showed up I was so happy I was ready to kiss him, as if I were French too and he was my long-lost buddy. He noticed and there was an amused glitter in the hard black eyes, and the pinched mouth actually flicked me a brief smile.

"Where's Kross?" he asked, after refusing a drink. I told him I didn't know. I told him we'd run into some difficulties and had to split up. I asked him if he wanted the details and he said no. So I just said Kross had instructed me to find Raymond and get him to help me.

"With what?" he said. "You have a return ticket, correct?"

"With this," I said. I took the diamonds out of my pocket and handed them to him, sock and all.

"Careful," I said. "There's a hole in the plastic."

"I'm always careful," Raymond said, and spilled the diamonds onto the night table. He poked them around with his forefinger, looking rather doubtful.

"Oh, I forgot," I said. "Kross instructed me to tell you something. He said to tell you that Giselle was right."

I was gratified to see Raymond exhibit some surprise. Most people probably never got to see that. He said:

"What was that again?"

"Giselle was right."

"I see," he said. He resumed poking the diamonds around, lips pursed. Then he kneaded his chin for a while. Eventually he said:

"All right. I can help you with that. It's not easy and it will put me to a lot of trouble. More than a lot of trouble if something goes wrong. Twenty percent."

"Okay," I said, without bothering to pretend I was thinking it over. He nodded, and said:

"Then this is what we do." And he outlined his plan with quiet assurance. He knew what he was talking about. He probably made much, much more money than his pilot's salary. It made me confident his plan was good.

I was to board the plane as planned, but disembark in Paris ('get your ticket rewritten at the office downstairs. Ask for Marlena'). Being Canadian, I didn't need a visa for a short stay. Then I was to wait for Raymond at a guesthouse called Pension Savarini, which was family-owned and discreet and inexpensive and had a good cook (Raymond stressed that last point). He promised to be in touch the very next day: we'd drive to Bruges, in goddamn Belgium—no visa needed there either. He knew someone up there who would not only buy the diamonds but also assist in the setting up of a respectable paper trail for the money.

"It's very important to have clean money," Raymond told me. "Dirty money means you're a dirty man."

I agreed. I agreed with everything he said that afternoon. I had just one question. I said:

"What if something goes wrong?"

Raymond grimaced, and waved a dismissive hand.

"You worry too much," he told me. "Everything will go fine."

And that was how it went. That was exactly how it went. Predictably I was nervous the next day: whatever arrangements Kross had made, I was leaving without paying for the room service and the rooms were booked in my name. It could mean trouble and I was resolved to send them more than enough money later. I took a sheet of hotel stationery for the address. Then it was just a question walking out with my bag without getting stopped by the admirals on door duty. I went the brazen route: I approached one of them and slipped him ten thousand francs and asked if he could get me a cab. He was glad to help me.

I left my military gear in the cab I took to the airport. I took it out discreetly while the driver was extra busy with traffic, and pushed it under the front passenger's seat with my foot. I arrived at the airport with nearly two hours to kill before my flight was due. I hung around in the waiting area for a while, hoping to see Raymond, until I realized how stupid that was. So I quickly went through passport control, successfully acting the happy tourist going home. For the first time in my life, I was happy to have a woman with a bawling infant standing in line right behind me. They got the attention that should've been reserved for me.

I felt enormous relief I when I seated myself in the plane, and then got increasingly tense when the plane kept squatting in its parking spot. Finally, five minutes past takeoff time, the engines roared—something could still go wrong—I gripped the armrests and didn't let go till Raymond flicked the plane off the runway in his trademark cavalier manner.

Eight hours later I arrived in France.

CHAPTER TWENTY ONE

France was great. France was fantastic. The guy that checked my passport even said: welcome to France. I subsequently cashed in my solitary remaining traveller's cheque and raided an automatic teller belonging to one of the networks listed on my credit card. I managed to get two 1,000 French franc payouts before a computer somewhere got wise.

Then I paid a small fortune for a cab to the Pension Savarini, which turned out to be located in a nineteenth-century apartment building on a narrow downtown street called Rue de Miromesnil. The six or seven assorted Savarinis lived on the bottom two floors, having converted one ground-floor room into a reception lounge and another into a small dining room. The remaining four floors contained the guest rooms, and the elevator had broken down; I was told it was always breaking down.

Predictably, I had the whole fourth floor to myself. My room had a hardwood floor and long white lace curtains, antiquated wooden furniture and a shower to match: it hardly worked at all. But there was an agreeable, homely smell about the place, tinged with butter-fried onions around dinner time, and having washed, rested, and consumed a very nice steak with a bottle of good red wine I went straight to bed.

I woke up at six the next day which was a good thing: Raymond called at quarter past seven to warn he'd be arriving at nine. I was standing on the pavement outside the Pension Savarini when he swooped down the narrow street in a big black ugly Citroen and swung it to a stop inches from the tips of my globetrotting desert boots.

He wordlessly dropped the sock with the stones into my lap the moment I was seated and we zoomed away. It made me trust him implicitly (though he could've taken a few stones and I'd have never known), and some time later, when we stopped to pay a motorway toll, I confessed the sorry state of my finances. I also asked if he thought Kross would make it to safety wherever he was doing the making.

Raymond Best told me not to worry about Kross ('he'll manage. He always does.') He went on to advise me not to worry about money ('you'll be rich soon'), and not to worry so much in general ('it gives you bad dreams and it's bad for the digestion.'). Then he concentrated on driving very fast.

We arrived in Brugges at three in the afternoon, having been impatiently waved through a Belgian customs post. Raymond Best and I took rooms at a respectable middle-class hotel overlooking the medieval town square, whereupon I savoured the view from my window while reviewing the contents of the mini-bar. I also did a a lot of self-congratulating. Just a few days earlier I'd been walking through the African bush, scared shitless. It all felt as if it had happened in a different life.

While I was happily engaged in mental masturbation, Best was busy making calls. At seven that evening we drove off to see a lawyer he knew. The lawyer's name was Theodore Sanis and did business out of a home office on the outskirts of the city. I was glad I'd had my black Italian suit freshly pressed by one of the enterprising Savarinis, in exchange for a small sum. Raymond was impressed enough to comment on its cut.

Mr. Sanis also showed signs of being impressed, and he didn't look like a guy who would be impressed easily. He was very fat, very bald, and in his late fifties, with a Levantine swarthiness and sensuousness in those face features that were discernible between folds of fat. He wore spectacles, thick lenses framed with gold wire, and his plump hairy fingers sported two rings set with expensive stones.

He looked more like the prosperous owner of a carpet shop than a lawyer. But when we'd sat down in his study and he began asking questions and making comments I realized there was a very fine and devious brain hidden in this egg-shaped, mottled head. He asked me what I proposed to do with the money I got for the diamonds—how would I take it home, how would I account for it to the authorities?—and I didn't know.

Raymond intervened, and told Sanis I needed the complete package as of yesterday. Sanis nodded sagely and observed it was going to cost; Raymond waved a world-weary hand and said we all knew nothing in life was free of charge. Then the two predators, the greying wolf and the fat octopus, exchanged glances of mutual admiration and Sanis told me to show him the diamonds.

They were still in their original sock, which caused merriment. Sanis scattered them on his desk top and poked among them thoughtfully ('this is rubbish,' he said at one point, sweeping a comma of diamond sand to the side with a fat finger). But many pieces clearly weren't rubbish—four were the size of very healthy peas—and after examining the loot with a jeweller's magnifying glass, a mildly excited Sanis told me to return the next afternoon, 'and I'll have the whole package ready. So much to do...' He rolled his eyes dramatically to illustrate the point. He asked me to leave the diamonds with him. I looked at Raymond, and Raymond nodded. So what could I do? I nodded too.

"Don't worry about Sanis," said the observant Best when we emerged from the building and were walking towards a taxi stand. "He's a good man. An honest man." I very nearly laughed.

"I'm past being worried," I told him. "I just want to eat."

I lied to him. I was worried all right—I worried all night. I'd kept all my fears under lock and key but the lock broke when I left the diamonds with Sanis. Raymond could increase his twenty percent cut radically with one tap, one thrust, one shot... Somehow this didn't fit my image of Raymond. Maybe he and Sanis would simply take everything and tell me to fuck off. What could I do? Go to the cops and tell them that the diamonds I'd robbed had been stolen?

"You're worried," commented Raymond that afternoon, as we sped towards Sanis in the black Citroen.

"No, I'm just a bit off. Africa's fucked up my stomach. You know—different water, different food."

302

"You had a healthy appetite yesterday. Never mind. I think I have to explain something to you. You're Kross's partner, okay? That means something. Though why..." He shrugged, and added:

"I'm a serious man and Sanis is a serious man. We don't fuck around. Understand? I like having a good digestion and nice dreams."

"So do I."

"Good," he said. "Good."

Sanis was waiting for us in a green silk dressing gown over white shirt and evening trousers. The pouches under his eyes were a very dark brown and he was refreshing himself from a family-sized tumbler containing what looked like whisky on the rocks. He had at least five ounces of booze in that glass. He shepherded us to his study and briskly proceeded with what he called 'the business'.

He lived up to Raymond's claim that he was an honest man. He said right away the diamonds were worth almost fourteen hundred and fifty thousand American dollars—he slid over a five-page estimate I couldn't read: the tightly typed columns jumped and swayed. Nearly one and a half million dollars! Kross had estimated the whole lot was worth a little over two million, and my share was less than a third of that! It shook my faith in Kross's expertise.

This faith was quickly restored when Sanis said my stones would fetch only half their estimated worth. This was in accordance with the time-honoured rules governing payment for hot merchandise. Of course Kross would have factored that in when he told me how much the diamonds were worth.

My money, after expenses, would amount to six hundred and twenty-six thousand American dollars, payable any way I wanted. I had acquired most of this minor fortune by winning a prize in a lottery held three months earlier—here Sanis picked up a lottery ticket stub and remarked that this alone had cost him five thousand American. In the unlikely event someone would get curious he was prepared to swear before any court that he'd known me for years, and had personally purchased the ticket for me (he added 'that's what lawyers are for', and laughed).

As for the money itself, he proposed investing it in a private subscriber-only mutual fund he was running with great success. He guaranteed a flat ten per cent return ('you *always* get at least ten percent, even if I have to make up the difference out of my own pocket, and sometimes you'll get fifteen or twenty'), and would be only too happy to supervise my account. He advised me to register a company in Luxembourg and open a corporate bank account ('this way the money comes as salary from this company that is retaining you as consultant. Of course I'm the company president—I'll deduct a symbolic salary from your payments when they exceed ten percent—and everything runs very smoothly.')

I still had to pay Raymond his cut: twenty percent. I really hoped that it was twenty percent of what I netted, not twenty percent of the diamonds' estimated worth. So I asked Raymond, and it was. I immediately instructed my new lawyer to pay Raymond his cut out of the money I was about to receive. Both Sanis and Raymond beamed with approval; it was obvious that the two of them had already discussed this issue, including various unpleasant options to ensure my compliance. They were nice guys, they were both relieved it would not have to come to that.

All this left me with just over half a million American dollars. The payoff amounted to fifty thousand American per annum. This wasn't bad. In fact it almost felt too good. But a little while later, as I signed the numerous papers Sanis pushed my way, my remaining doubts dissipated.

Sanis had likely just made a profit of at least a couple of hundred thousand on the diamonds. He'd awarded himself a yearly salary that was supposed to be symbolic, but with a guy his size any symbols would have to be large. He'd also secured at least fifty thousand in annual income from the financial scam he was running—it was reasonable to assume he wouldn't pay me more than he paid himself, and I was to get a minimum of fifty a year. In the long run, he'd probably make more money out this whole thing than I would.

We spent another half an hour setting up a company called AG Design which immediately retained me as vice-president (I insisted). At the end of it all, Sanis clasped my hand in both of his and gravely asked if there was anything else he could assist me with, being my attorney. I told him about the unpaid room service bill at the Hotel Palais-Royal, and he immediately promised to see to it and forward me an itemized expense sheet. I also jokingly asked for five thousand American, half in French francs. Sanis listened gravely and said he'd have the money delivered to the Pension Savarini the next morning. Then he said:

"And now we have to celebrate. I have just become president of the twenty-seventh company under my wise guidance and you have just become a wealthy man. So I'd like to invite you two gentlemen to dinner, followed by entertainment. I would be proud to have you as my guests—and I'm absolutely at your disposal."

I believed him. If people came around to drop sacks of money on my doorstep, I'd have willingly served them dinner myself, dressed in a French maid's outfit if required.

And so, I spent a night on the town with Sanis and Raymond. We began with dinner at a fancy restaurant, whose moustachioed waiters visibly fawned over Sanis: he must have represented important income. The taciturn Raymond started smiling after the second bottle of champagne. I felt tired and out of sorts next to those two sharks. So I drank a lot of champagne, and it helped.

The evening ended at a brothel. I was drunk enough not to question this destination when we left the restaurant. It didn't make much difference: I'd left my libido behind in Africa, and I spent my time there sitting in the bar together with Raymond. Sanis the Nightlife Star was greeted with shouts of joyful surprise by a group of middle-aged, suited types that hung around the far end of the bar. He went to converse with them and then returned with a hooker dressed in an eighteenth-century costume, all shiny silk and lace. Her hair was a mountain of chestnut ringlets piled up high over her forehead, and she actually carried a tiny silk umbrella.

"I might not see you before you leave," Sanis said, breathing booze in my face. "Contact me the moment you get home. I need your bank account number and address so that I can start sending you money." He gave me a wink, and added:

"And now, as your attorney, I advise you to make merry." He went off with his courtesan. I turned to talk to Raymond and found that a whore in a red latex dress and matching elbow-length gloves had interposed herself between us. Raymond's hand was already resting on her ass. I caught his eye over her shoulder and said:

"Raymond. Who is Giselle and what did she say?" He looked at me reproachfully, patted the red rubber rump and said:

"Oh, she likes to say me and Kross get innocent people into trouble. Are you innocent and do you like trouble?" he asked the whore, in English for my benefit. She giggled and tousled his hair with one hand and put her cigarette out with the other, taking special care not to melt her red glove.

"Who is Giselle?" I asked again. Raymond grinned at me, showing me his teeth for the first time ever. They were packed in dense yellowish rows and gleamed with spit and champagne. He said:

"She's my wife. We've been married nearly twenty years."

CHAPTER TWENTY TWO

Three days later I was home. My childhood home in Peterborough.

The trip back to Paris went fine. The flight from Paris to Toronto went fine. The woman who was my immigration officer said she hoped I'd had a great holiday. But as I stood on the pavement outside the Toronto airport, I found the notion of returning to my room next to the toilet impossible. I ended up renting a car and driving to Peterborough. I arrived at three in the morning, let myself in with the spare back door key hidden under the funny rock in the garden, and spent the rest of the night on the front room sofa.

I was woken up by the smell of coffee and the first thing I saw was my childhood mug standing within reach, issuing clouds of aromatic steam. I heard my old man move around in the kitchen and I sat up on the sofa and reached for the steaming mug. I drank coffee and massaged my temples and reviewed the story I'd prepared. When I felt it contained enough truth to conceal the lies I went to join my father:

SON: (enters kitchen)

FATHER: (looks up from plate with remains of scrambled eggs, grunts)

SON: (grunts)

FATHER: There are fresh eggs in the fridge.

SON: I'm all right for now. I'll join you with another coffee if I may.

(pause while SON pours a coffee and joins as advertised)

FATHER: Nice tan. Did you go on a holiday?

SON: Actually it was a kind of a working holiday. Got a gig to do a complete ad and promo package for a luxury hotel in Africa. Manager of the hotel is a friend of a friend. They flew me down there for a week to take things in. But I meant to apologize for crashing in like that.

FATHER (somewhat doubtfully): It's all right.

SON: I spent a week living in the so-called lap of luxury and couldn't face the shitty room I'm renting presently. But now I'll be able to afford something better.

FATHER (still somewhat doubtfully): That's good.

SON: And I'll be able to give you your money back.

FATHER: (dismissively) The money... It's good you showed up. I needed to talk to you.

SON: You needed to talk to me? What about?

FATHER: Frieda's worse. So I'm going to join your mother. We'll stay there as long as necessary. (checks the weather outside the window while computing Frieda's life expectancy) Maybe until the summer.

SON: Dad... Why do you always refer to her as 'your mother', not 'my wife'?

FATHER: Because she's your mother and I'm talking to you.

SON: I see. Listen, would it be okay if I moved in for a couple of months? This way I could look after the place when you're gone. I don't need to be physically present in the city for this gig.

FATHER (deeply puzzled, issues the official press release): You're always welcome.

And so, two days later I drove my old man to the airport in his Oldsmobile. As we were saying goodbye he asked if I could grant him a favour.

"Sure," I said. "Sure."

"When it gets warmer, can you paint the fence? It needs a fresh coat."

"Oh sure," I said. "Sure."

After his flight left, I drove my rented car back to Toronto to see the Natarajan, settle outstanding rent, then give notice and collect the few odds and ends that constituted my current belongings. Natarajan literally exploded with joy when he saw me, grew suspicious, then joyful again when I paid him what I owed. I also told him I was vacating the room and that was when he told me that someone had been around, looking for Mr. Hansen. He didn't deal with the mysterious visitor, one of the tenants did, so he couldn't even give me a description.

I didn't hang around. I gathered everything up and was out of there. I refused to give the insistent Natarajan my new address on grounds of an impending move, and announced I'd be back to collect mail before slipping him a conciliatory twenty. He was standing on the front path and waving when I drove away.

I dropped off the rental and subsequently went through the pain of a bus journey back to Peterborough. I did a lot of thinking during that journey. I didn't like the fact that there had been people asking about me. I suspected it could be connected with Hercules Moving & Storage. But it might have been the cops too, alerted that an advertising art director was running around Africa shooting at people. It was good that I'd moved out.

When I got back to Peterborough I finally called my answering service. I had three messages. Two were from Donna. Her first message told me she'd received a visit from the manager and owner of Hercules Moving and Storage. He was stupid enough to threaten a lawsuit. She immediately threatened a lawsuit of her own. When the manager and owner discovered Donna was a hotshot lawyer, he retreated mumbling apologies.

Her second message informed me that there was a court hearing scheduled for our divorce case. Her lawyer would handle it, and send me my copy of the papers. Clean break, no fighting over possessions or alimony.

I drank brandy and coffee in the kitchen until three in the morning. Then I called Sanis. He was very pleased to hear from me. He'd already taken care of the Palais-Royal business and was ready to transfer the first monthly retainer from AG Design into my bank account; he wanted the number. I told him to FedEx me a banker's draft instead. He liked that. He said he'd take this opportunity to send me some literature on my investments.

I received the FedEx envelope four days later. The draft amounted to just under thirty-six hundred American and was accompanied by an itemized expenses statement. That worked out to around four and a half thousand Canadian dollars. Not exactly go-wild money, but enough for a pain-free existence. It struck me that I now had the financial freedom to get into painting in a serious way.

I suspected my monthly retainer would somehow always amount to less than expected, and that it would be always accompanied by some sort of an expenses statement. Sanis was smart. He knew that cheating someone rudely meant you only got to cheat that person once. But I was reassured to see that the money scam he'd persuaded me to invest in turned out to be a perfectly respectable operation backed by a Belgian merchant bank. At least that was what it looked like on paper.

I immediately went and sold the draft at my parents' bank branch. Then I visited a computer store and acquired a mid-range Pentium with a 56k modem. Having been spoiled by my Mac, I spent a couple of days struggling with assorted Windows idiocies. I signed on with a new provider, using my father's name, address, and credit card number. I only needed that account for a month or two, and only for one specific purpose: to check on Kross.

When I typed his name into the search engine and tapped return, I was rewarded by a small electronic blizzard: over 1000 hits. It was a popular name in cyberspace, mostly through the efforts of one Kross, Bentley who specialized in churning out books about computer games. I tried going through the list but surrendered at Kross Kuts, a hairdressing salon in Hawaii. I decided to start with the Nazi father, and ran a search for Kross within World War II context.

There still were over three hundred hits, well over half pointing to illiterate Nazi-lovers who fawningly mentioned the Iron Kross. But I did find a Kross in the Kriegsmarine: the wartime German navy. However, this particular Kross drowned with his destroyer in a Norwegian fjord in 1940, curiously enough right next to Narvik and just a few miles away from my parents' current residence. I persisted and unearthed another Kriegsmarine Kross who in turn drowned with the *Bismarck*. Neither of them had been a submariner.

The next day, I tried a different tack: I ran a search on Kriegsmarine war criminals. It seemed there had been quite a few. I read about them for nearly four hours and came close to giving up when I came across oberleutant-zur-see Rudolf Krossman.

His name was on a list of naval war criminals who had never been prosecuted for various reasons. The most common reason was that they were dead by the time war ended. But Krossman wasn't one of those. He was listed as missing.

The list was prefaced by an appeal by Dr Alfred Bonner to send him all and any information on war criminals in the German wartime navy. It included his e-mail address. I wrote him right away, asking about Krossman. I told Dr Bonner that I had heard a story about a German naval officer of that name who had served on a submarine off the coast of West Africa. The story had him appropriating a small fortune in diamonds from a British freighter. Could that be the same Krossman who was named as a war criminal?

Dr Bonner wrote me back the very next day. It was a very long e-mail and I anticipated interesting news. I wasn't disappointed, quite the opposite. Frankly, I was blown away.

Yes, my Krossman and Dr Bonner's Krossman were most likely the same person. Oberleutant-zur-see Rudolf Krossman was on officer on U-122. The U-122 was an ocean-going submarine of the IXB class. In late 1941, it was patrolling the approach to Takoradi, a port on the Gold Coast that was an important link in the supply chain set up to keep the British army in Egypt alive and fighting. A long supply chain, because at that time the Germans and the Italians controlled the Mediterranean Sea.

The U-122 laid a few mines in the shipping lanes, then continued lurking in the area hoping to ambush merchant ships. On the 11th of December, 1941, it intercepted a British freighter called *SS Cadogan*. It was sailing back to Britain, loaded with timber and cocoa beans. The captain's safe contained a special cargo: nearly five pounds of diamonds, mostly industrial-grade.

The commander of the U-122 was a gentleman. He followed the rules of war: the U-122 surfaced, and ordered the *SS Cadogan* to stop its engines. When it did, a boarding party from the submarine led by oberleutnant Krossman searched the ship. Krossman ordered the freighter's captain to open his safe. The captain refused. Krossman threatened to kill one of his crew, and to keep killing his crew until the safe was opened. The captain refused. Whereupon Krossman killed leading seaman Arthur Roe, shooting him in the head from his pistol. The captain changed his mind—a little late for leading seaman Roe, but better late than never—and opened the safe.

The newly-minted war criminal collected the diamonds, advised the captain he had twenty minutes to abandon the ship before it was sunk, and left. Exactly twenty minutes later, the submarine's deck gun put a few holes into the freighter's waterline, and that was it for *SS Cadogan*.

The reason for this amazing amount of detail was explained in Dr Bonner's concluding paragraph. He was fascinated by the U-122, he wrote, because shortly after the described events the U-122 disappeared. Its last radio transmission took place on December 18th, 1941, and put it two hundred miles south of Canary Islands, sailing home. Eventually, it was listed as missing in action.

There was no record of any German submarine being sunk in the relevant time frame and geographical area. Of course, it could have sunk as a result of an accident: many subs did. But there was a persistent rumor after the war of a U-boat whose crew had deserted *en masse* relatively early in the war; hard to believe, because Hitler and company were winning at the time. Dr Bonner had traced that rumor to Brazil. The IXB-type boats had a very long operating range. The U-122 had more than enough fuel to sail west across the Atlantic instead of returning home.

Would I be so kind as to find out more from my friend, and report whatever I found out? Dr Bonner told me he would be overjoyed if I could help him. He was a naval historian, he wrote, and the mystery surrounding U-122 had really gotten its hooks into him.

I didn't write Bonner back. Instead, I ran a search on Dr Alfred Bonner and found that he was who he claimed to be: a naval historian specializing in the wartime German navy. He'd published three books on the subject.

I thought about what I'd just learned. Takoradi was almost literally a stone's throw from Dixcove: I'd seen it on the map, just forty or fifty miles east. It wouldn't take long for the U-122 to reach the coast. It would be easy to go ashore in one of those motor-powered dinghies big German subs carried. Then it was a matter of slipping ashore and finding a good spot to hide the diamonds—or at least part of them. The spooky noises emitted by the rocks would be like a homing beacon. A German naval officer who shot people in the head was unlikely to be afraid of ghosts. It would be the perfect spot to hide the loot.

But there was a snag that made all that implausible. Krossman was an officer aboard the U-122, but not its commander. He would have to get his approval to take the diamonds, and hide them ashore. More than that: his commander had to be in on the whole thing from the start. Okay, but why?

And suddenly I had it. That story Kross had told me about the *Swallow*: mutinous crew, Connacher and Avery leaving the ship with Connacher's diamonds—all I had to do was substitute a few names. U-122 instead of *Swallow*, Krossman for Avery... It all fit perfectly. But why would the crew of the U-122 want to mutiny? Hitler was winning the war.

I reread Bonner's long letter. U-122 intercepted *SS Cadogan* on the 11th of December, 1941. It made its last radio transmission exactly a week later; by then, it was nearing the Canary Islands. So the diamonds had to be hidden ashore immediately following the encounter with the freighter. Would the submarine's crew turn mutinous just because an officer shot a British sailor in the head? Doubtful.

In the end, I had the bright idea to run a search on the date: December 11, 1941. And I saw the reason why the entire crew of a German submarine, captain included, could decide that as far as they were concerned, the war was over. On the 11th of December, 1941, Germany declared war on the United States. And the crew of the U-122 would have learned that when they radioed in their report about SS *Cadogan*.

Up to that moment, there might have been a chance that Hitler could win. But it instantly ceased to exist. True, on that date German tanks were on the outskirts of Moscow, and the Japanese had just sunk most of the American fleet in the Pacific. But only a madman could think he could win a war against the combined might of Great Britain, the Soviet Union, and the USA. Great Britain was truly great at that time. It wasn't limited to the British Isles. It ruled over a big chunk of global real estate, including all of India. Taking on the Big Three was tantamount to suicide.

So yes, the crew of the U-122 had every reason to suddenly feel disenchanted. And maybe Krossman was the odd man out, a true Nazi, as proven by the murder of leading seaman Roe. Maybe they abandoned him on the shore of a British colony, giving him part of the diamonds because after all he was the one who had found them. Maybe later they sailed home for a while, sent that final signal to base, then turned west. Sank their sub off the shore of Brazil and dispersed, everyone carrying a small handful of diamonds in his pocket. Five pounds of diamonds was a hell of a lot. What Kross had shown me was much less than half a pound, I was sure.

Maybe, maybe, maybe. I spent the rest of that day going round in fucking circles. I knew just enough to invent many different scenarios, and not enough to choose the correct one. I didn't even know for sure Krossman was Kross's father. But the sum of coincidences was just too great.

It was somewhat surprising, therefore, that when I woke up the next day I was convinced that whole Krossman business was bullshit. The simplest explanation was almost always the correct explanation. And the simplest explanation for the diamonds' origin was presented on the Wanted poster I saw at the police station in Dixcove. Kross had stolen the diamonds while a military coup was underway.

He knew that sooner or later, he would be meticulously searched—deserting mercenaries were likely asked to bend over and cough while naked. So he hid his loot among the haunted rocks. Maybe that was what had happened.

Maybe. Maybe. Maybe.

I'd told Kross I didn't give a fuck where the diamonds came from. It was true at the time. All I cared about then was getting out of Africa in one piece. But now that I'd made it home, the diamonds' provenance began to bother me.

It got worse as time went on, most likely because I didn't really have anything to do. My carefree existence, living off those diamonds, was turning into a horror. And after only a few weeks! I couldn't imagine living my whole life like that.

I attempted to be active and organized. I wrote Dr Bonner thanking him for all the information he'd sent me. Unfortunately my friend was unreachable at present, but I'd ask a few questions when that changed, and immediately convey what I'd learned.

Writing all those lies made me sweat as if I'd been working out. I set the thermostat lower and took a shower and began hitting Peterborough bars. My automatic pilot must have been in top nick, for I woke up in the middle of the night on the front room sofa.

I had a dim memory of actually talking to people while in one of the bars—I fancied I'd visited more than one. I was terrified that I might have blurted out everything I'd been through to someone in a rush of alcoholic honesty, and I spent the long hours until dawn drinking coffee, swallowing painkillers, and shivering with paranoia. I kept hearing the shots, the screams of the men Kross killed. Three dead, Mireille had told me. She'd probably reported me in the end. She just had to. She was one of those people who couldn't live with a dirty conscience. Unlike myself.

By the afternoon I was convinced that the only thing to do was to go and confess everything to the cops. They'd be knocking on my door sooner or later; maybe they already did. I was tired and hungover so I decided to turn myself in the next day. I got very lucky there.

What happened was that around six in the evening the telephone rang, and when I answered I found out I was speaking to someone called Samantha. Someone called Samantha told me we'd become friends the previous night and that I insisted on getting together the next evening. This was the next evening. And so I got together with Samantha, hungover as I was, although I dreaded it. In particular, I dreaded finding out what I'd told her the previous night.

It turned out I'd talked very little apart from an impassioned speech about taking up painting again. I liked her—she was a very attractive woman—and she liked the fact that I'd listened to her, instead of talking about myself all the time, like most of the men she'd met. She'd also liked my outburst about taking up painting in a serious way.

"You said you might fail, but at least you would die trying," she told me.

"That sounds about right," I said, making her laugh.

Samantha and I met several times over the next couple of weeks. She was a lifesaver, she kept me sane, because I spent those weeks practically in hiding, tortured by paranoia. I ventured out after nightfall to buy sundry items, and greatly boosted the business of a nearby Chinese takeaway. I could see Sam was favourably impressed by my preference for taking long, romantic walks in the woods, but puzzled over my refusal to meet her friends. 'But you already met them the night you met me!' That exactly was yet another reason why I didn't want to see them again: I'd been really drunk that night. And that whole business of pretending to remember names...

The arrival of another FedEx envelope from Sanis jolted me into the realization that I'd changed my mind about turning myself in. I would try and get away with it. It was time to cut all connections with my past. I called the Natarajan and found out there was mail waiting for me: a large envelope sent from a law office, and a small package mailed in Canada. Most importantly, no one had come looking for me again. Kross? No, Kross hadn't returned. Didn't I know he'd given notice the day before we left?

"What about his things?" I said, shocked.

"He said we could keep whatever he was leaving behind. It wasn't a lot. A few books and magazines, and a hammock. He slept in a hammock! He never used the bed! Maybe he was a sailor."

"Maybe," I said.

I told Natarajan I'd be around to collect the mail. I disconnected and then stood next to the phone, collecting my thoughts. The sneaky bastard! And he'd told me that if he failed to show up in time, we'd meet at home! He likely told me that lie on purpose. If I was caught and spilled the beans, the forces of law and order would be expecting him in Toronto. Meanwhile, he'd hide out somewhere else.

I didn't want to think about Kross and Krossman any more. So, since I was standing next to the phone anyway, I called Tad.

He answered on the first ring and it was obvious he was eagerly awaiting a call from someone he liked a whole lot better than me. The instant change in his tone the moment he heard my voice was very unpleasant. So I just told him I saw him being wheeled out on a stretcher last time I tried to pay a visit, that I was glad he was all right, and lied that I'd call again.

I made the trip to Toronto in my father's Oldsmobile, on an early March day that couldn't decide whether it belonged to spring or winter. I hit a snow blizzard soon after I set out, but kept crawling determinedly and was rewarded by an explosion of near-tropical sunshine an hour later.

I parked the Oldsmobile on my old street around three in the afternoon feeling irritated—I'd counted on wrapping everything up by two. I quickly became even more irritated, for it turned out Natarajan was absent from the premises. Another tenant let me in, so at least I waited indoors.

Natarajan appeared after an extremely long half an hour. He'd been on a small shopping expedition. After he'd disposed of his bags, he gave me my mail. There was the expected envelope from the lawyer handling the divorce. And there also was a large flat package wrapped in brown paper that had gotten wet, so wet that the handwritten address of the sender and the postmark were illegible. Natarajan reacted to my frowning silence by explaining that he'd dropped the package in the snow on the way back from the post office—'I went to collect it personally!' He pouted until I gave him twenty dollars along with my thanks.

I didn't get back home until ten that night, having stopped for a meal along the way. After I'd poured myself a drink and made some coffee, I turned my attention to the mail. As expected, the envelope from the lawyer's office contained my divorce papers. I poured myself a second drink to celebrate. Then, armed with a big kitchen knife, I tackled the package.

I slit the taped paper along the edge and tore it aside to reveal a two-week-old front page of the Vancouver Sun. It was wrapped around a big album-sized book which was quite heavy. I put it in the middle of the table and unwrapped it.

My heart began to pound the moment I saw the cover. Here and there, I could see it had once been green leather; now it was mostly greyish brown, furred where someone had roughly removed the mold. The spine creaked as I lifted the front cover and stared at the yellowed front page. It featured the title and the author in slanted, embellished script, the ink purple with age: *The Life Well Led. A Collection of Thoughts and Esseys. Horatio Greenbottle, Vicar of Rye, Sussx.*

I had to step back and get another drink and walk around the kitchen to calm down. When I did, I walked up to the book and opened it at random and instantly saw my random opening wasn't random: there was a bookmark attached to the spine, a long twisted leather thong, and someone had placed it almost exactly halfway through the book. It would take a real effort to read that far: the big stiff pages were filled with Greenbottle's slanting, cramped script. His esses looked like efs and he capitalized nouns, verbs and adjectives as he thought appropriate.

My mother used a magnifying glass to read the tiny type on food packaging. I got it from the drawer and examined the bookmarked spread. There was a small x pencilled halfway down the margin of the left page. It marked the beginning of a sentence, and I slowly slid the glass over these words:

For God is Infinitly Mercifull; yet he who Lives by Falsehood will even Lie to Him, and seek to Caress His Mercie with False Gifts. As His Humble Servant I had many a Time Prepared a Sinner to Meet His Maker, and recieved many Pledges of Property and Monneys from the Deathbed. Had They all been Earnest, my Humble Vicrage would Possess more

Wealth than the Vatican, for these Empty Promisses included viz. a Gold Mine in Brasil, one Isle in the West Indies and another in the Greek Seas (tho' the Benefactor knew these Seas remain under Infidel Rule), and a magnificent Mansion whos Dying Master was pleass'd to call his Glasgow Castle. But of all the Wretched Souls seeking to Appeaz Gods Rightful Wrath, none were more Elaborate and Cunning than a certain James Avery, by his own admittance a very Sad Dog indeed, who Claimed to Know of Treasure Hidden Well out of Reach viz. on the Coast of Guinney, buried under Stones he called the Weeping Sisters, and whos Compleat Story I shall now Recount for My Readers Edification.

I put the glass aside, sat down, and began to read.

Don't miss out!

Visit the website below and you can sign up to receive emails whenever Michael Rymaszewski publishes a new book. There's no charge and no obligation.

https://books2read.com/r/B-A-GNTY-BJAOC

BOOKS 2 READ

Connecting independent readers to independent writers.

Did you love *SS Glasgow Castle*? Then you should read *The Bewildering Effect of Cabbages*[1] by Michael Rymaszewski!

The Bewildering Effect
of
Cabbages

Michael Rymaszewski

2

Do You Really Know What Will Happen Next?

A young man lands the job of his dreams and discovers dreams can come only half-true.

An orphan inherits a million dollars from a mother he'd never met.

A corporate executive who specializes in firing people loses his job.

A wedding goes awry, waking up a ghost.

---

1. https://books2read.com/u/38W0VB

2. https://books2read.com/u/38W0VB

Four stories told in four distinct voices, but with a common theme: the magic unpredictability of life.

Also by Michael Rymaszewski

The Bewildering Effect of Cabbages
SS Glasgow Castle

About the Author

Michael Rymaszewski was born in Poland, grew up in Ghana, and spent most of his working life in Canada. He writes in not just one but two difficult languages: Canadian English, and Polish.